D0910017

DISCARDED

PUBLISHED BY KaBOOM!

ROSS RICHIE ~ CEO & Founder

MATT GAGNON ~ Editor-in-Chief

FILIP SABLIK ~ VP-Publishing & Marketing

LANCE KREITER ~ VP-Licensing & Merchandising

PHIL BARBARO ~ Director of Finance

BRYCE CARLSON ~ Managing Editor

DAFNA PLEBAN ~ Editor

SHANNON WATTERS ~ Editor

ERIC HARBURN ~ Editor

CHRIS ROSA ~ Assistant Editor

ALEX GALER ~ Assistant Editor

WHITNEY LEOPARD ~ Assistant Editor

JASMINE AMIRI ~ Assistant Editor

STEPHANIE GONZAGA ~ Graphic Designer

MIKE LOPEZ ~ Production Designer

DEVIN FUNCHES ~ E-Commerce & Inventory Coordinator

BRIANNA HART ~ Executive Assistant

AARON FERRARA ~ Operations Assistant

A catalog record of this book is available from
OCLC and from the KaBOOM! website, www.
kaboom-studios.com, on the Librarians Page.

BOOM! Studios, 5670 Wilshire Boulevard, Suite
450, Los Angeles, CA 90036-5679.

Printed in China. First Printing.

ISBN: 978-1-60886-343-3

ADVENTURE TIME™

EYE CANDY

VOLUME ONE

kaboom!™
CARTOON NETWORK. FREDERATOR

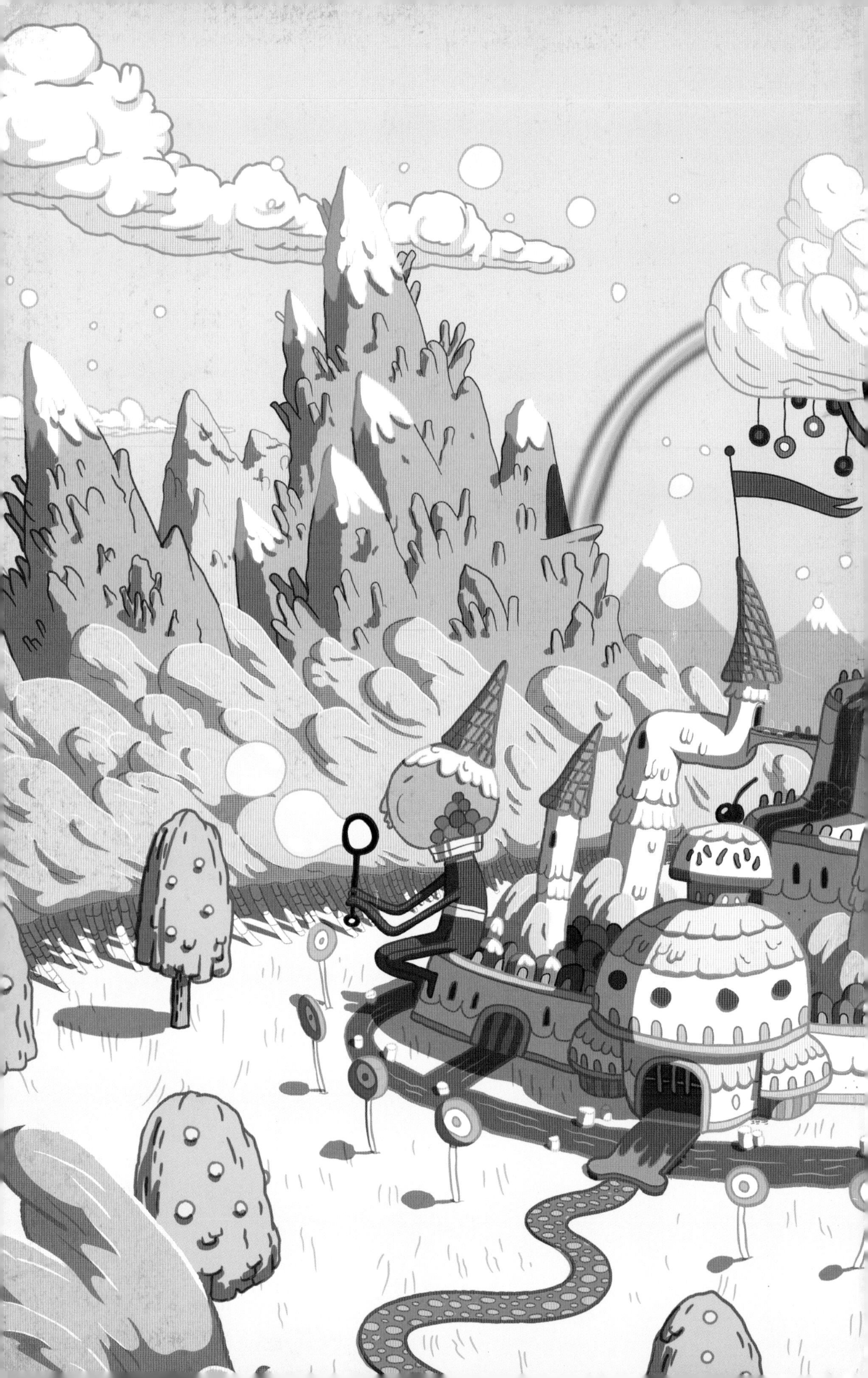

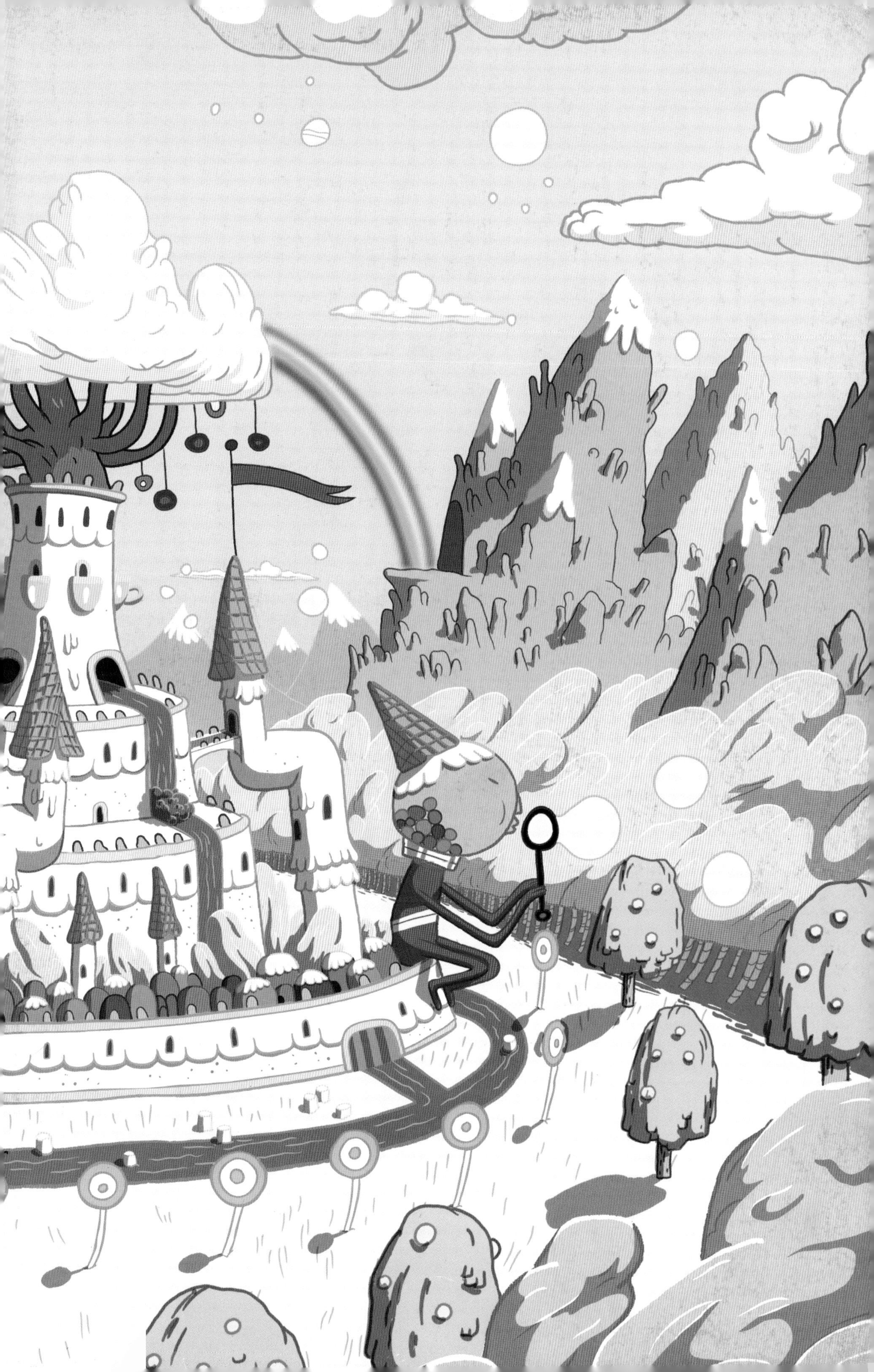

CREATED BY
Pendleton Ward

ASSISTANT EDITOR
Whitney Leopard

EDITOR
Shannon Watters

COVER ILLUSTRATION AND TRADE DESIGN BY
Stephanie Gonzaga

ENCHIRIDION EDITION COVER BY
Zack Sterling

With special thanks to
Marisa Marionakis, Rick Blanco, Curtis Lelash, Laurie Halal-Ono, Keith Mack, Kelly Crews
and the wonderful folks at Cartoon Network.

CONTENTS

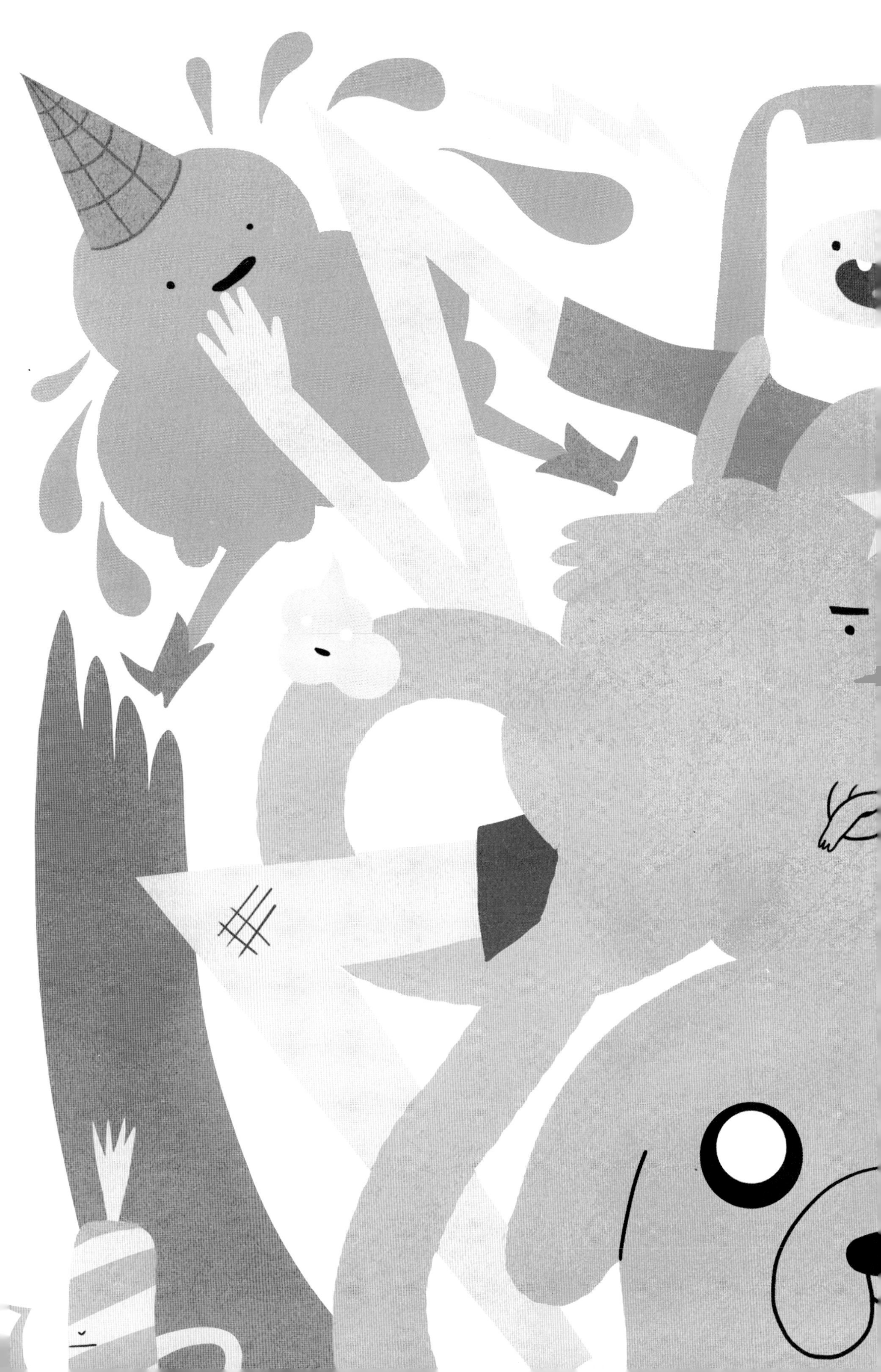

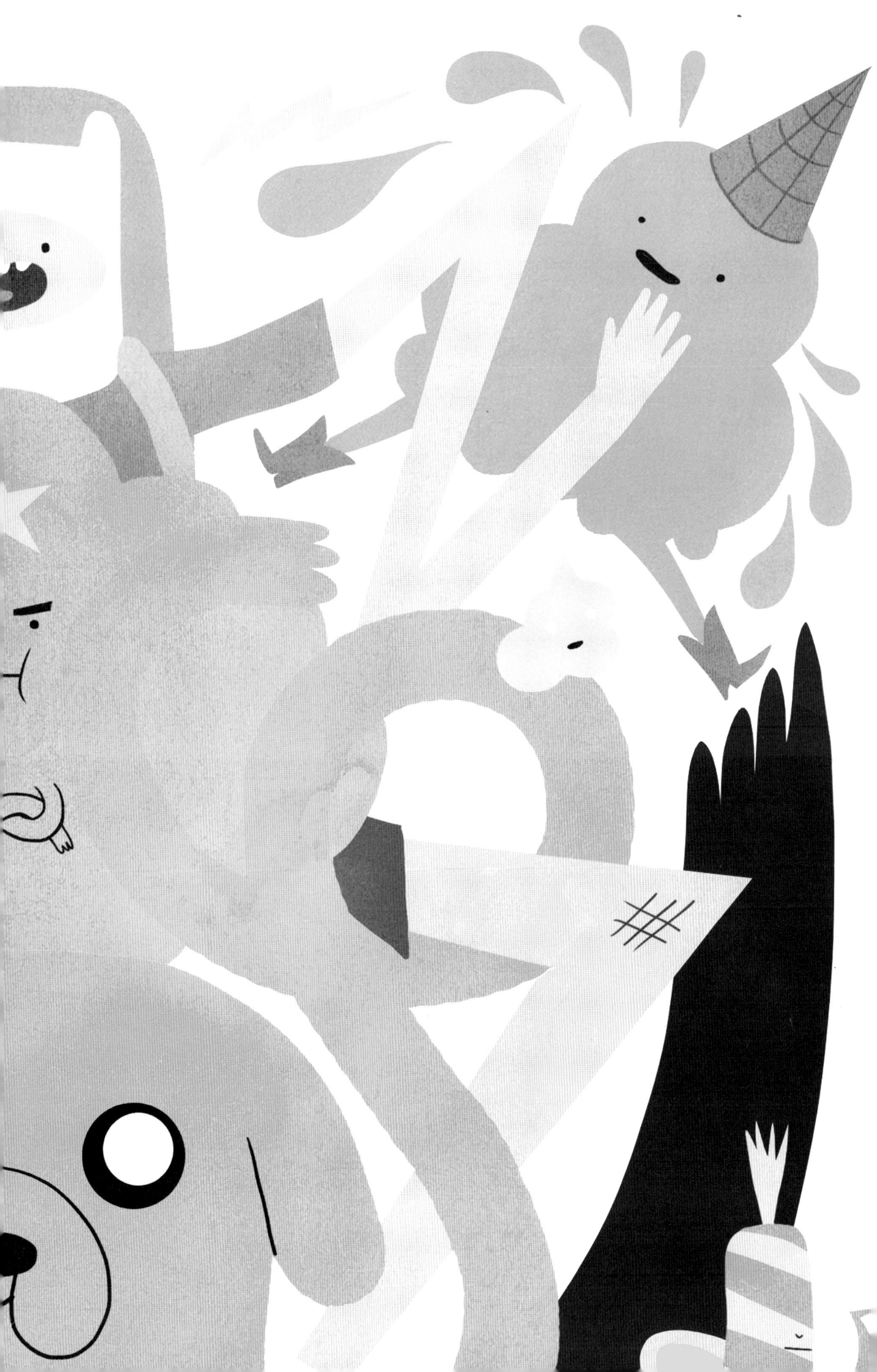

ISSUE ONE

"MAN, YOU KNOW I DON'T JUDGE.
I KINDA LIKE WEARING
JEWELRY TOO SOMETIMES."

-JAKE

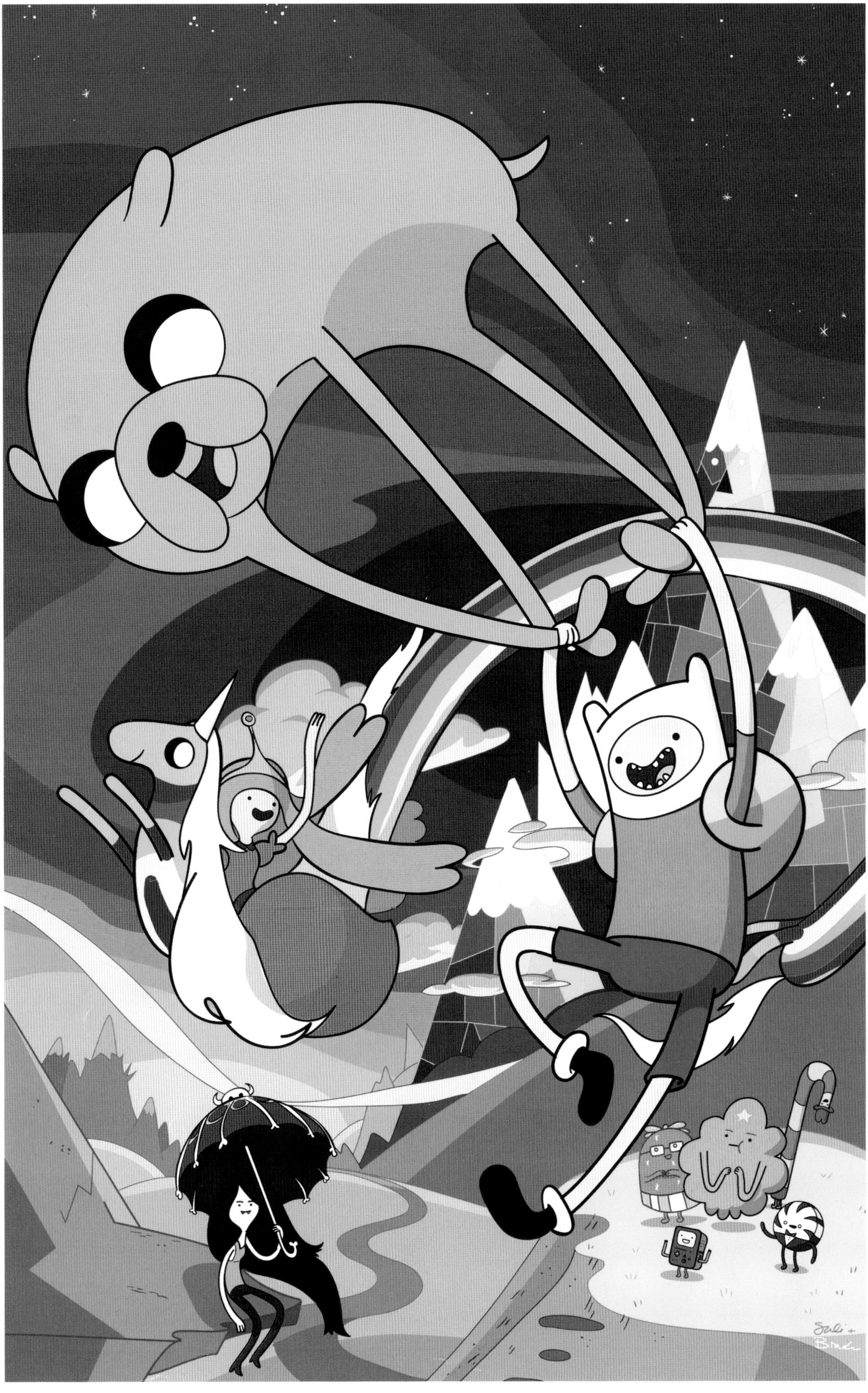

ISSUE ONE | SHELLI PAROLINE & BRADEN LAMB

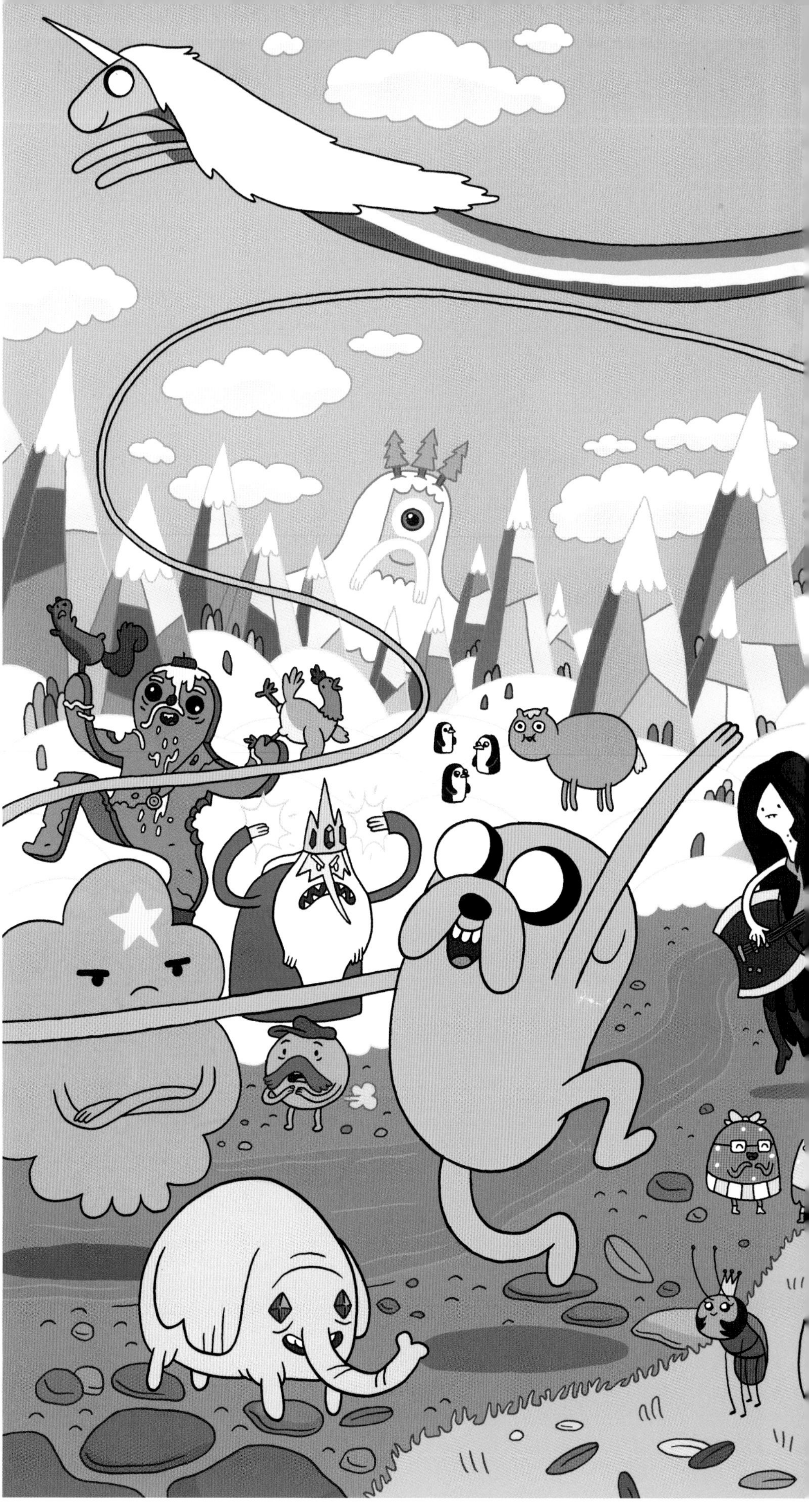

ISSUE ONE
CHRIS HOUGHTON
COLORS BY KASSANDRA HELLER

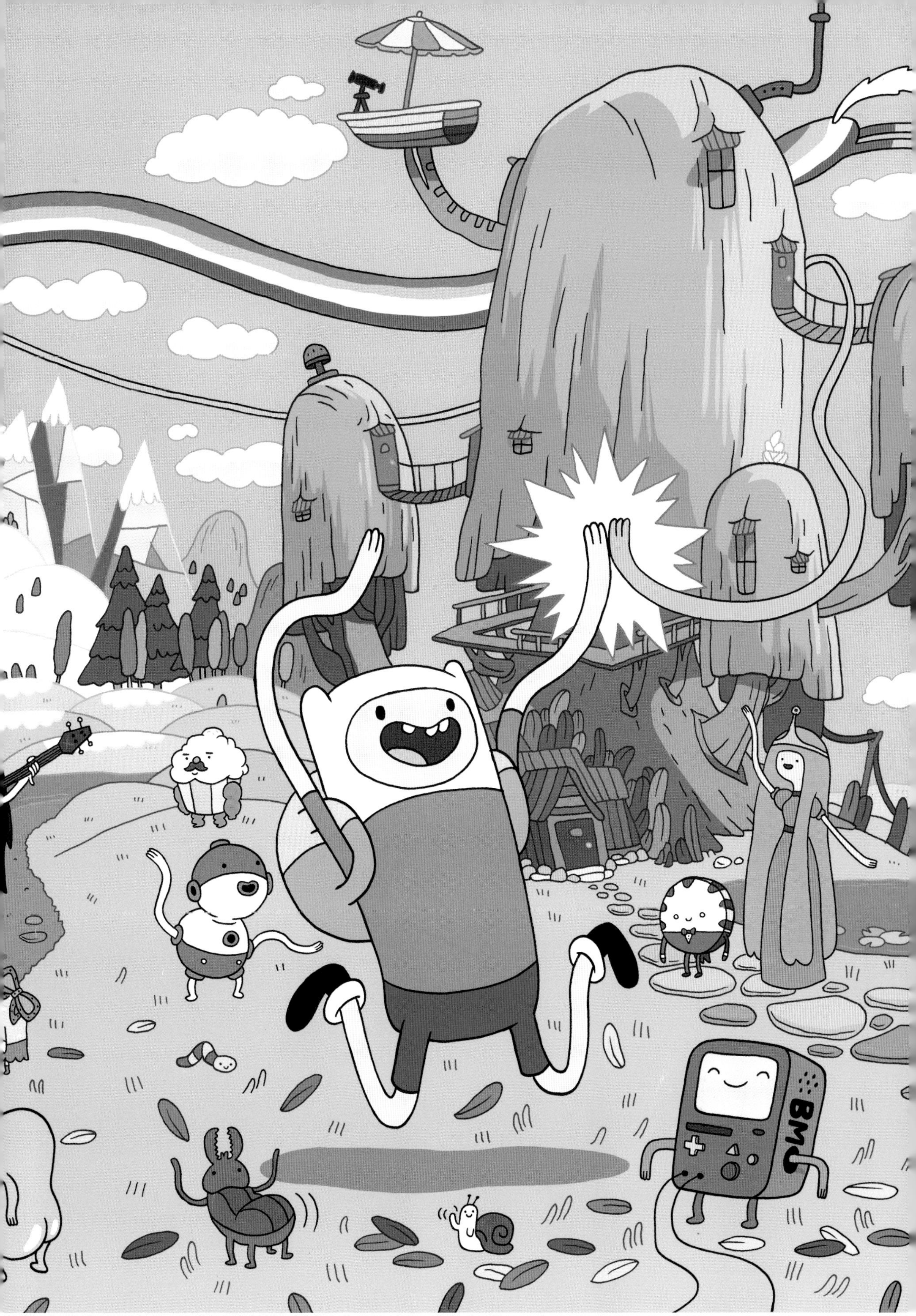
BMO

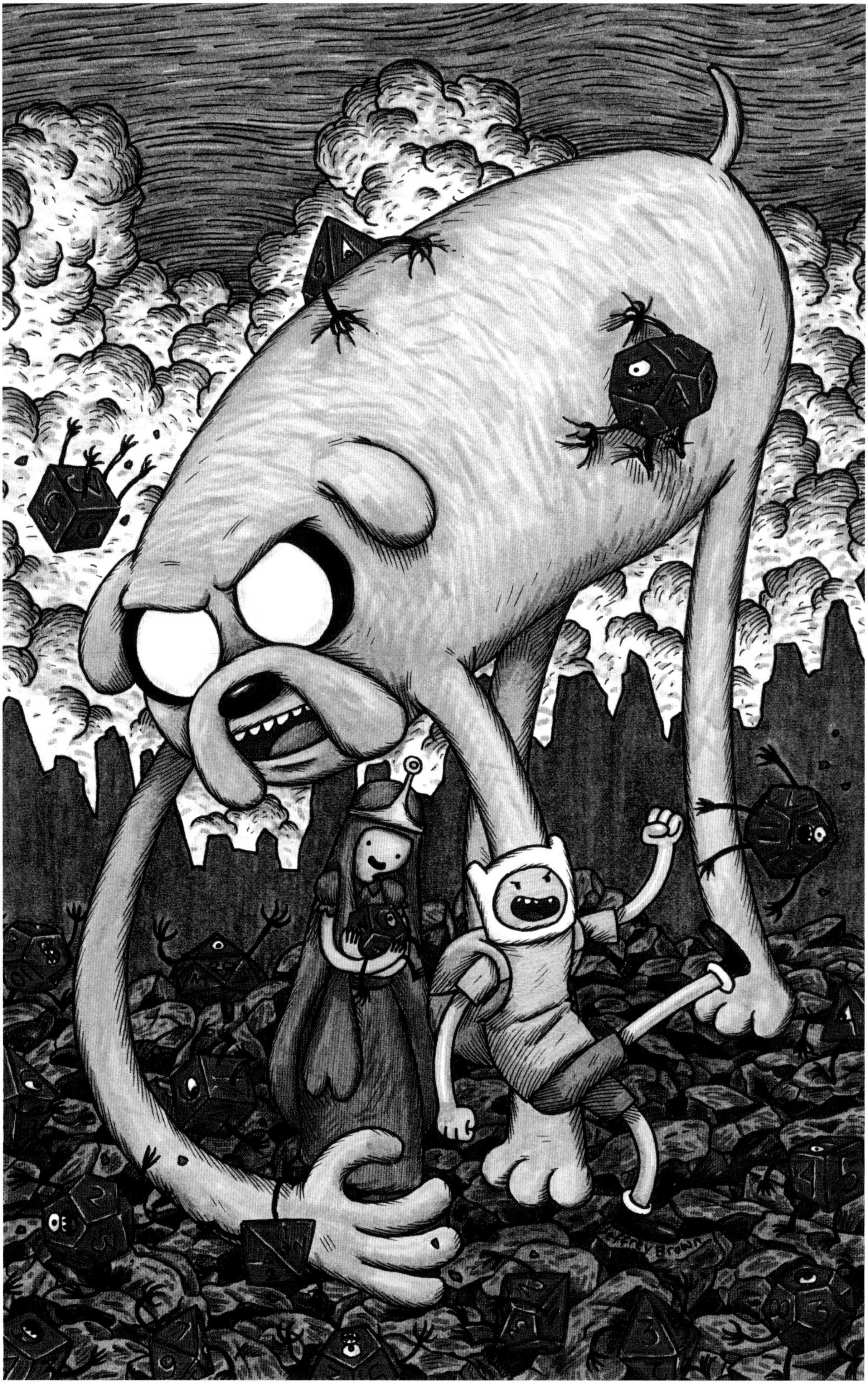

ISSUE ONE | JEFFREY BROWN

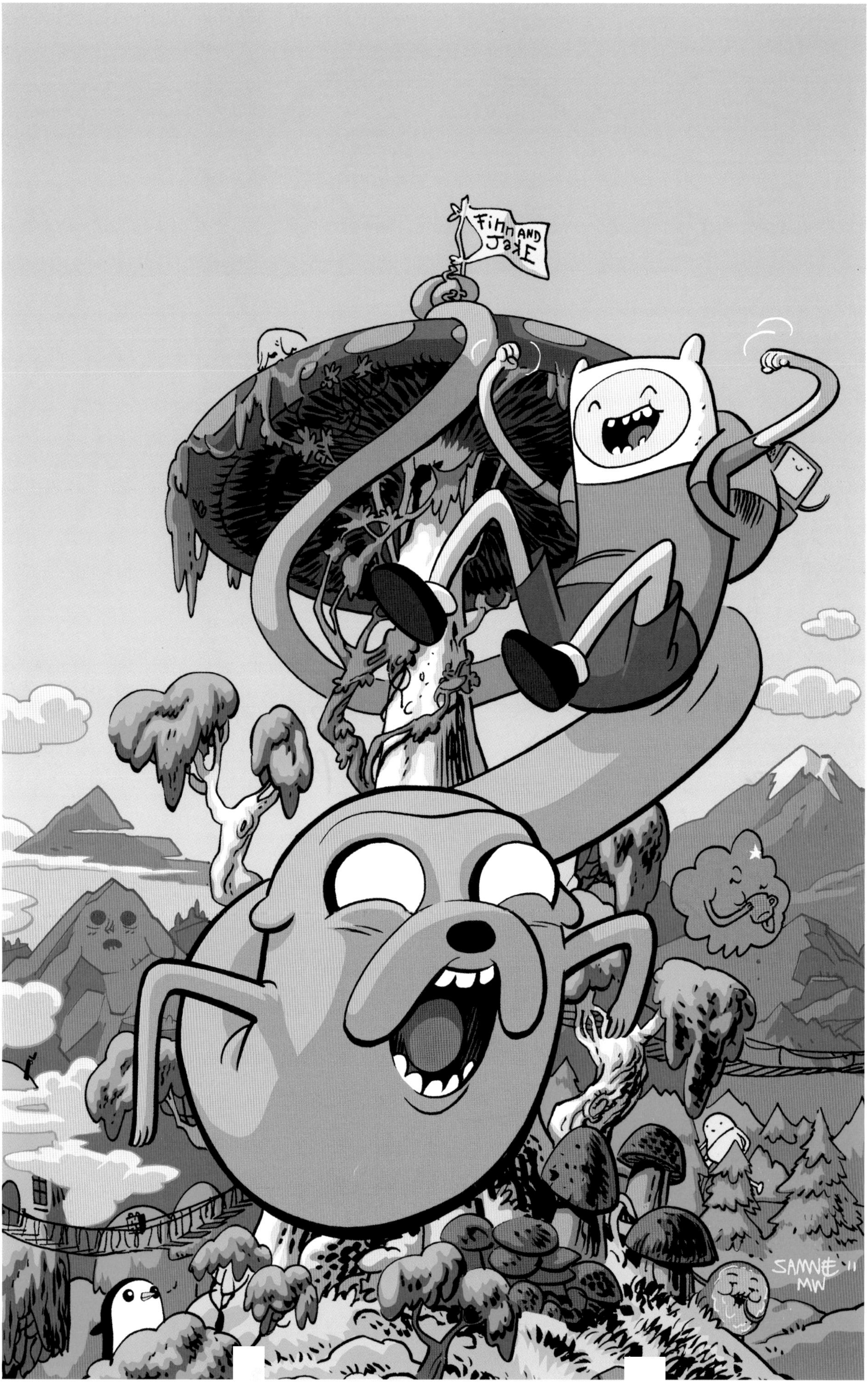
FINN AND JAKE
SAMNEE '11
MW
EMERALD CITY COMICON ISSUE ONE EXCLUSIVE COVER | CHRIS SAMNEE | COLORS BY MATTHEW WILSON

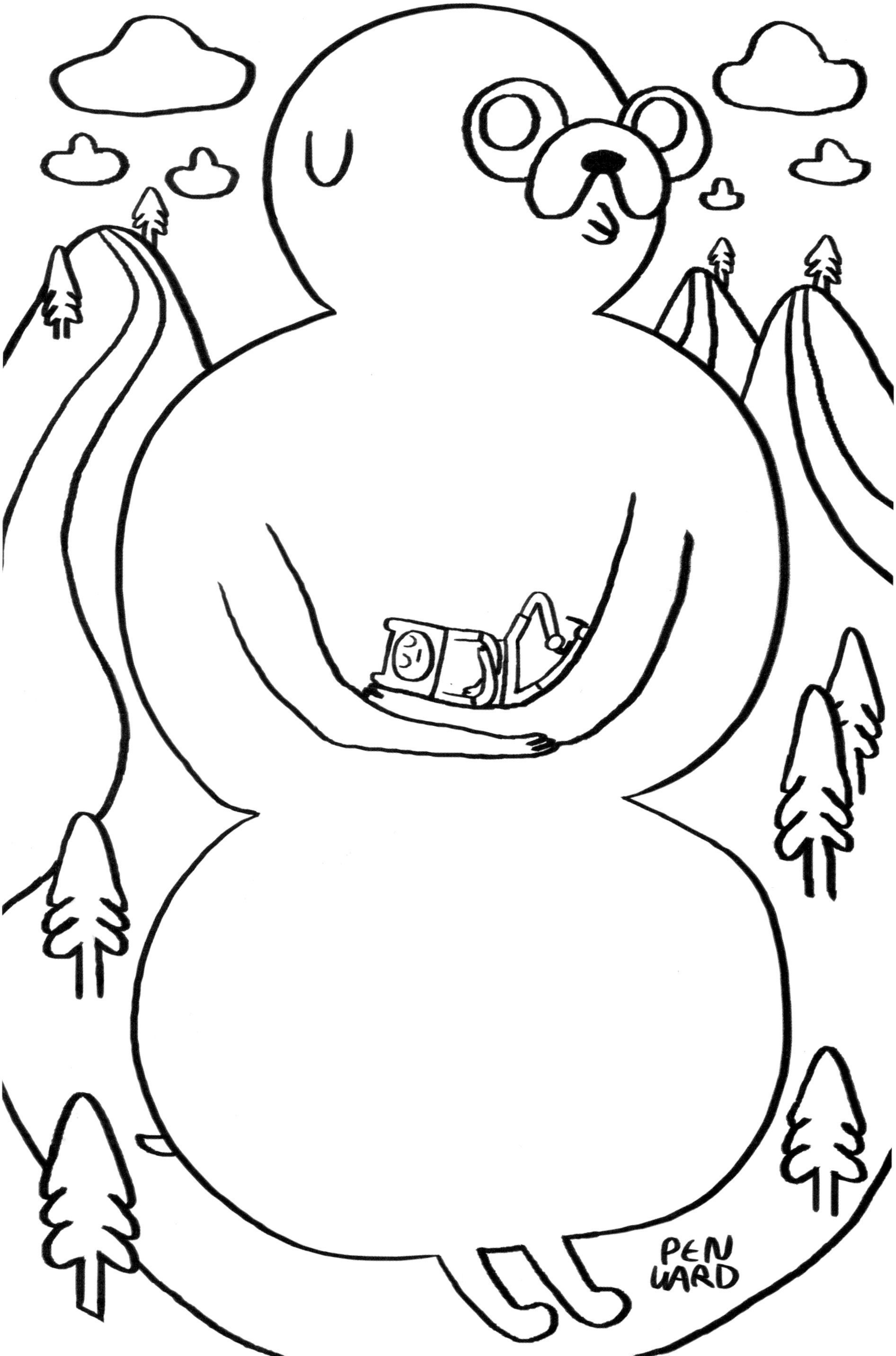
PEN
WARD
SAN DIEGO COMIC-CON ISSUE ONE EXCLUSIVE COVER | PENDLETON WARD

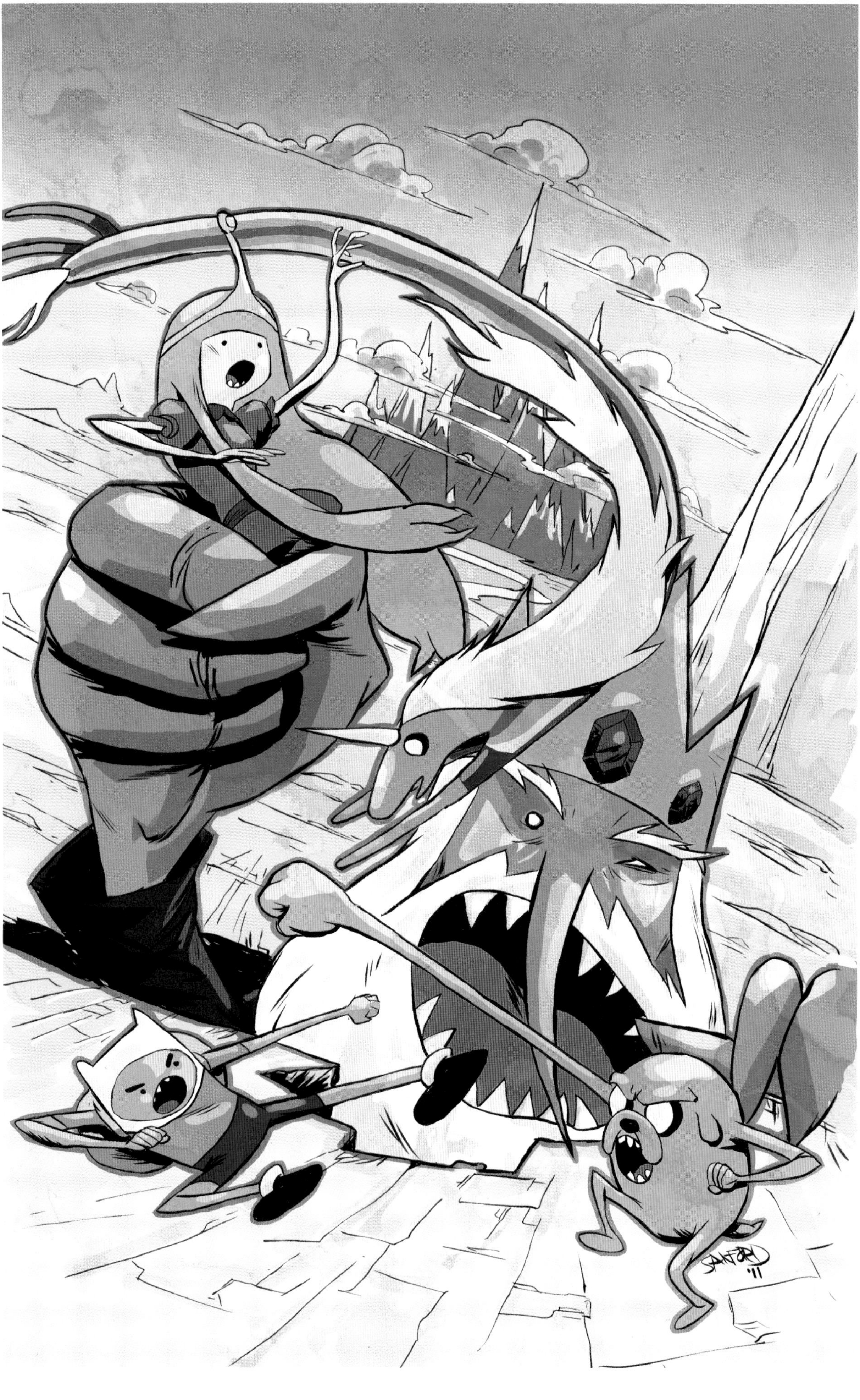
SANFORD '11

ANNAPOLIS COMIC-CON ISSUE ONE EXCLUSIVE COVER | SANFORD GREENE

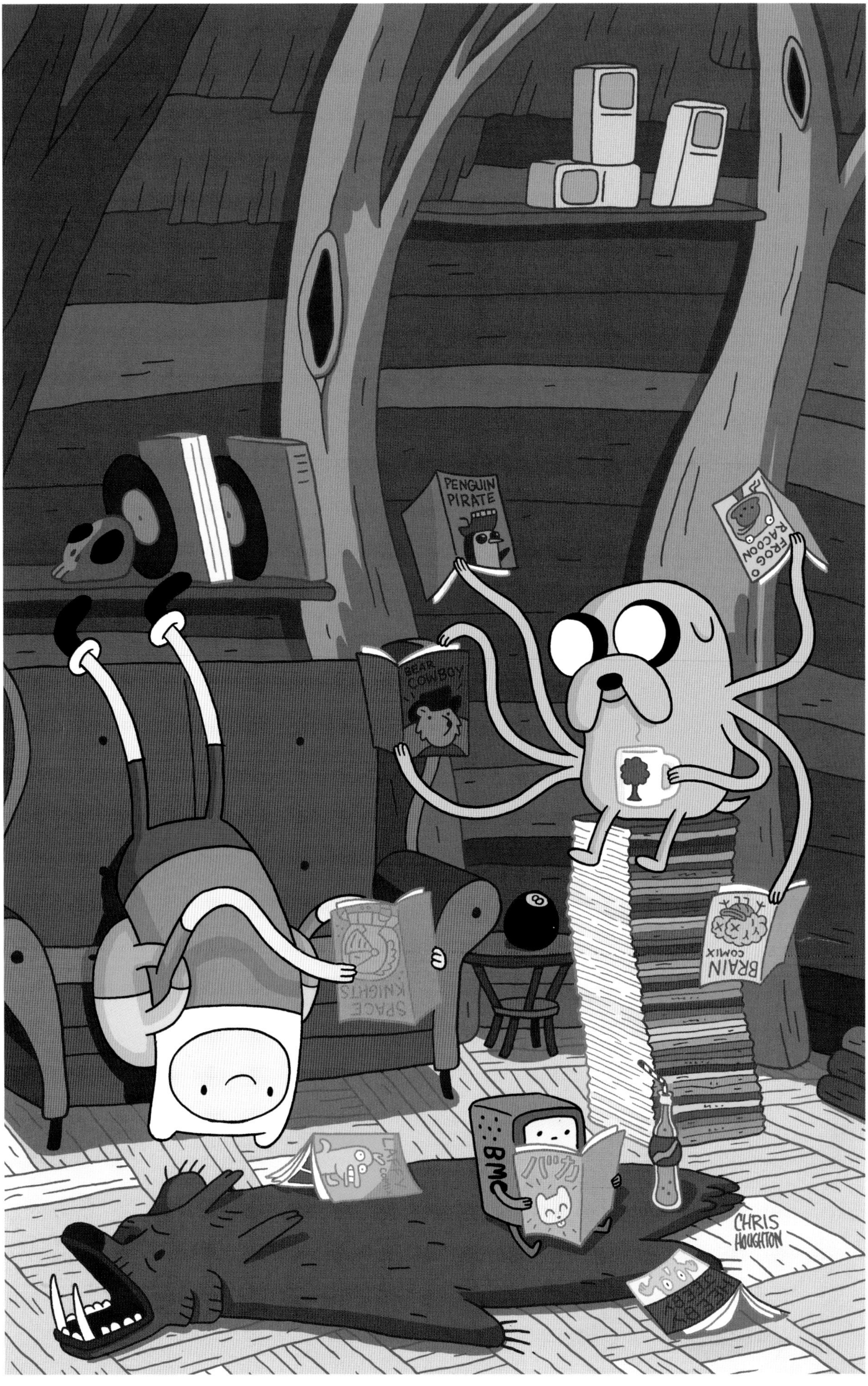
PENGUIN PIRATE
FROG RACOON
BEAR COWBOY
SPACE KNIGHTS
BRAIN COMIX
BMO
バカ
CHRIS HOUGHTON

ISSUE ONE | CHRIS HOUGHTON | COLORS BY KASSANDRA HELLER

ISSUE TWO

"I ACCEPT YOUR VERSION OF EVENTS."

- FINN

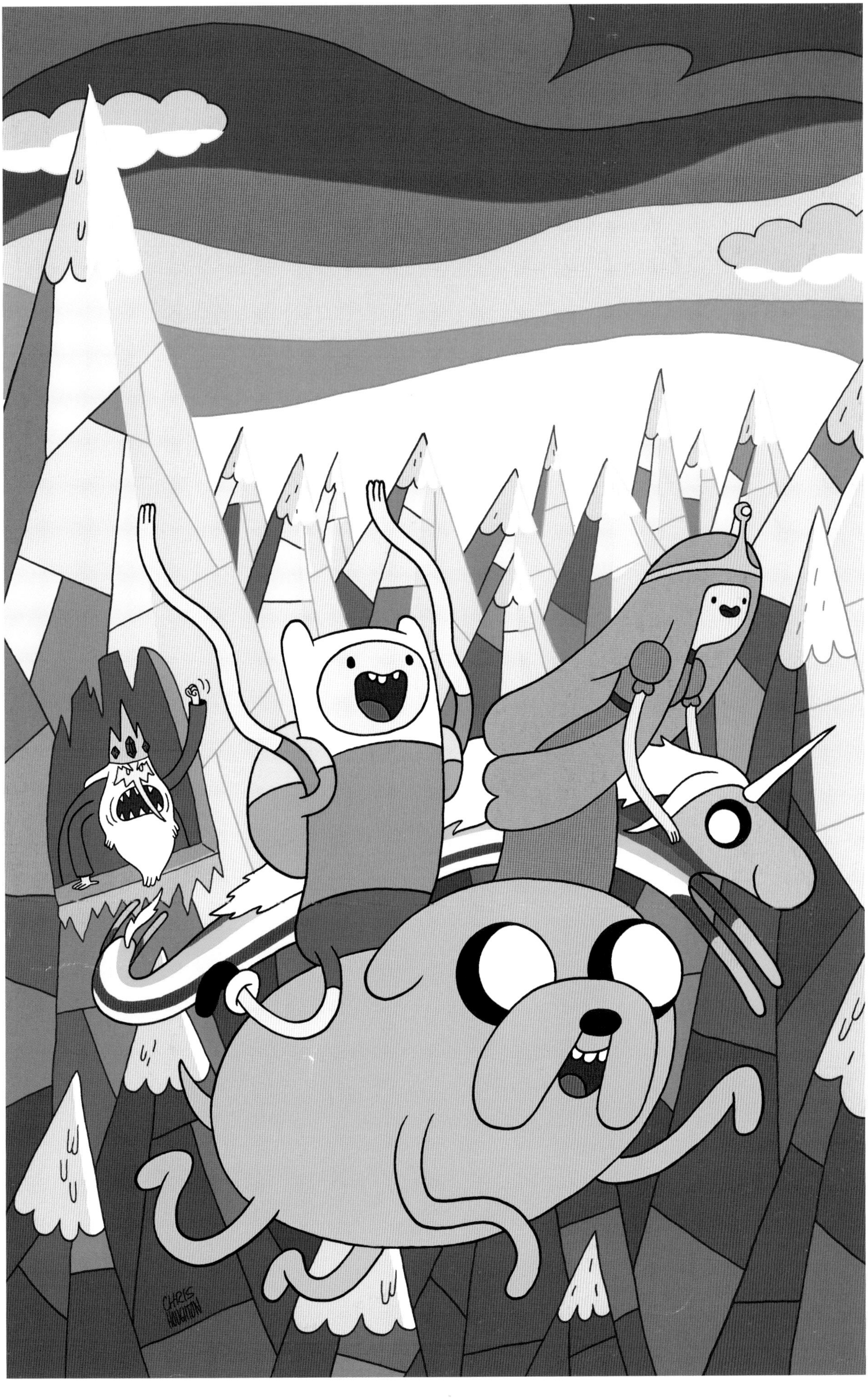
CHRIS
HOUGHTON

ISSUE TWO | CHRIS HOUGHTON | COLORS BY KASSANDRA HELLER

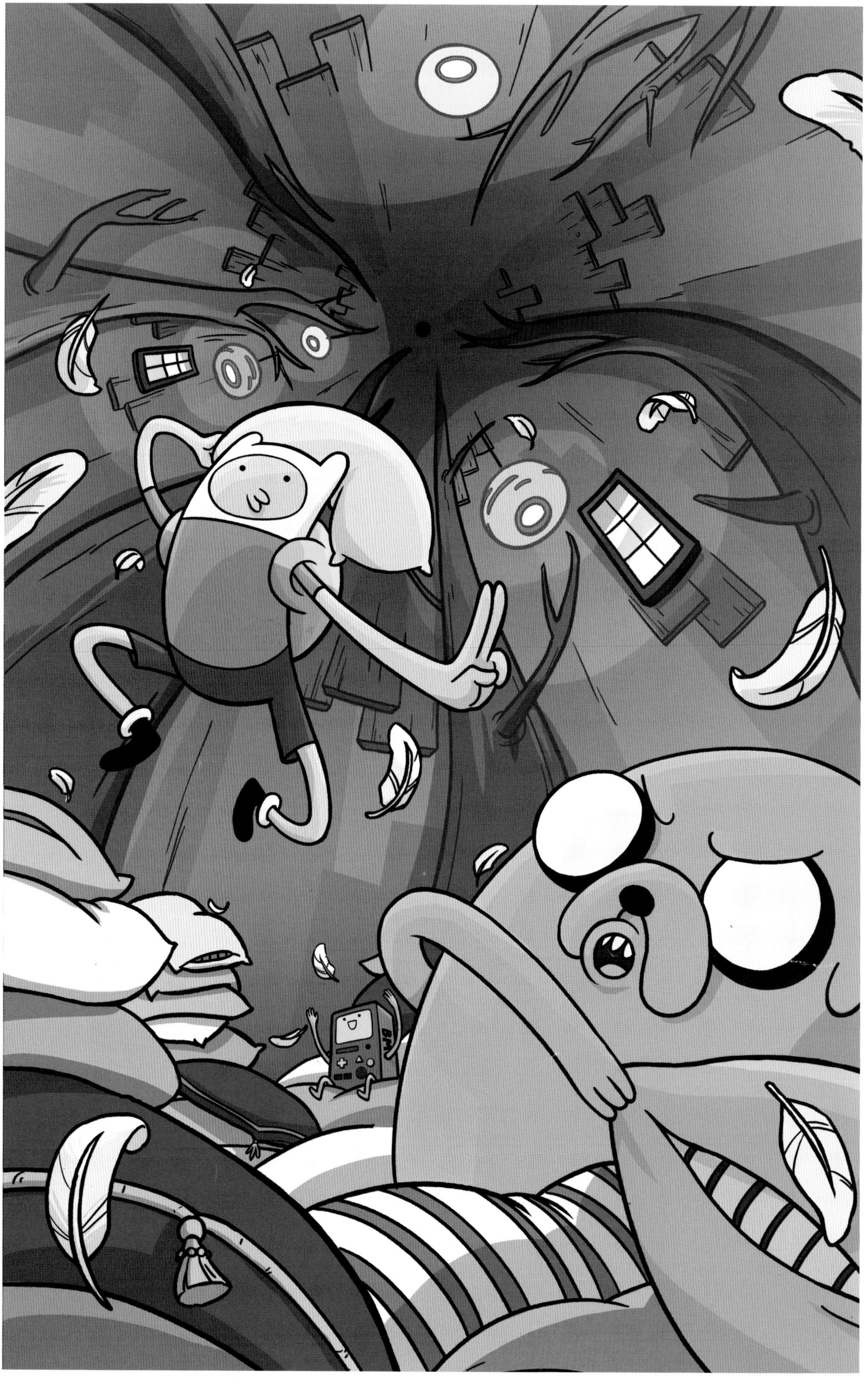
BMO

ISSUE TWO | JEN BENNETT | COLORS BY BRADEN LAMB

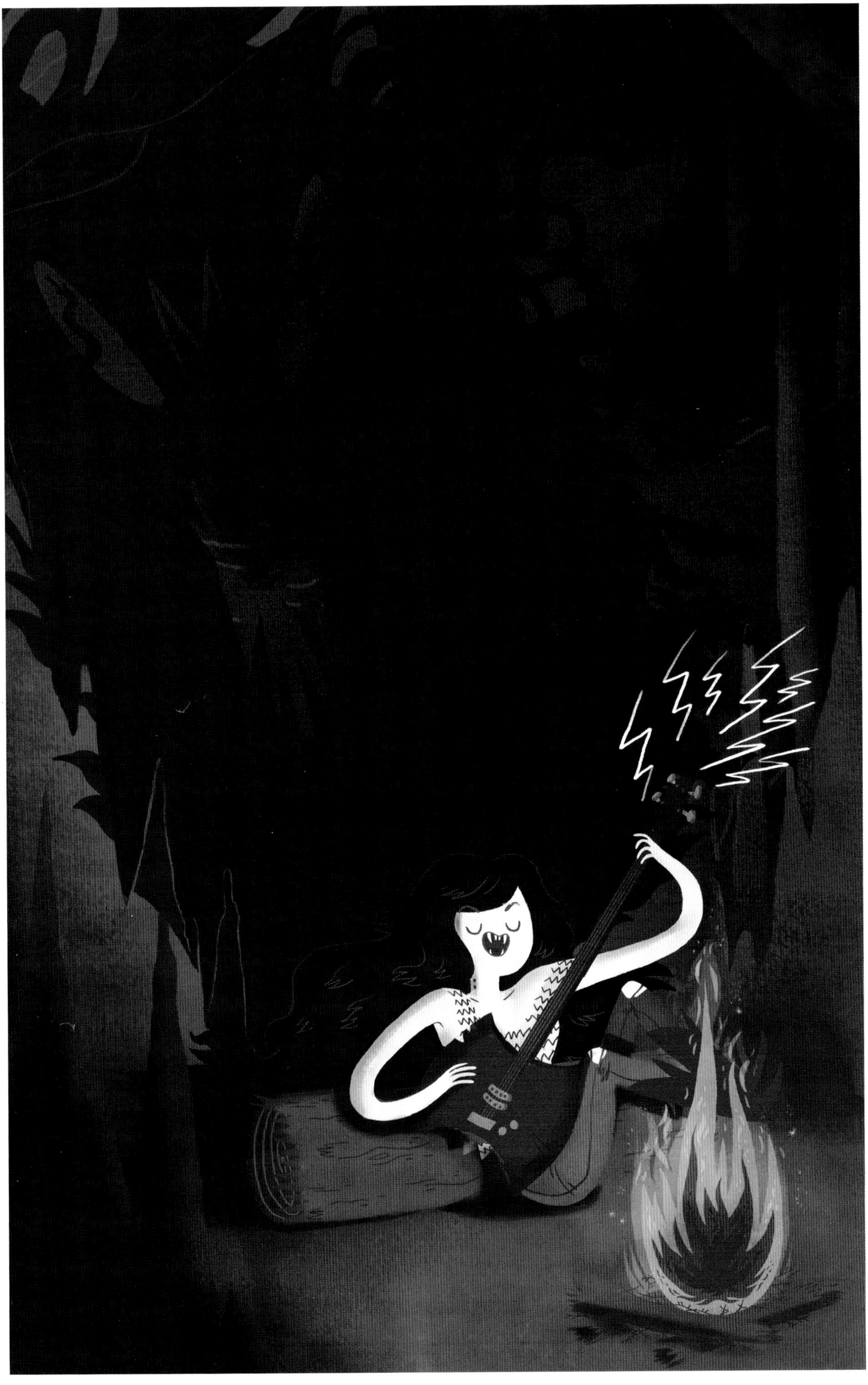

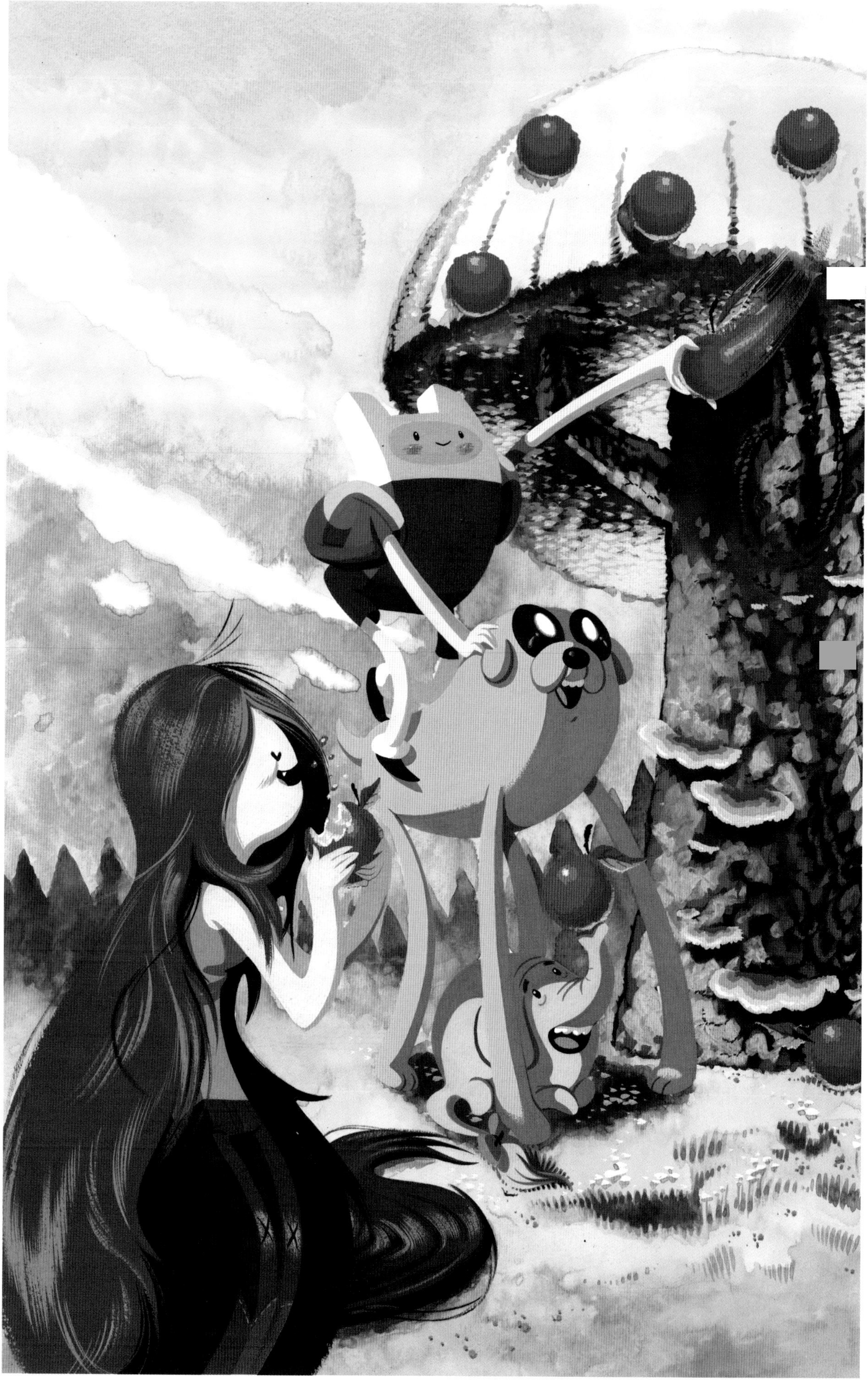

ISSUE TWO | BECKY DREISTADT & FRANK GIBSON

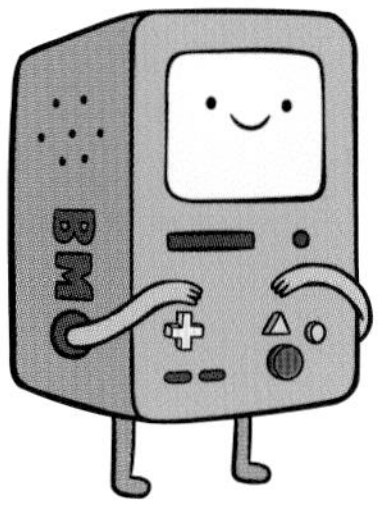
BMO

ISSUE THREE

"THAT DIDN'T GO NEARLY AS WELL AS IT DID IN MY IMAGINATION."

- FINN

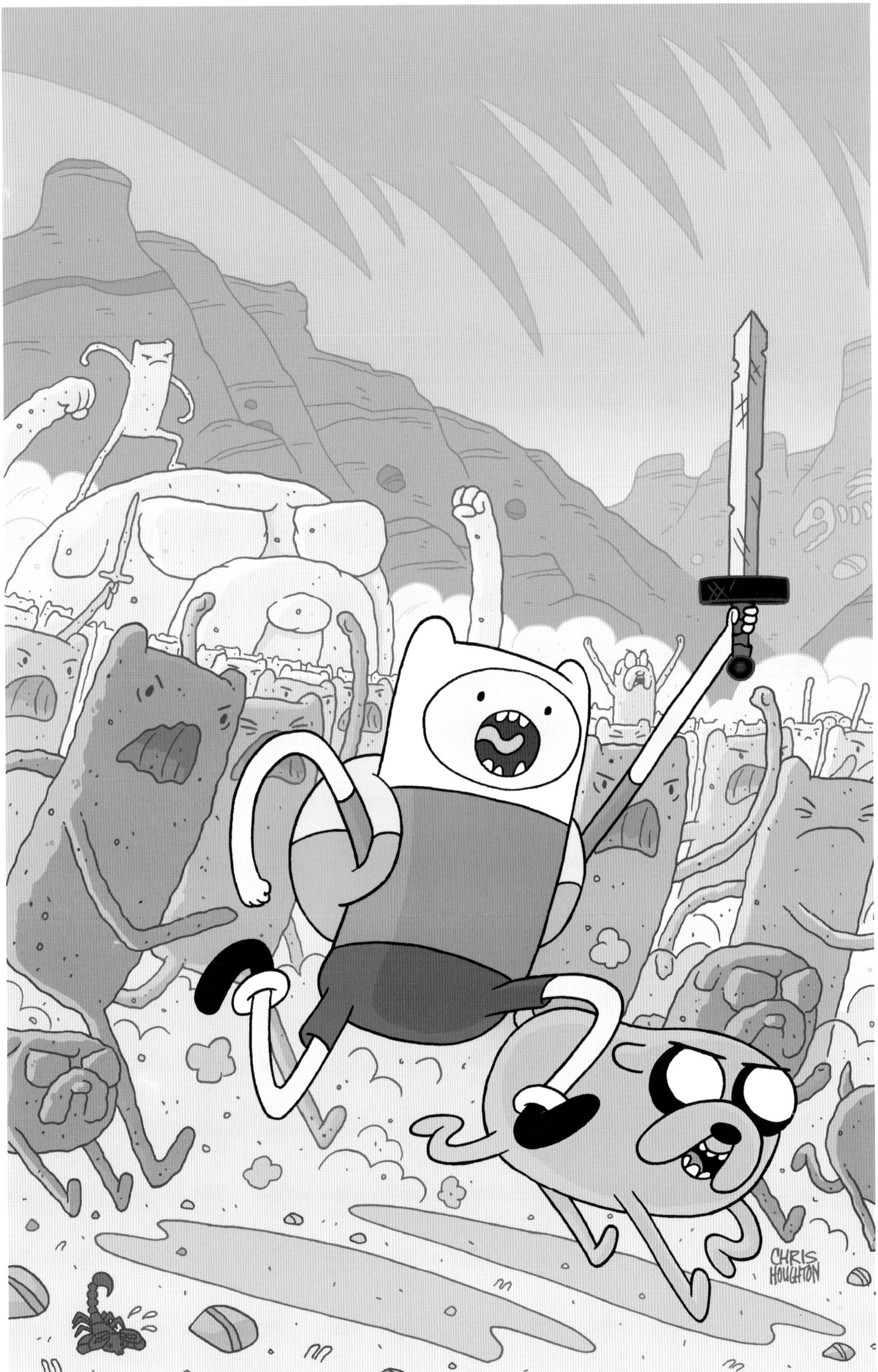
CHRIS HOUGHTON

ISSUE THREE | CHRIS HOUGHTON | COLORS BY KASSANDRA HELLER

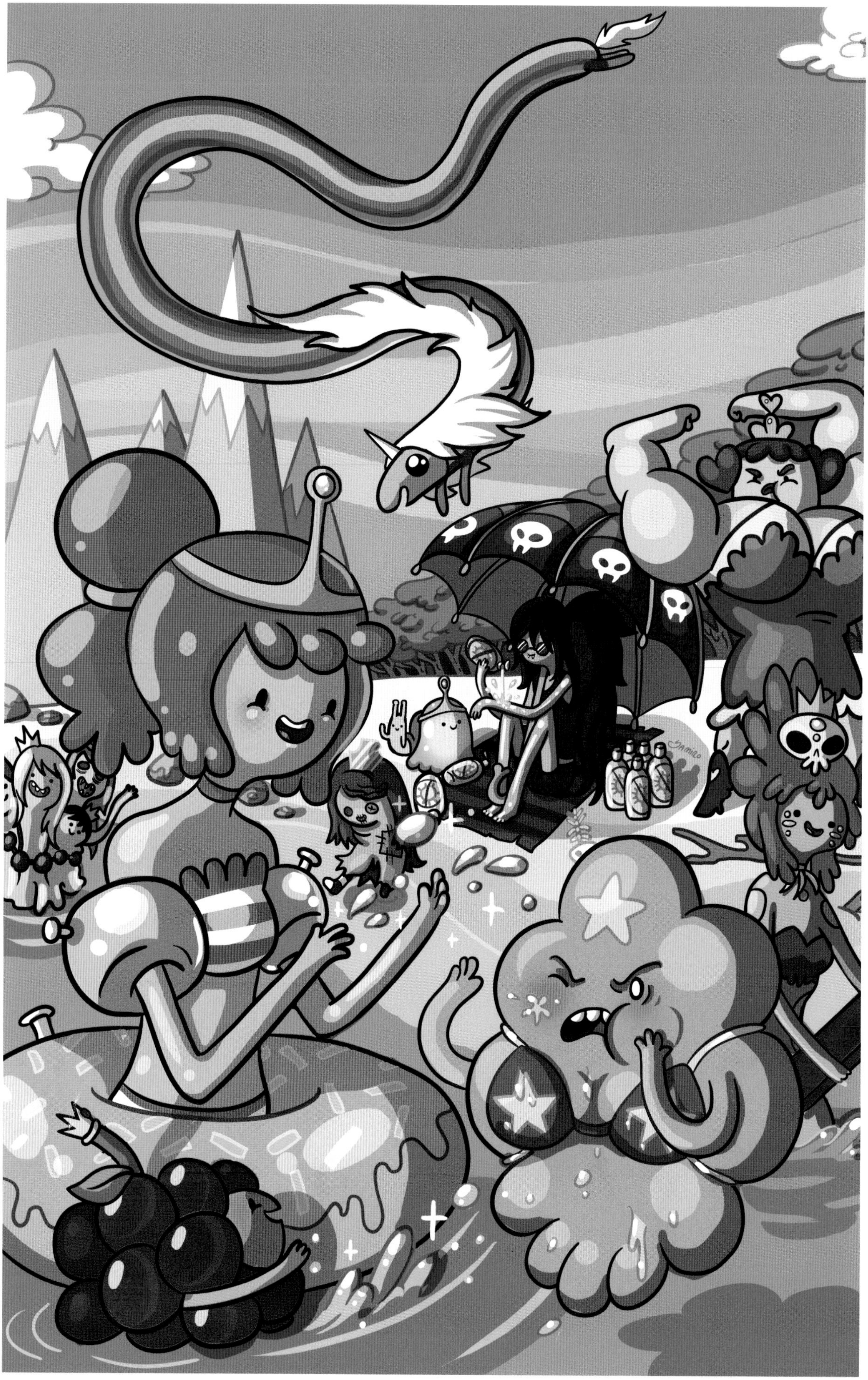

ISSUE THREE | ELENA BARBARICH

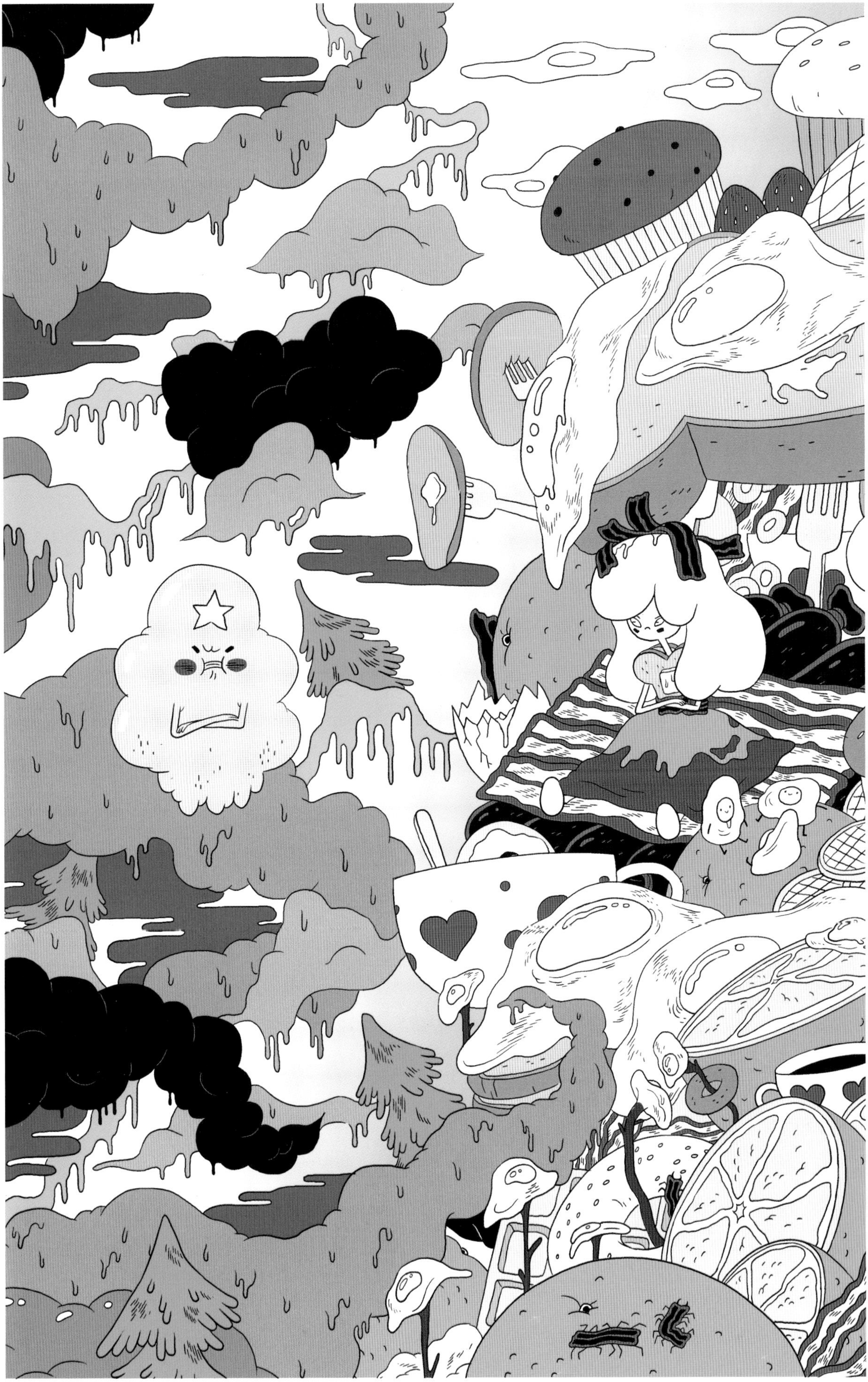

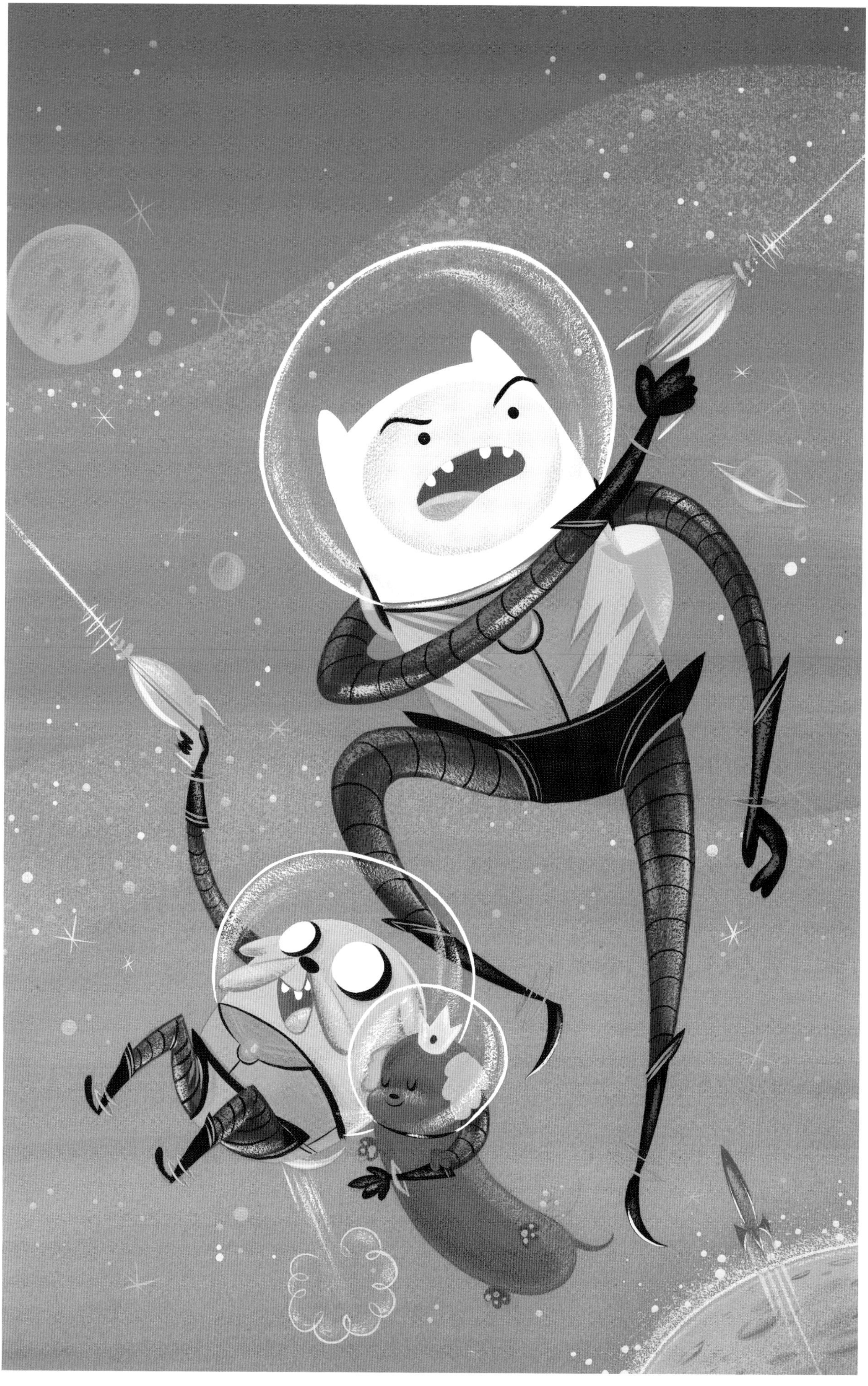

ISSUE THREE | STEPHANIE BUSCEMA

ISSUE FOUR

"WELP, I'M OUT. THAT'S MY
LIMIT OF CRAZY FOR TODAY!"

- ICE KING

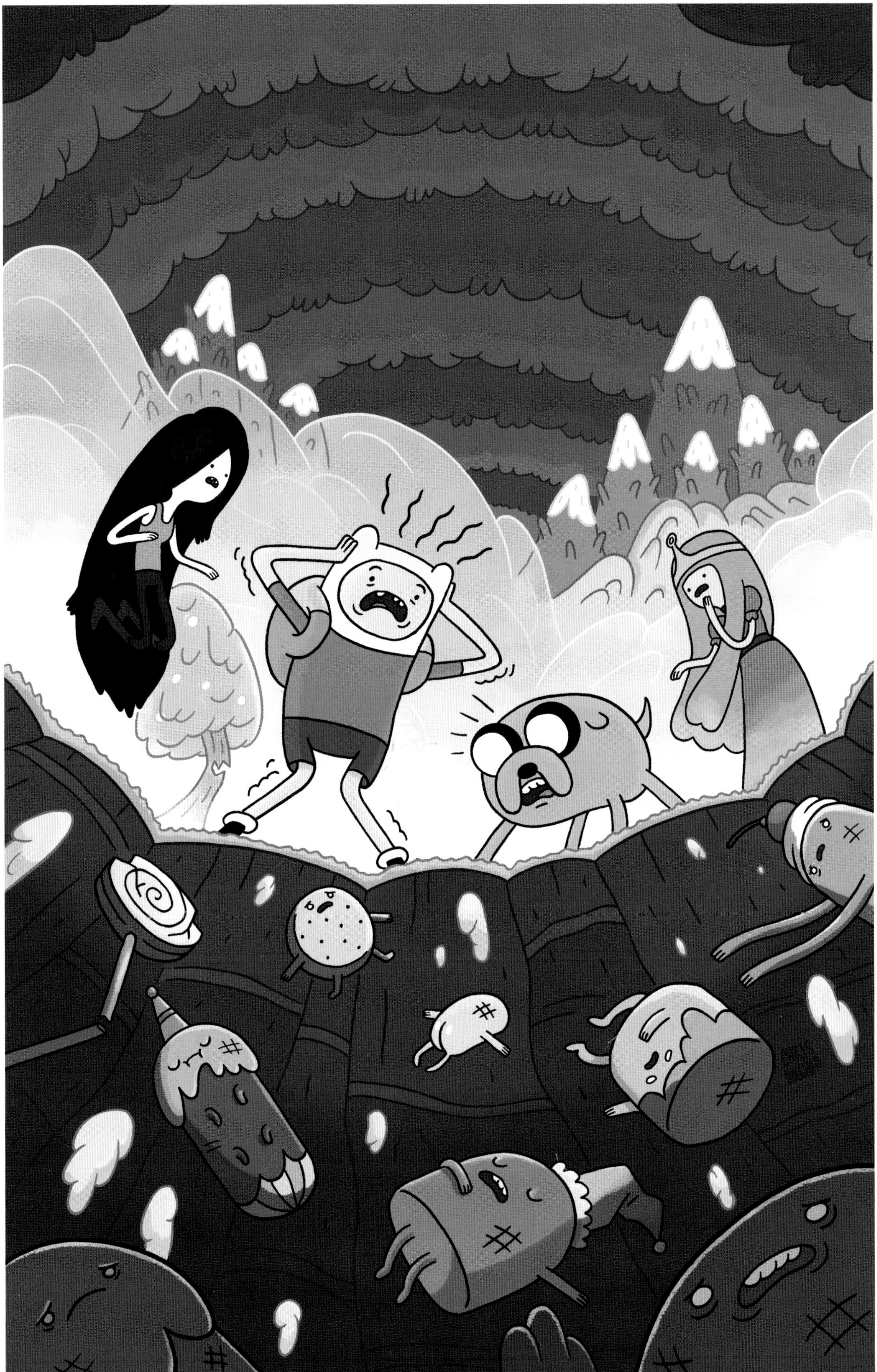

ISSUE FOUR | CHRIS HOUGHTON | COLORS BY KASSANDRA HELLER

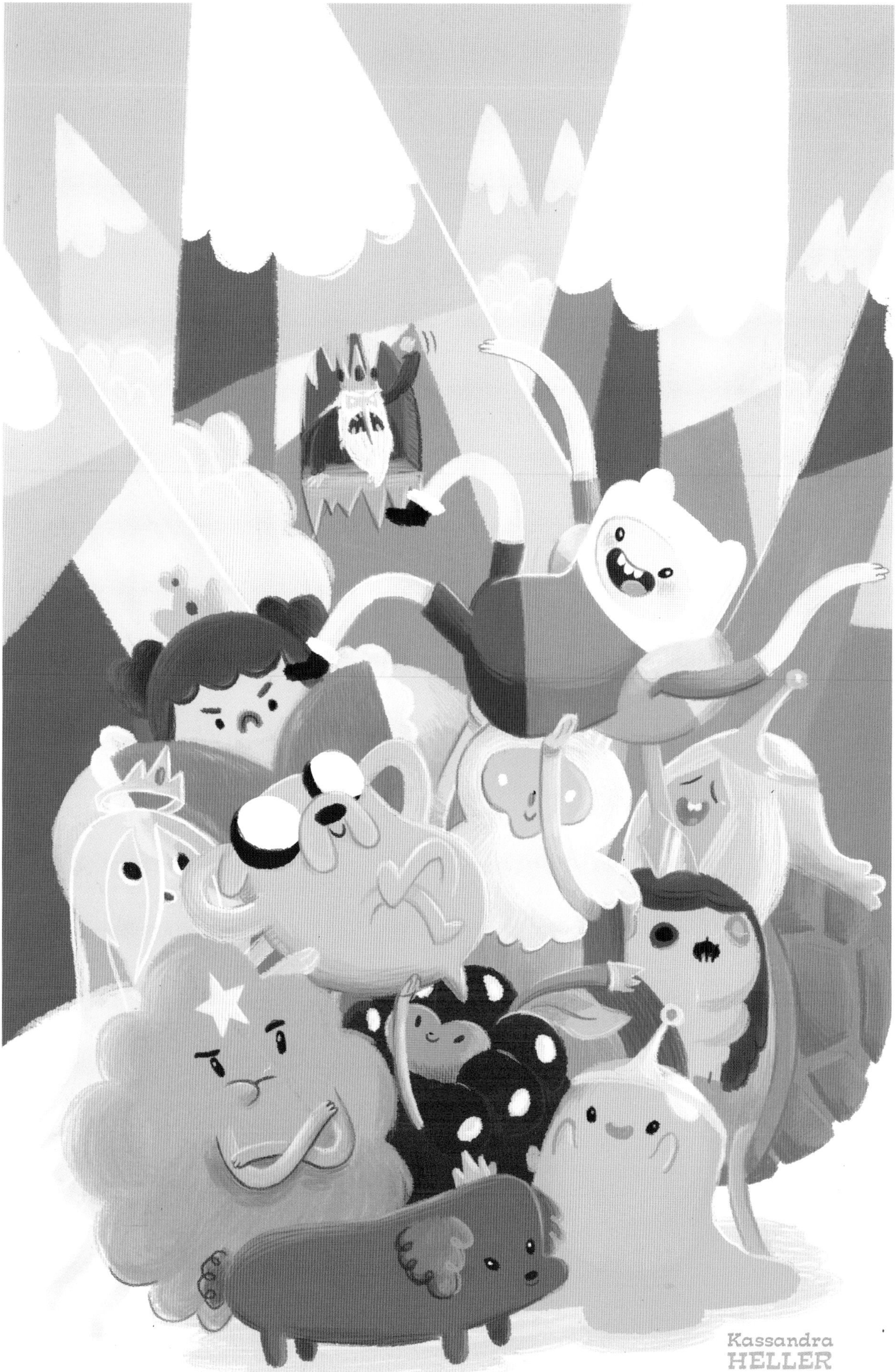
Kassandra
HELLER

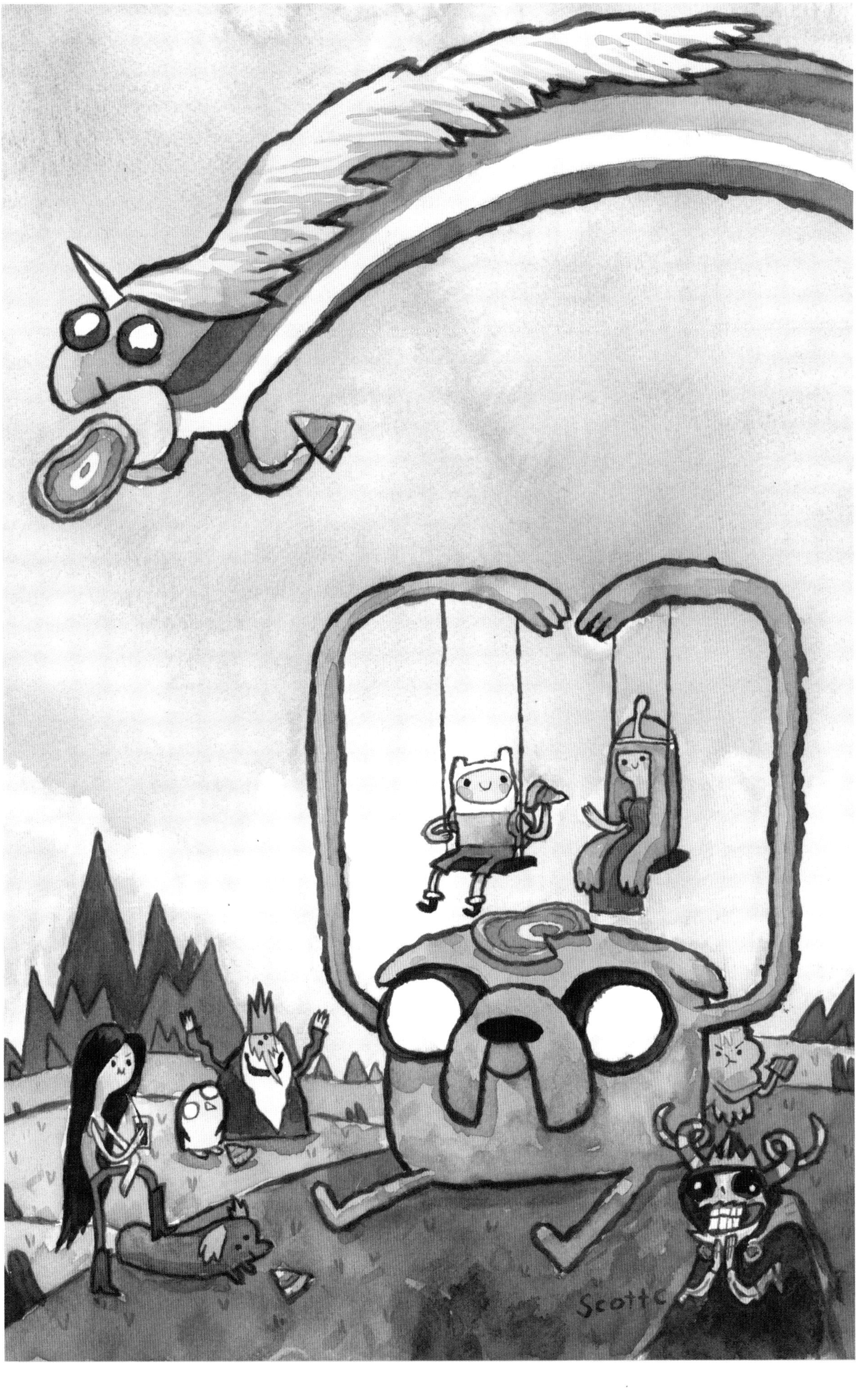
Scott C

ISSUE FOUR | SCOTT C.

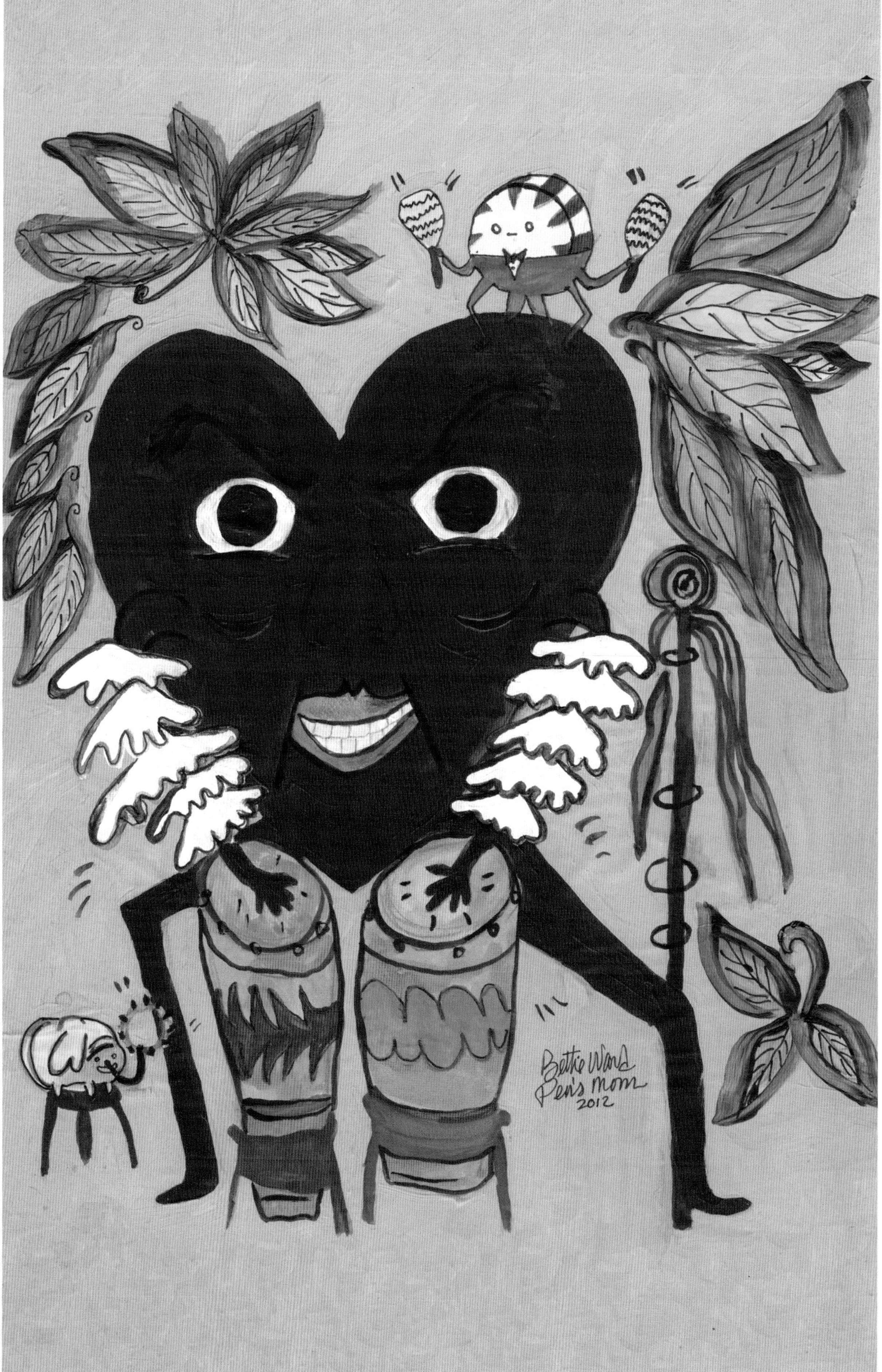
Bettie Ward
Pen's mom
2012

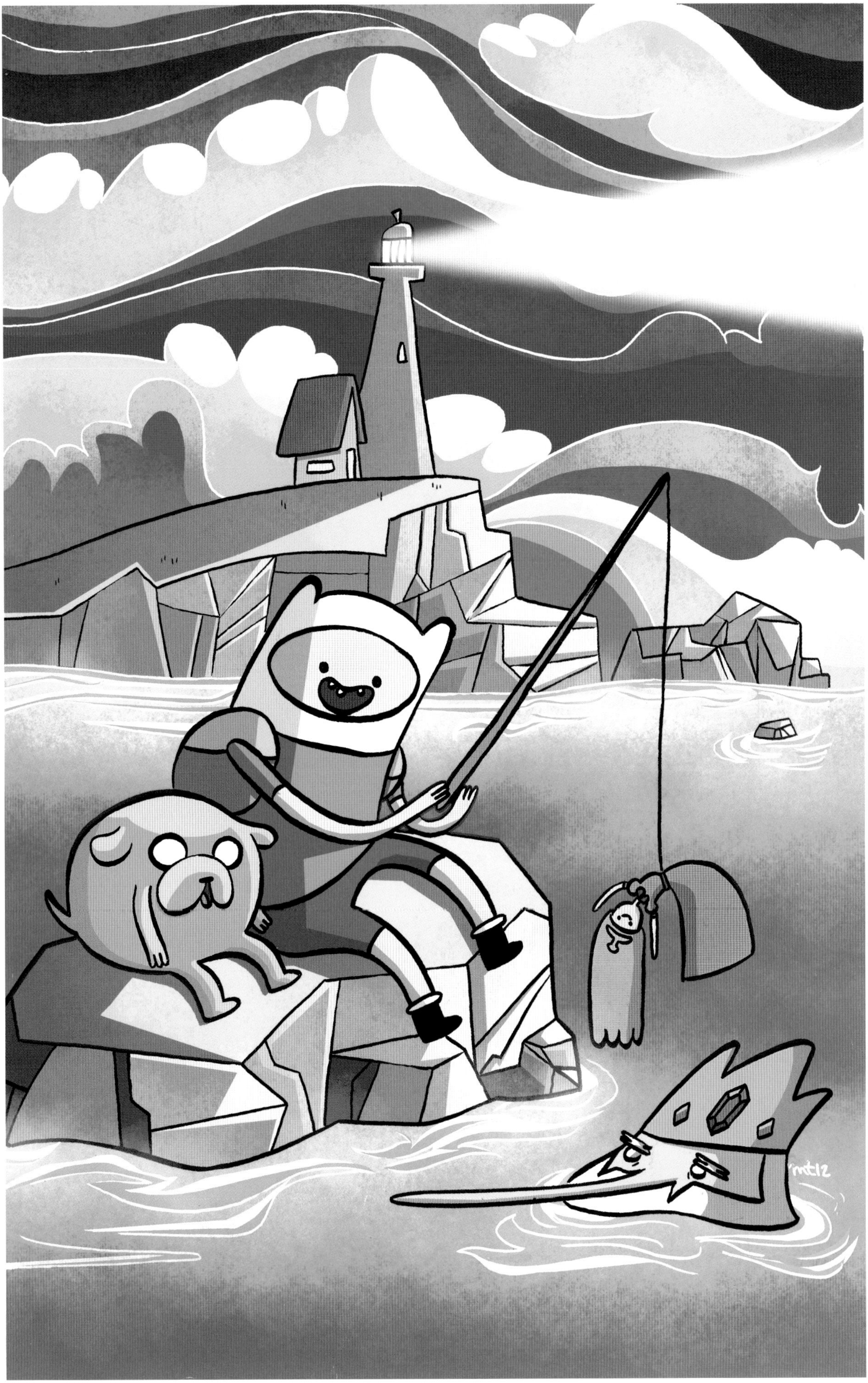
mt12

MAINE COMIC ARTS FESTIVAL ISSUE FOUR EXCLUSIVE | MELANIE TINGDAHL | COLORS BY LISA MOORE

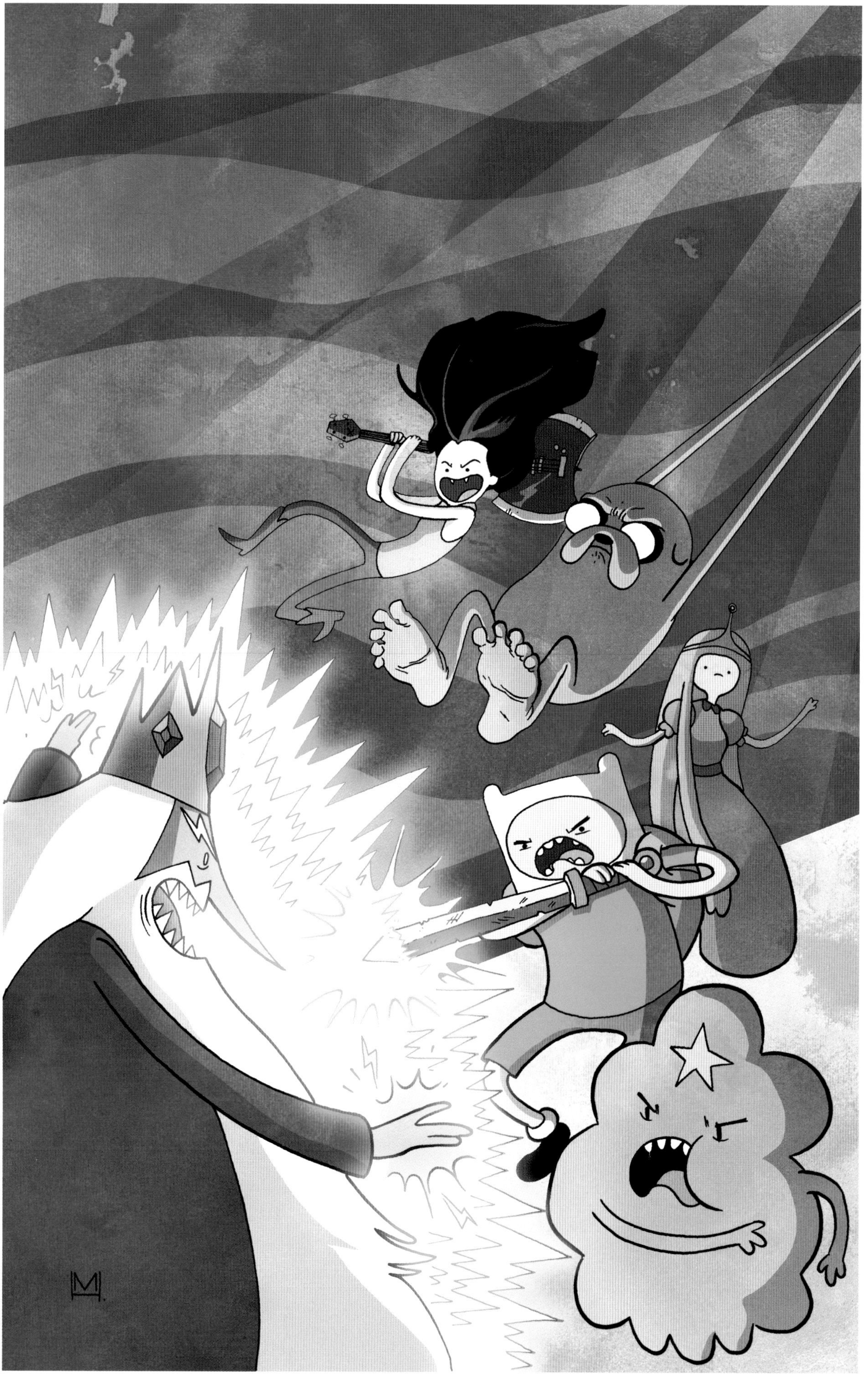

DOUBLE MIDNIGHT COMICS ISSUE FOUR EXCLUSIVE | MIKE HOLMES | COLORS BY LISA MOORE

ISSUE FIVE

"WELL, YOU'RE JUST LUCKY
THAT WALL DIDN'T GO UP INFINITY HIGH."

- FINN

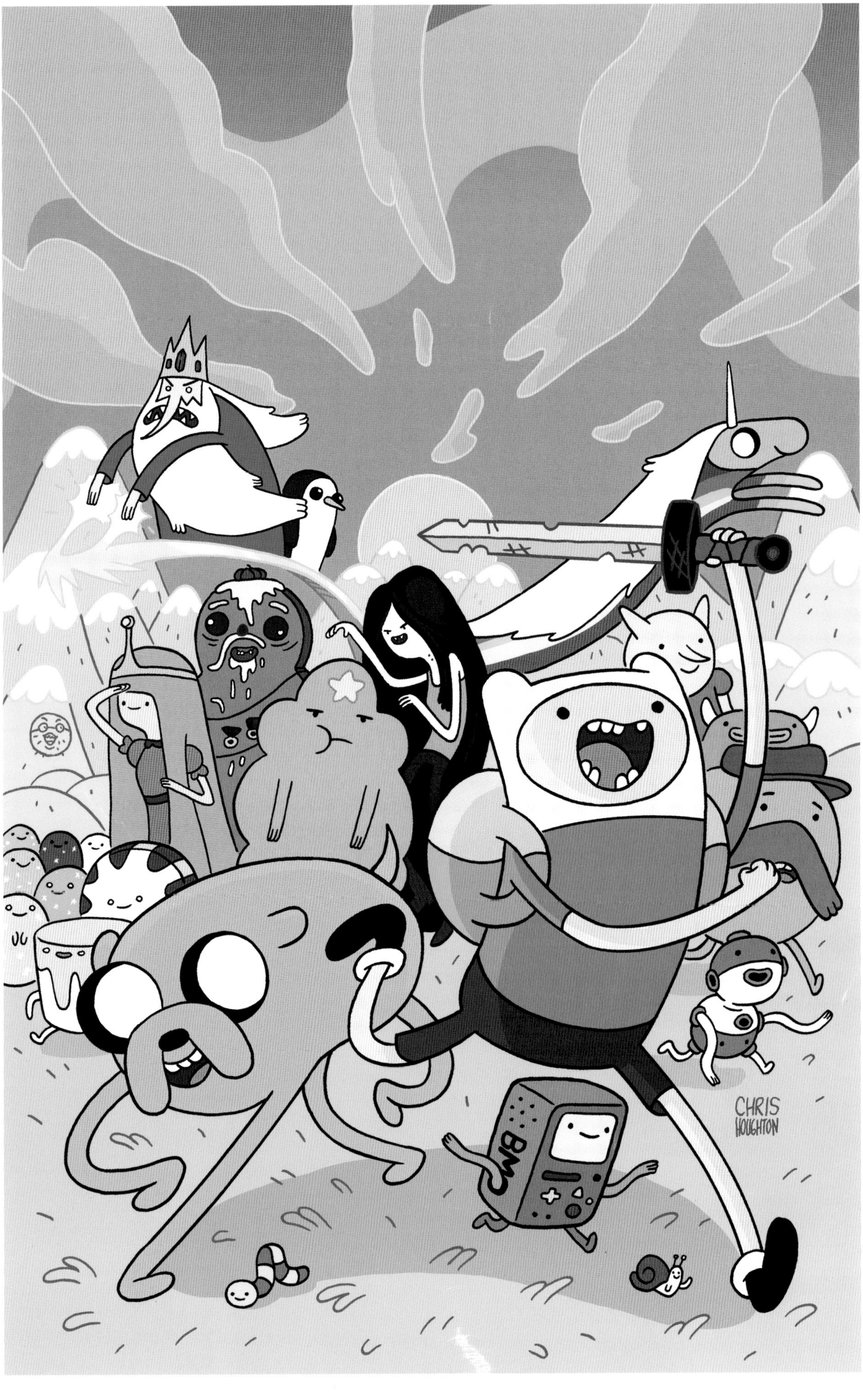
BMO
CHRIS
HOUGHTON

ISSUE FIVE | CHRIS HOUGHTON | COLORS BY KASSANDRA HELLER

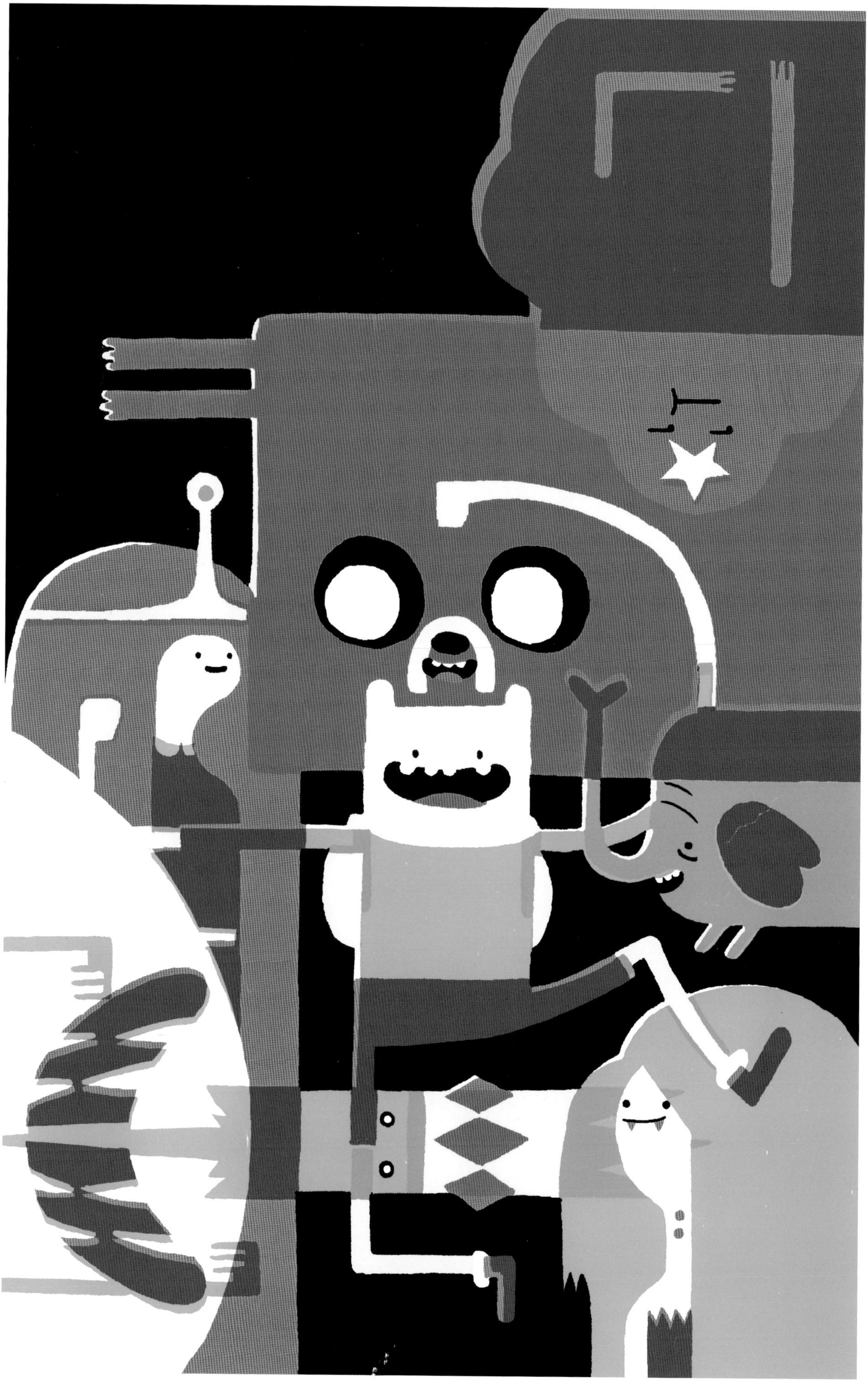

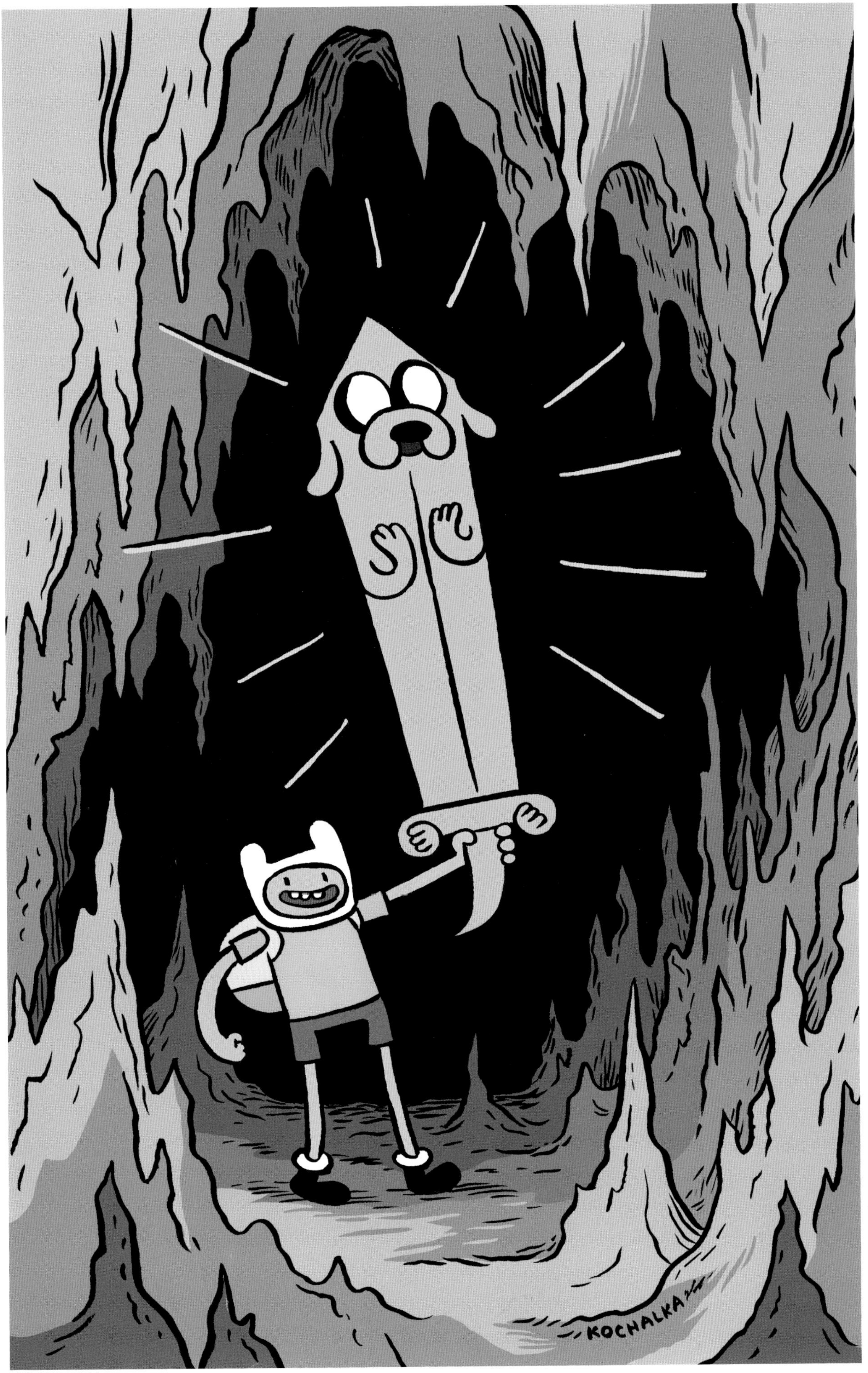
KOCHALKA

ISSUE FIVE | JAMES KOCHALKA

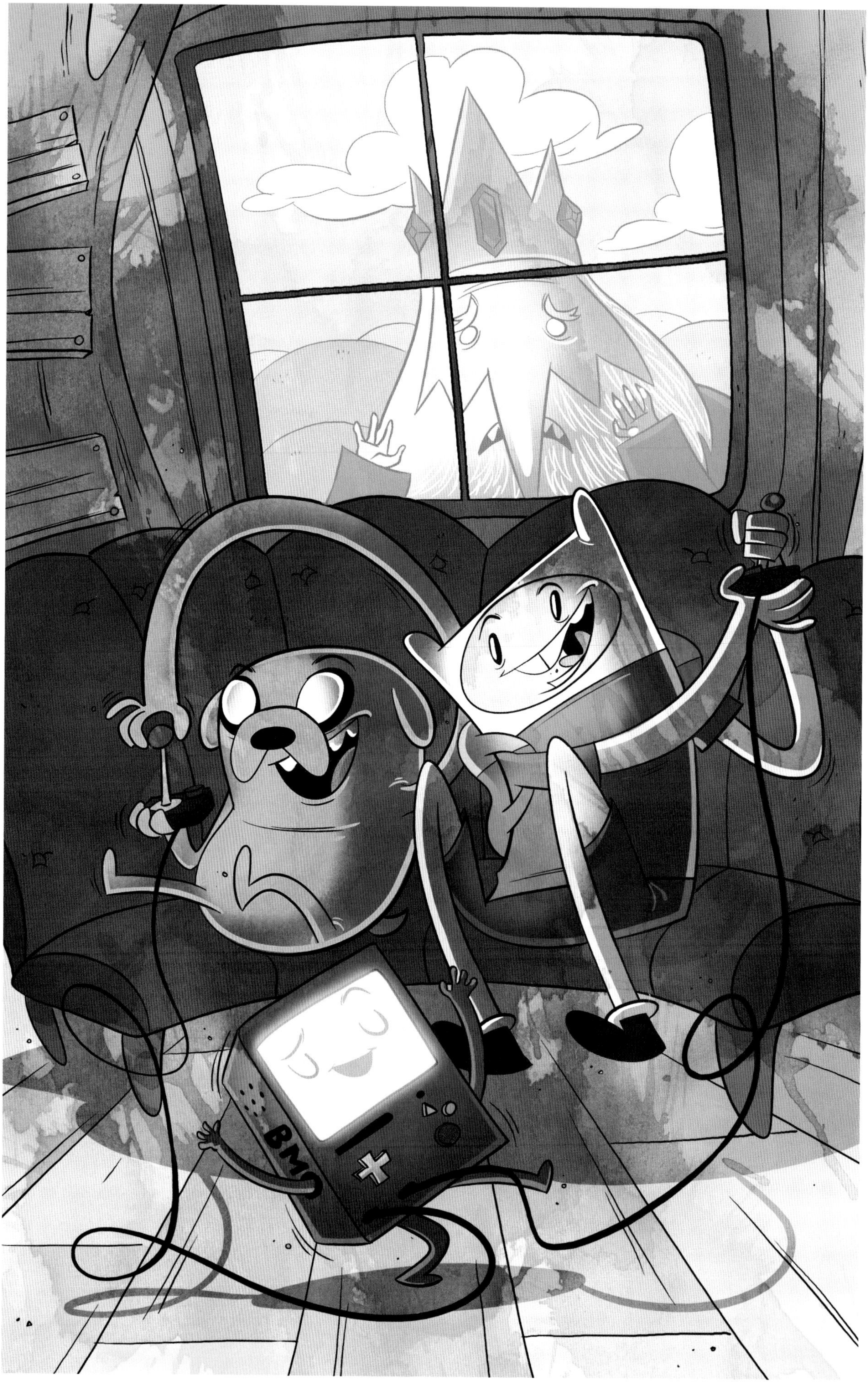
BMO

ISSUE FIVE | MIKE "GABE" KRAHULIK

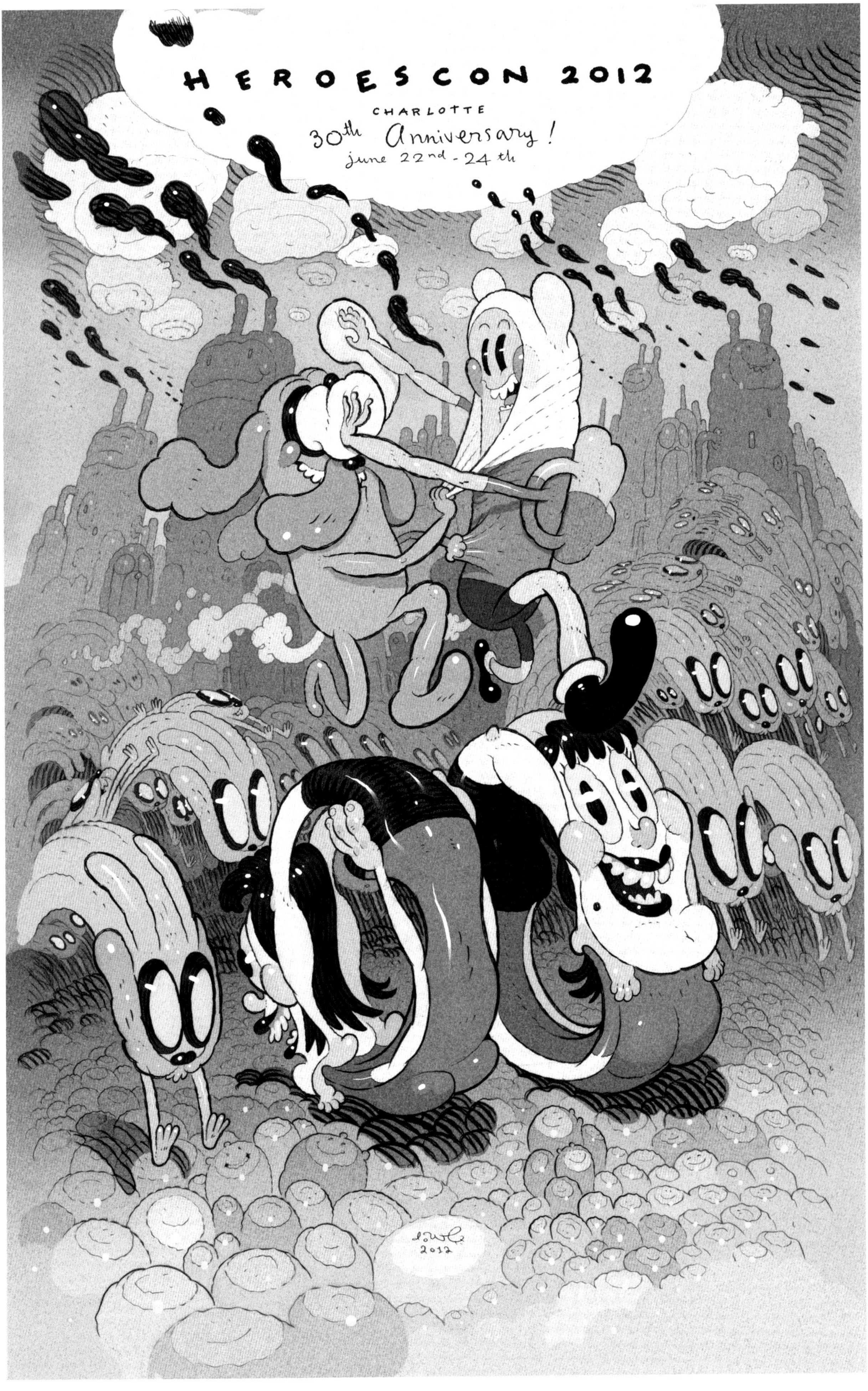
HEROESCON 2012
CHARLOTTE
30th Anniversary!
june 22nd - 24th

HEROESCON ISSUE FIVE EXCLUSIVE | DAVE COOPER

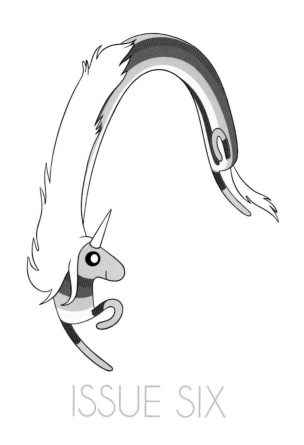

ISSUE SIX

"BUT UM, IF I HAD A FRIEND WHO
DIDN'T GET IT AT ALL, COULD
YOU EXPLAIN IT AGAIN?"

– FINN

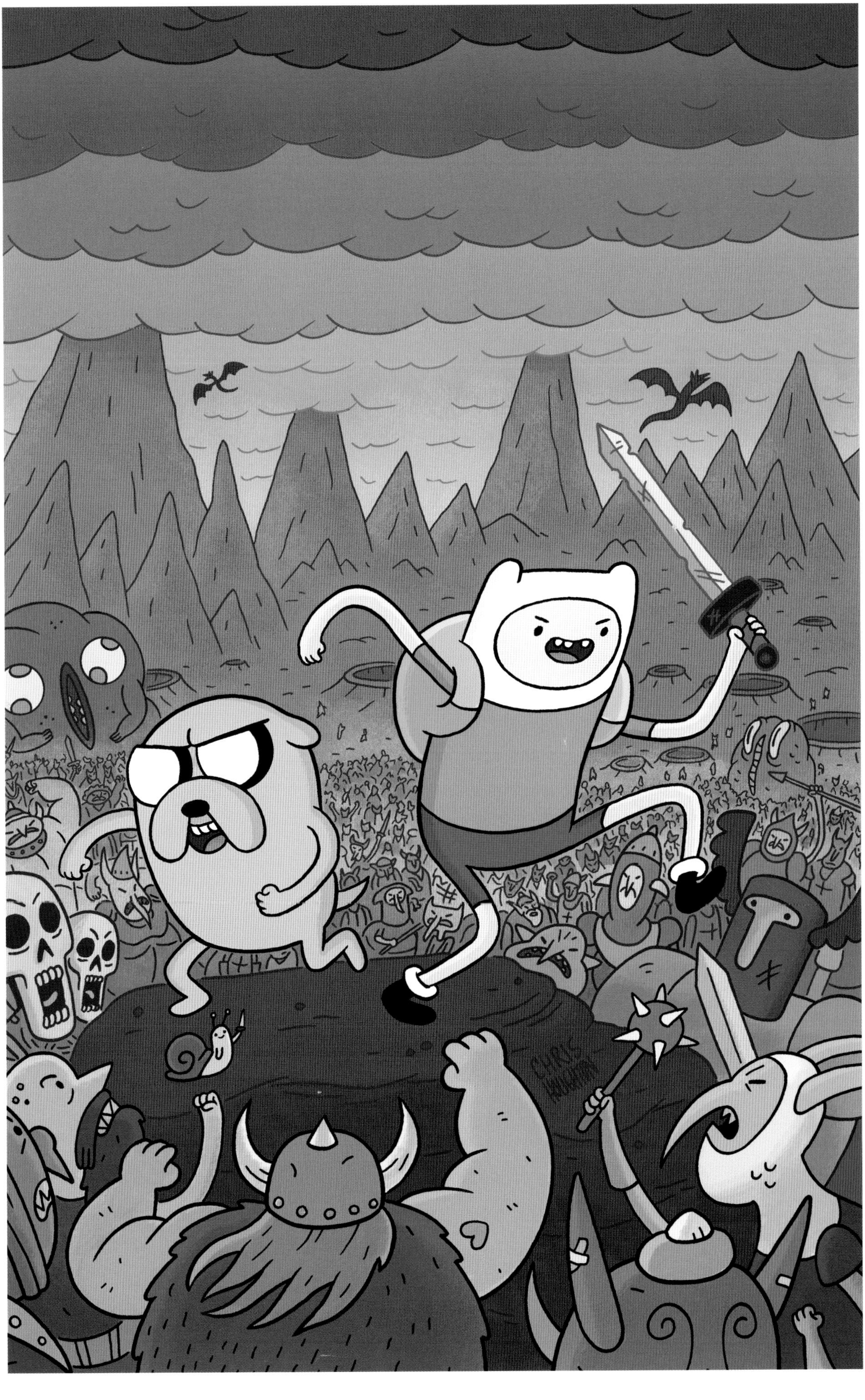
CHRIS HOUGHTON

ISSUE SIX | CHRIS HOUGHTON | COLORS BY KASSANDRA HELLER

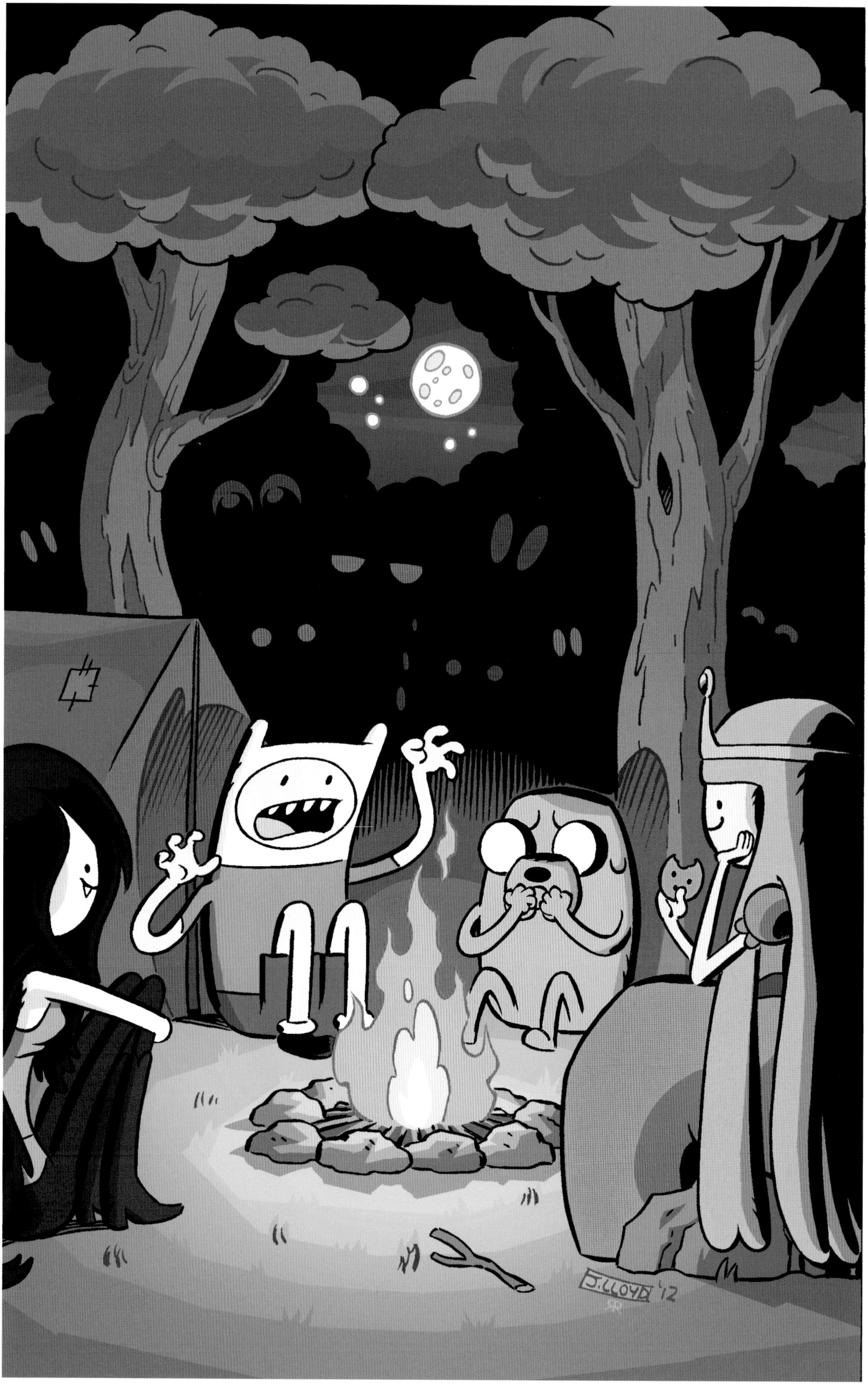
J. LLOYD '12

ISSUE SIX | JAMES LLOYD

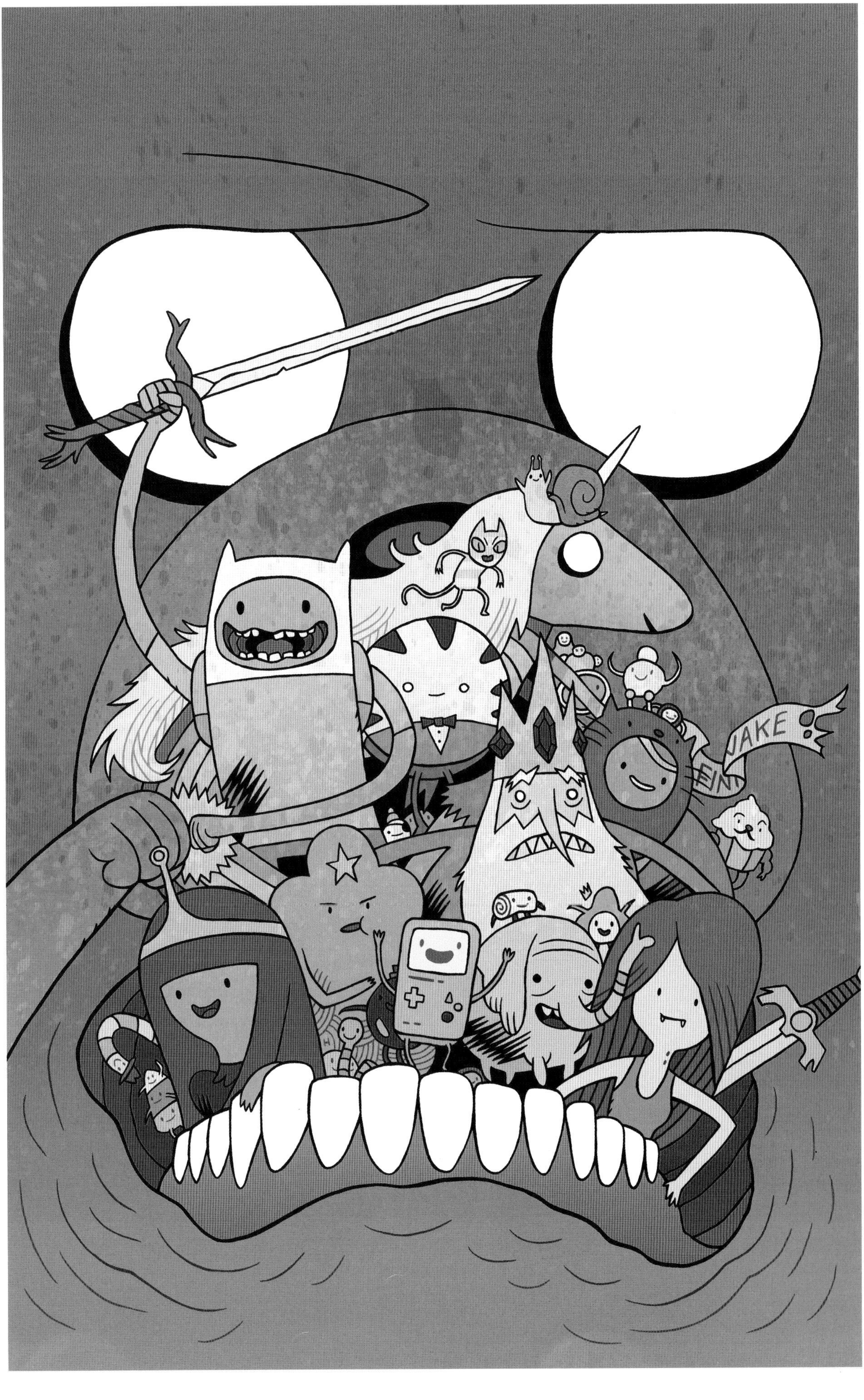
JAKE

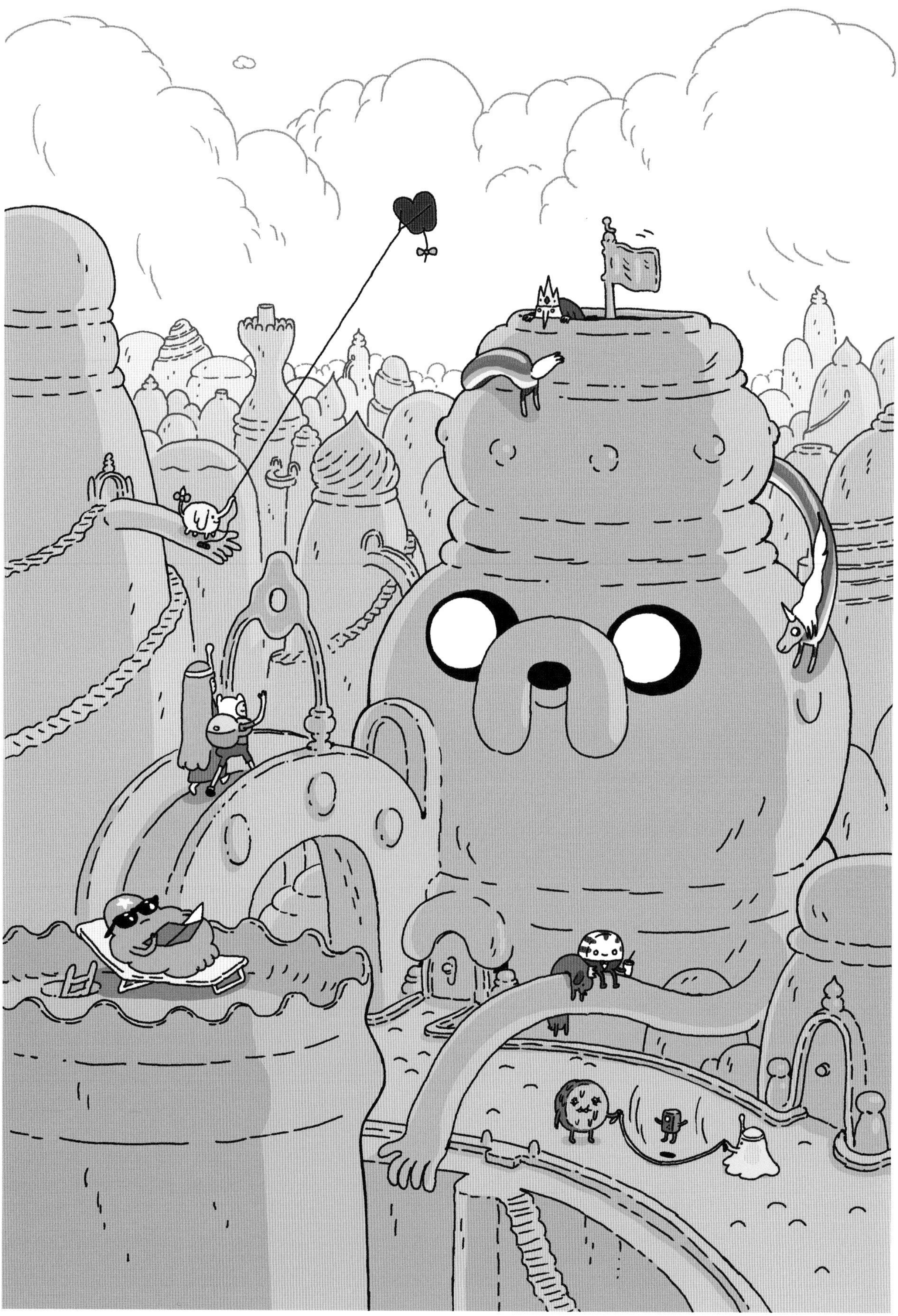

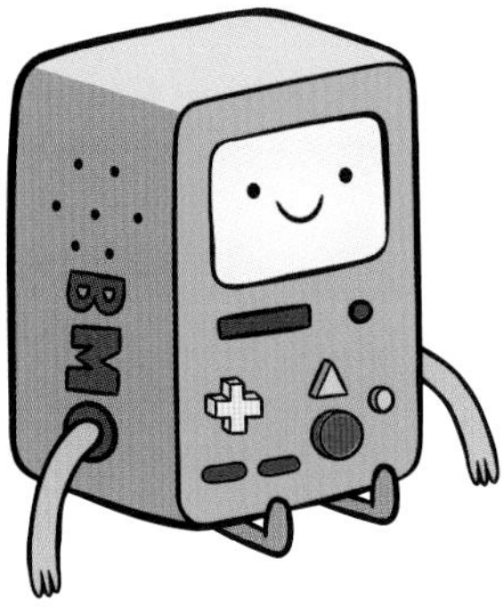
BMO

ISSUE SEVEN

"MAN, I BET THIS PIECE
ISN'T THAT IMPORTANT ANYWAY!"

- JAKE

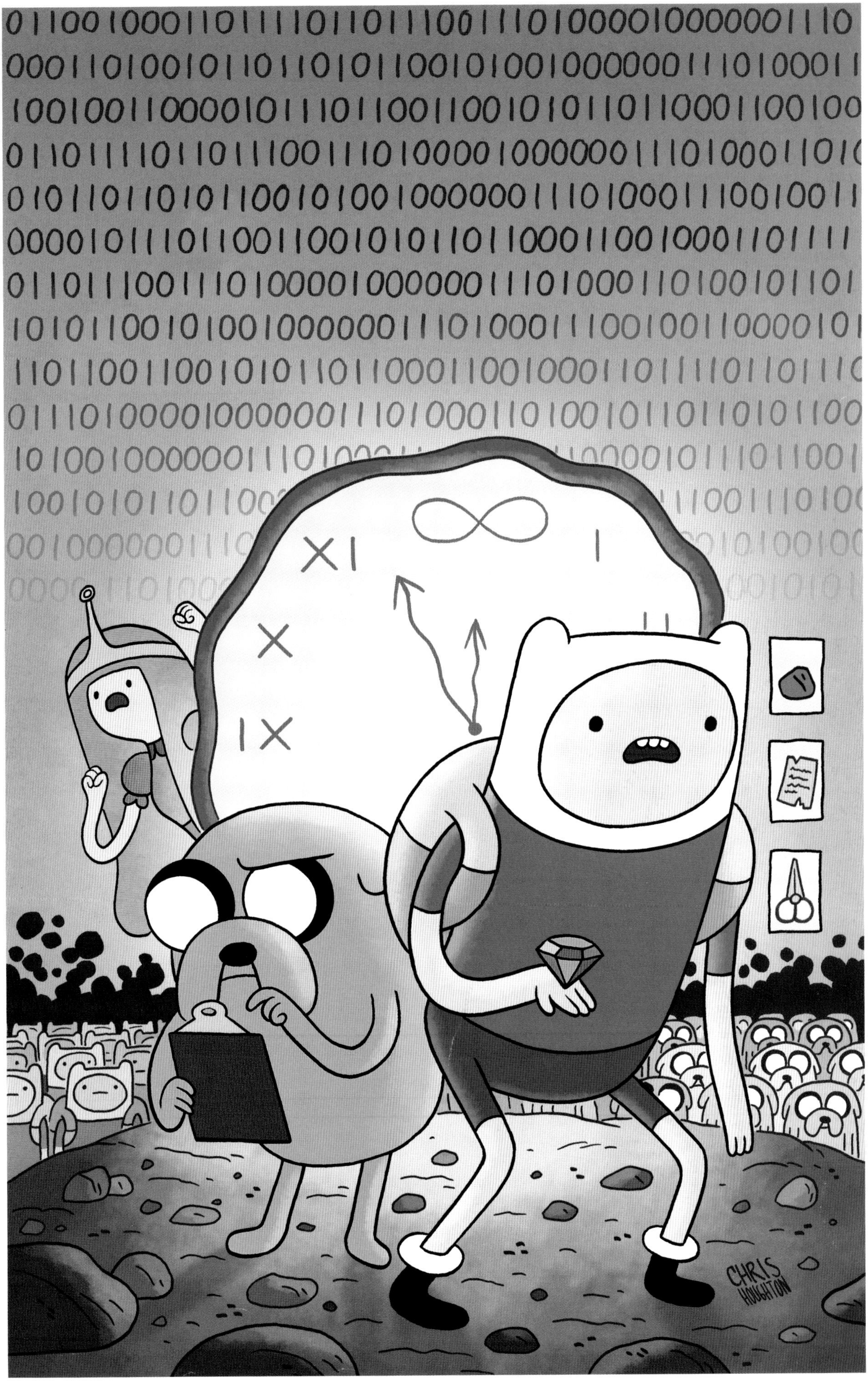

ISSUE SEVEN | CHRIS HOUGHTON | COLORS BY KASSANDRA HELLER

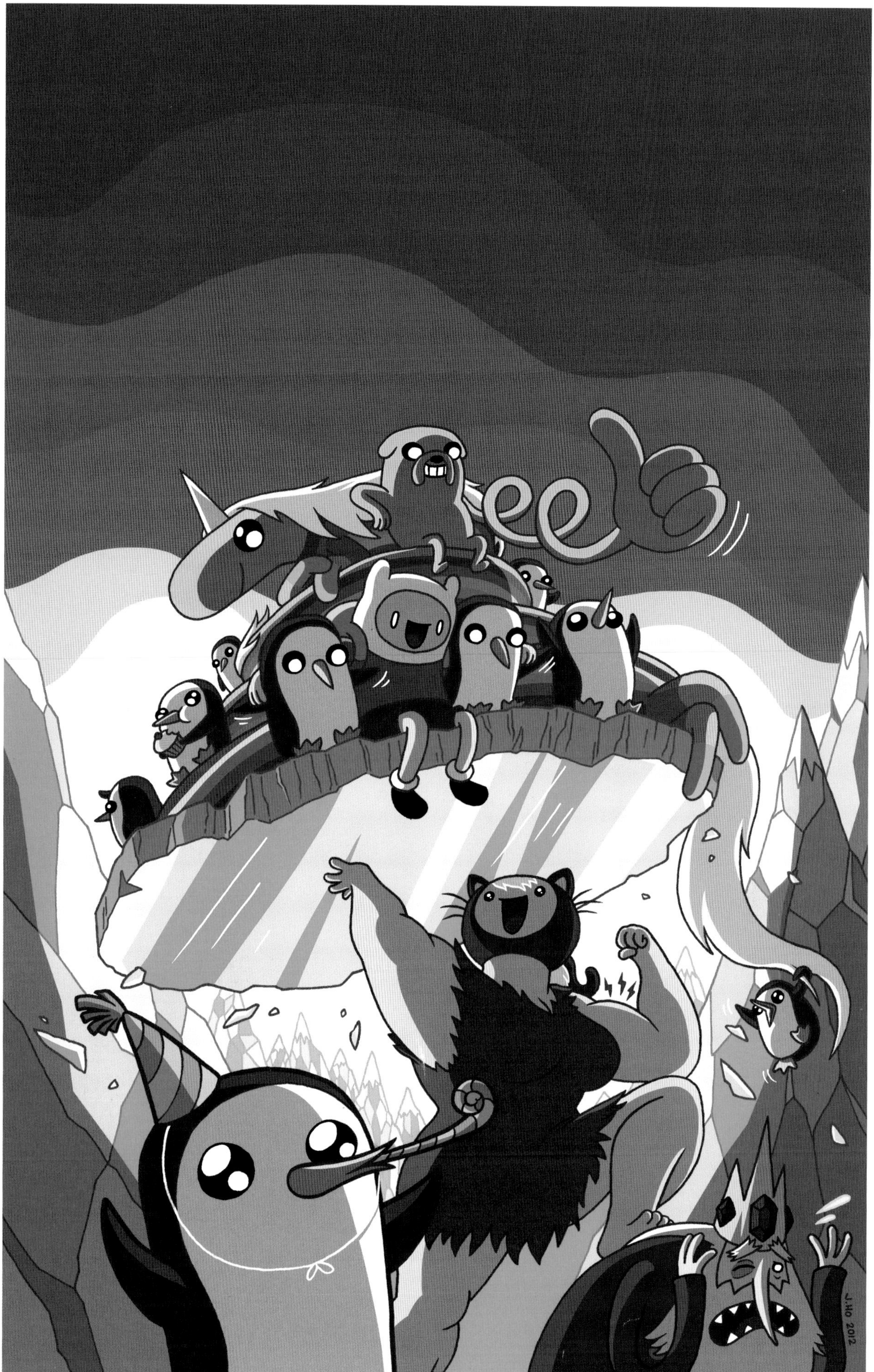
J. HO 2012

ISSUE SEVEN | JASON HO

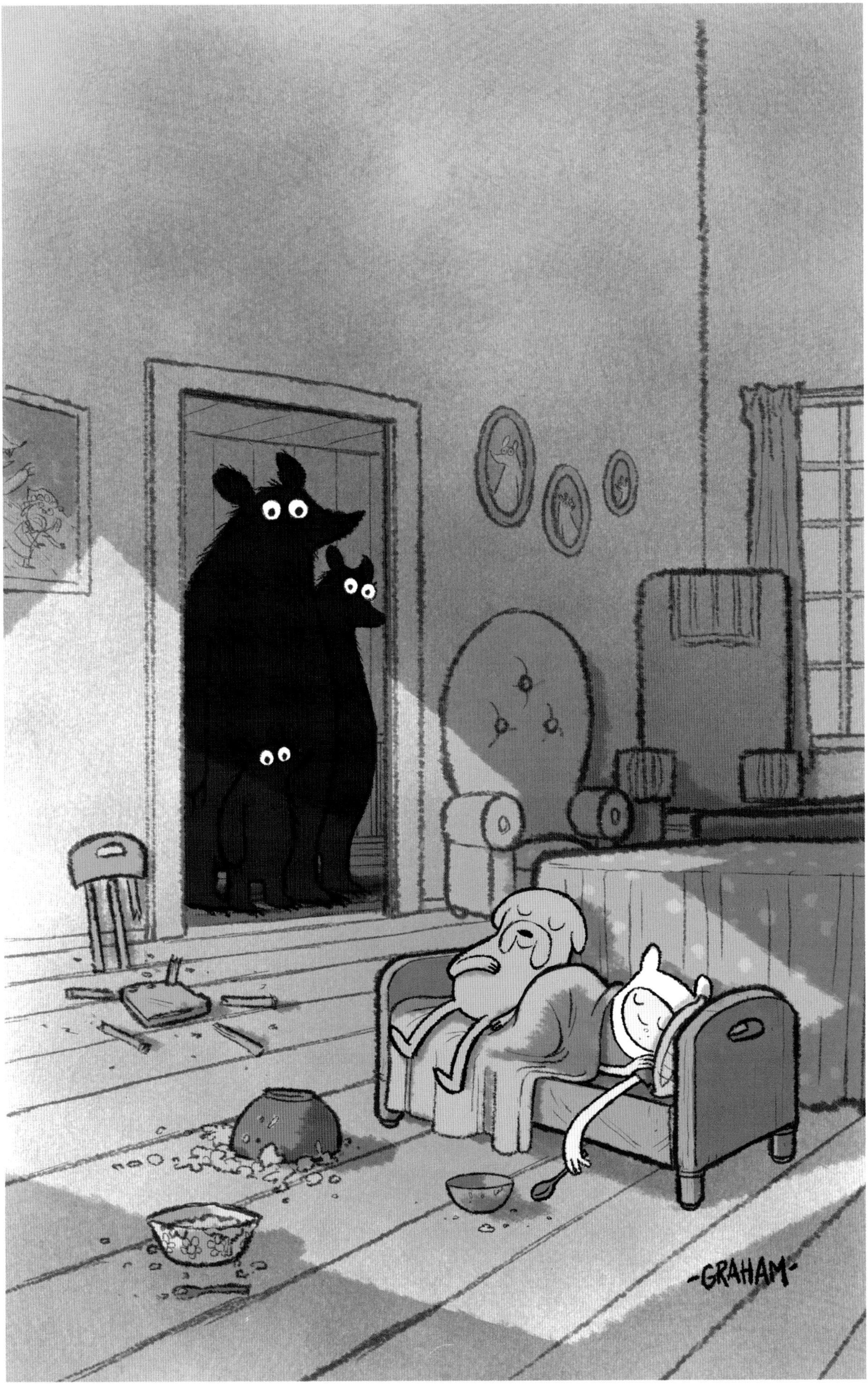
-GRAHAM-

ISSUE SEVEN | GRAHAM ANNABLE

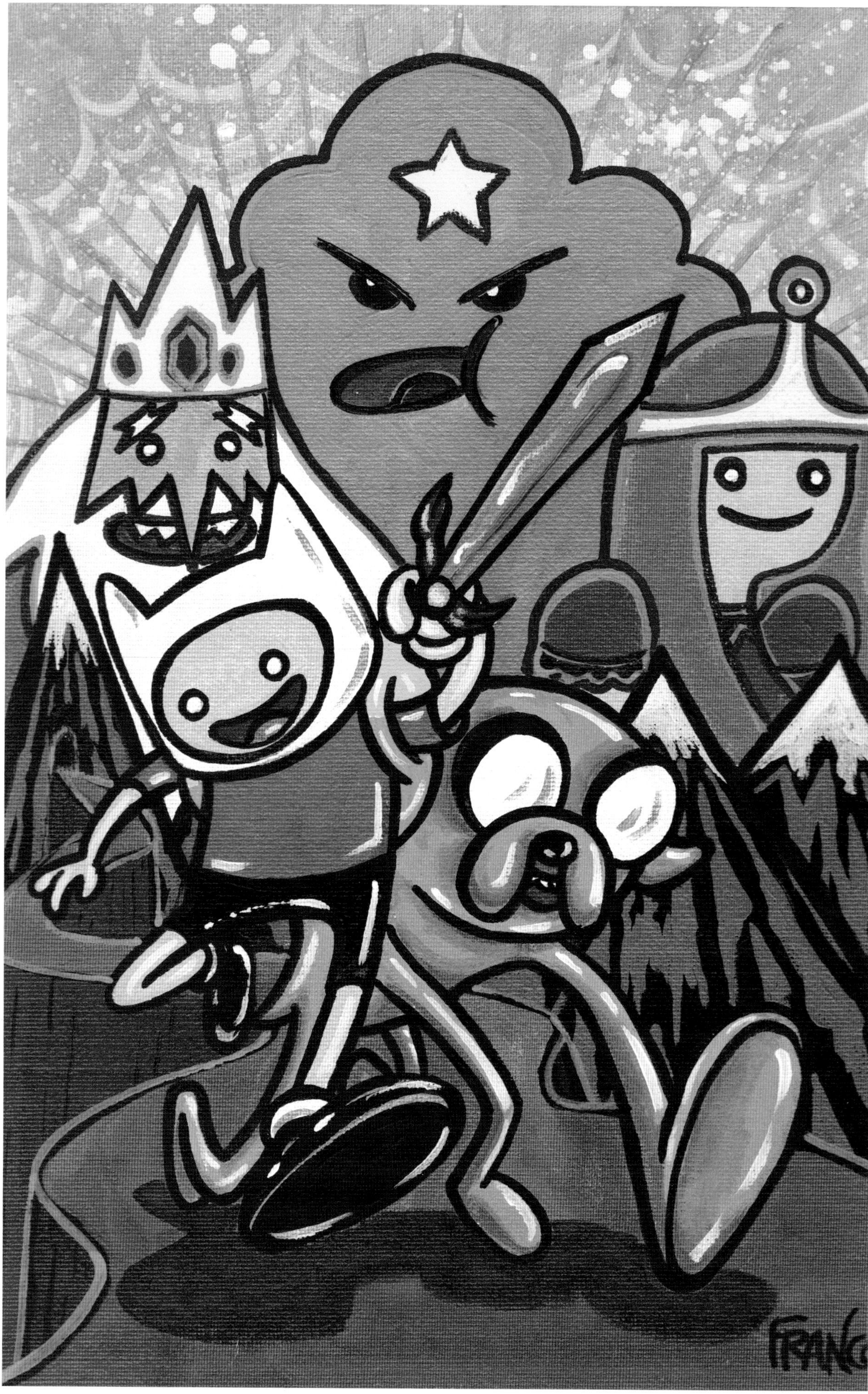
FRANCO

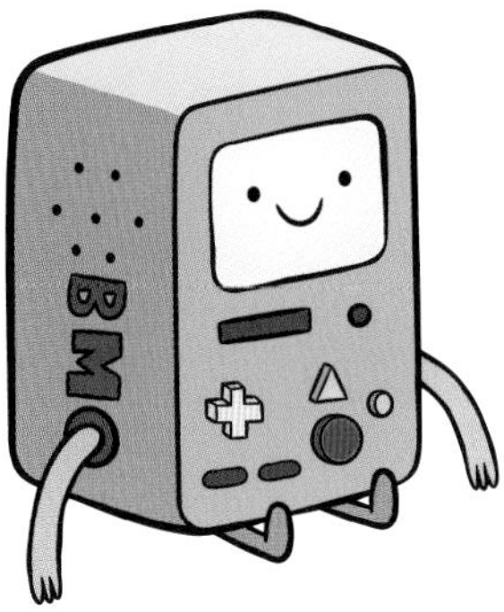
BMO

ISSUE EIGHT

"I DON'T KNOW IF YOU WERE
PROGRAMMED TO GET JOKES OR WHAT."

– JAKE

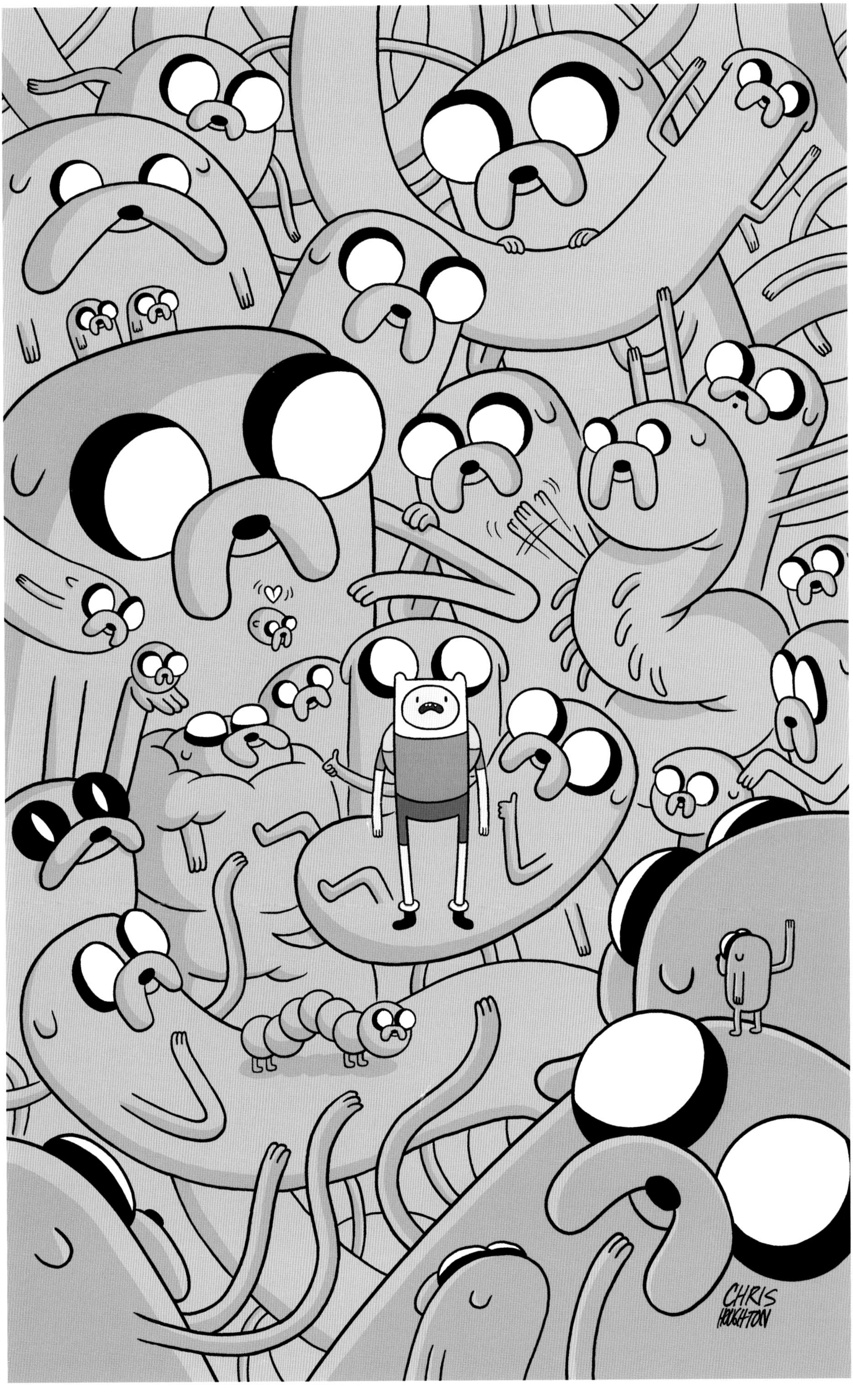
CHRIS
HOUGHTON

ISSUE EIGHT | CHRIS HOUGHTON | COLORS BY KASSANDRA HELLER

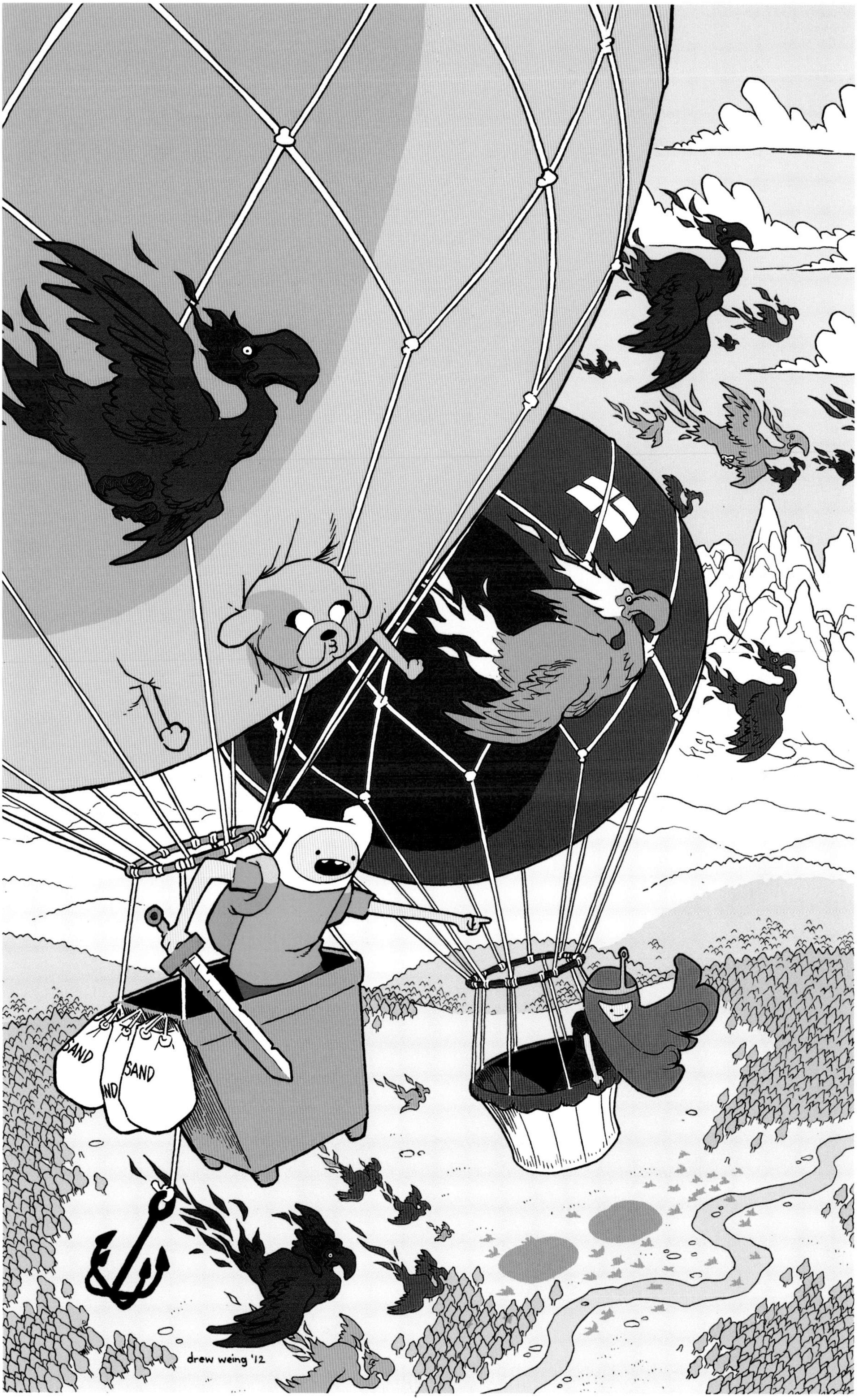
SAND
ND
SAND
drew weing '12

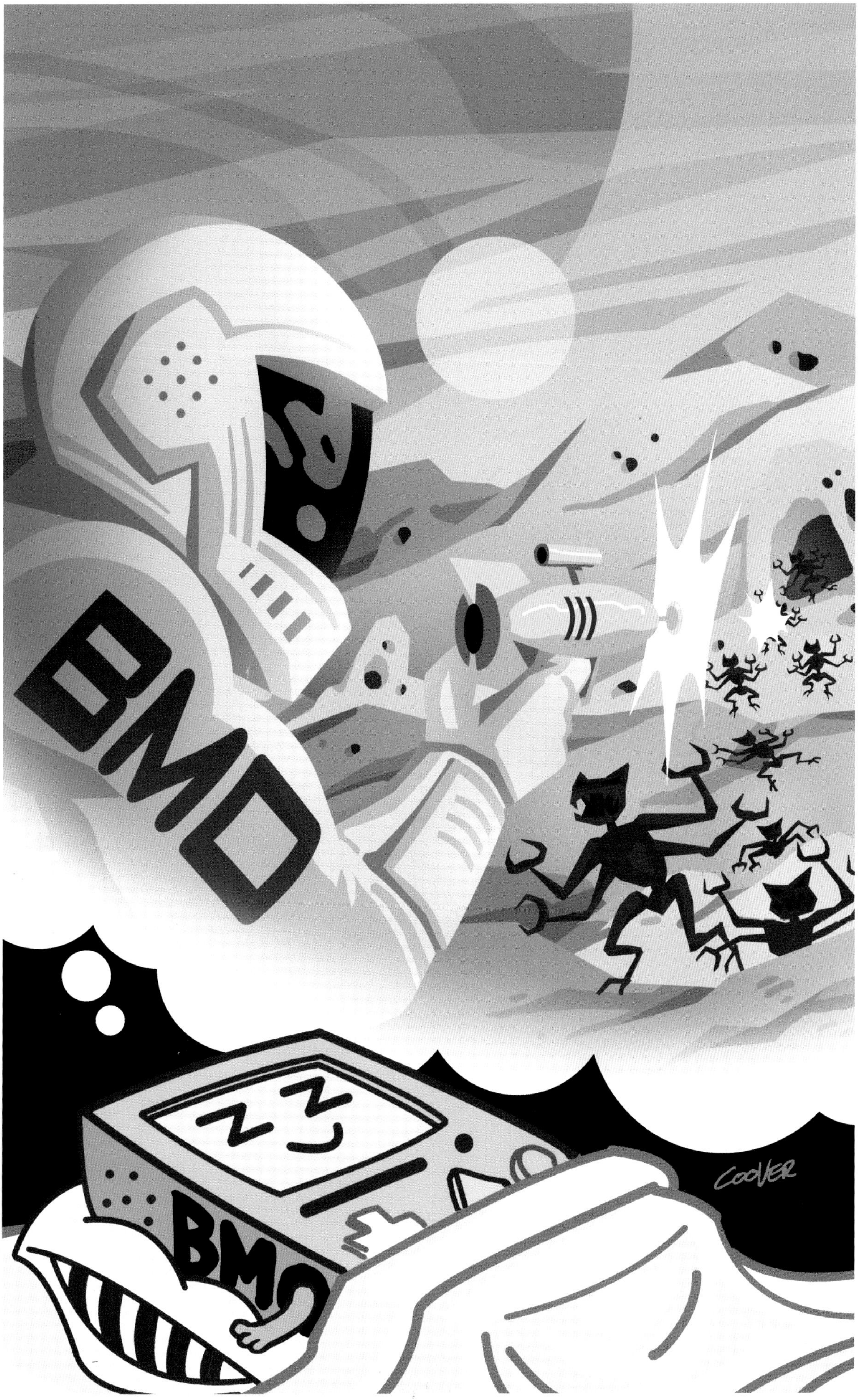
BMO
BMO
COOVER

ISSUE EIGHT | COLLEEN COOVER

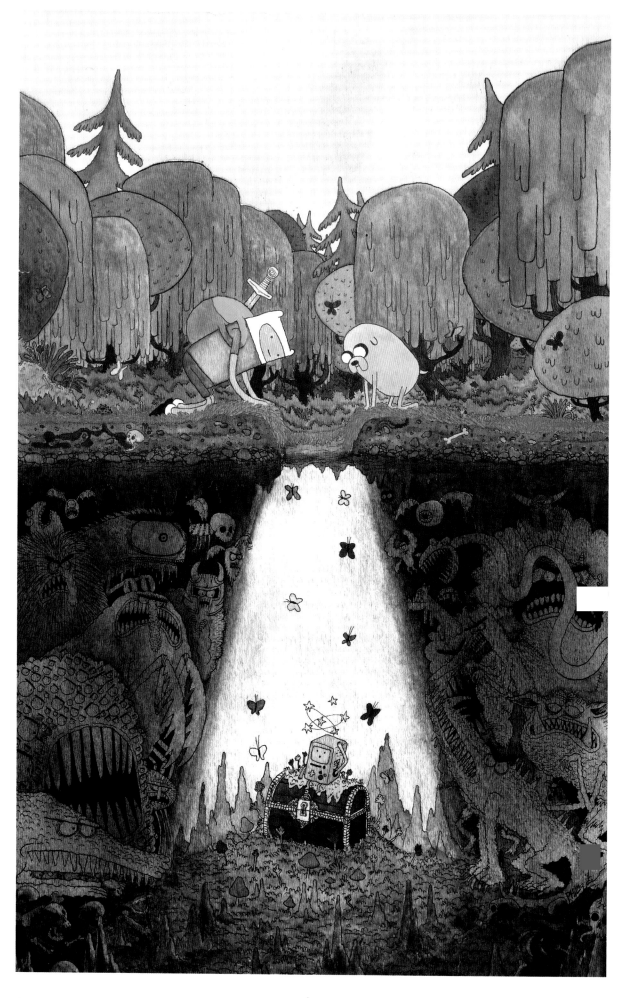

ISSUE NINE

"YES, YES, YOU BOTH HAVE AWESOME BODS."

- PRINCESS BUBBLEGUM

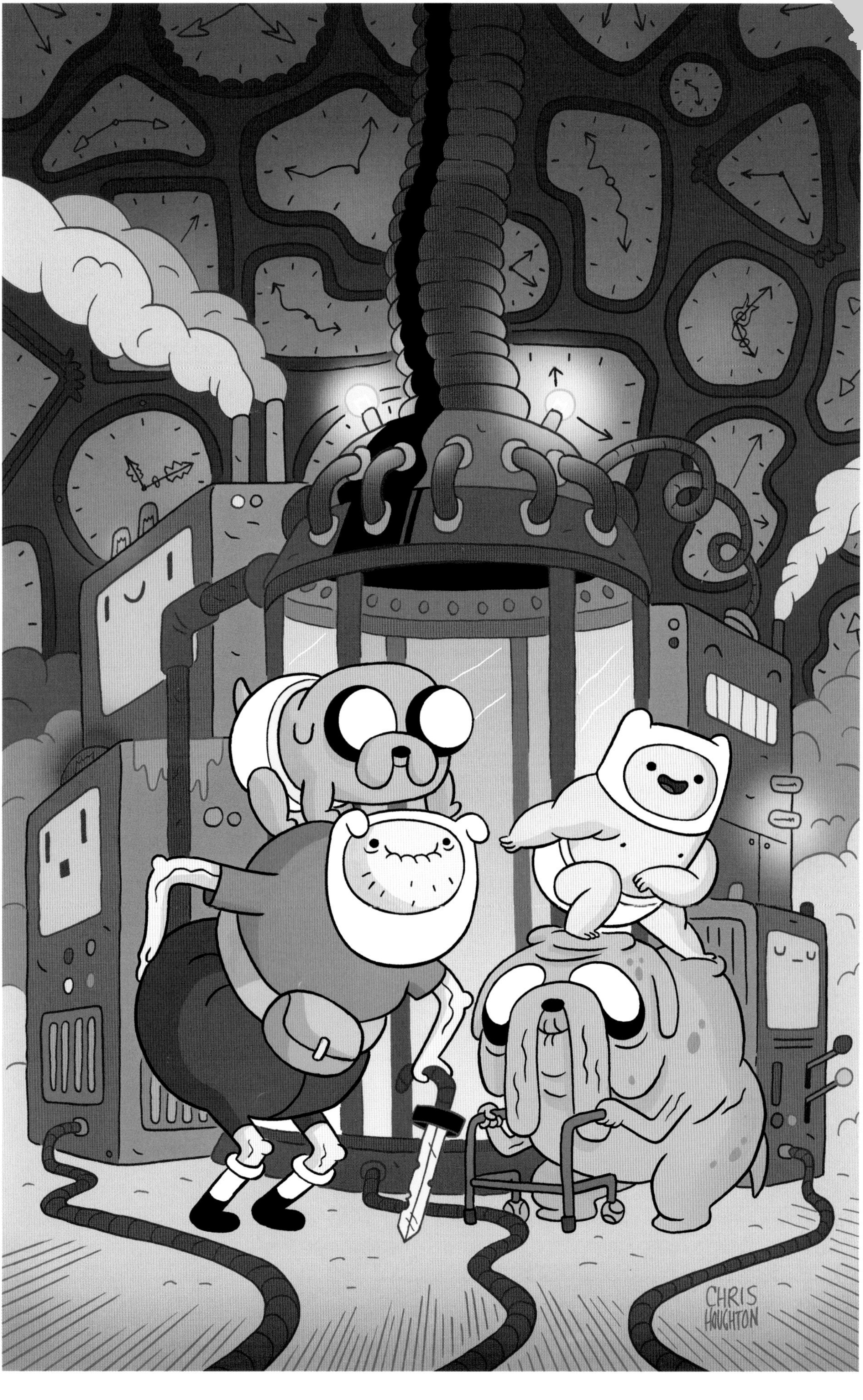
CHRIS
HOUGHTON

ISSUE NINE | CHRIS HOUGHTON | COLORS BY KASSANDRA HELLER

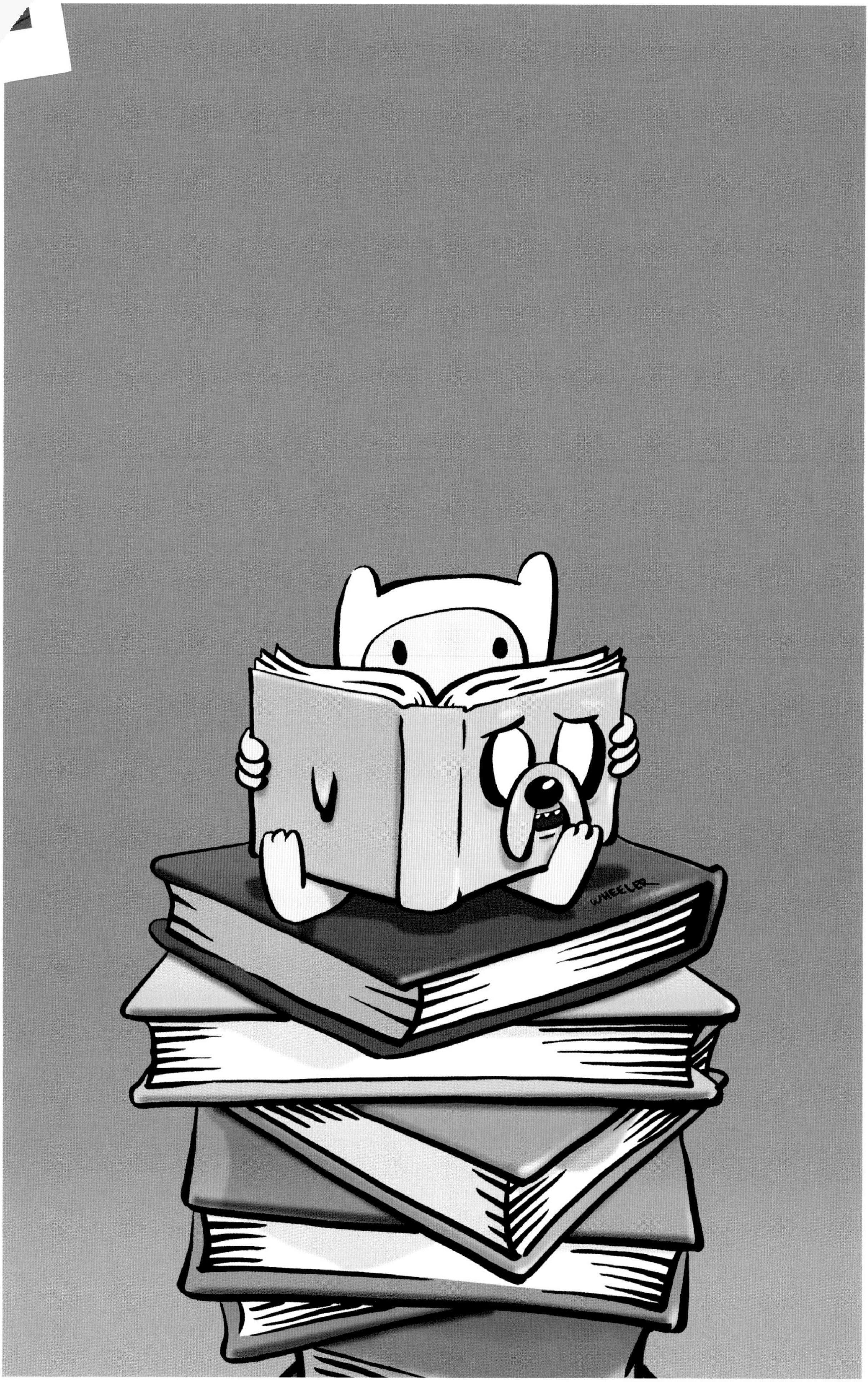
WHEELER

ISSUE NINE | SHANNON WHEELER

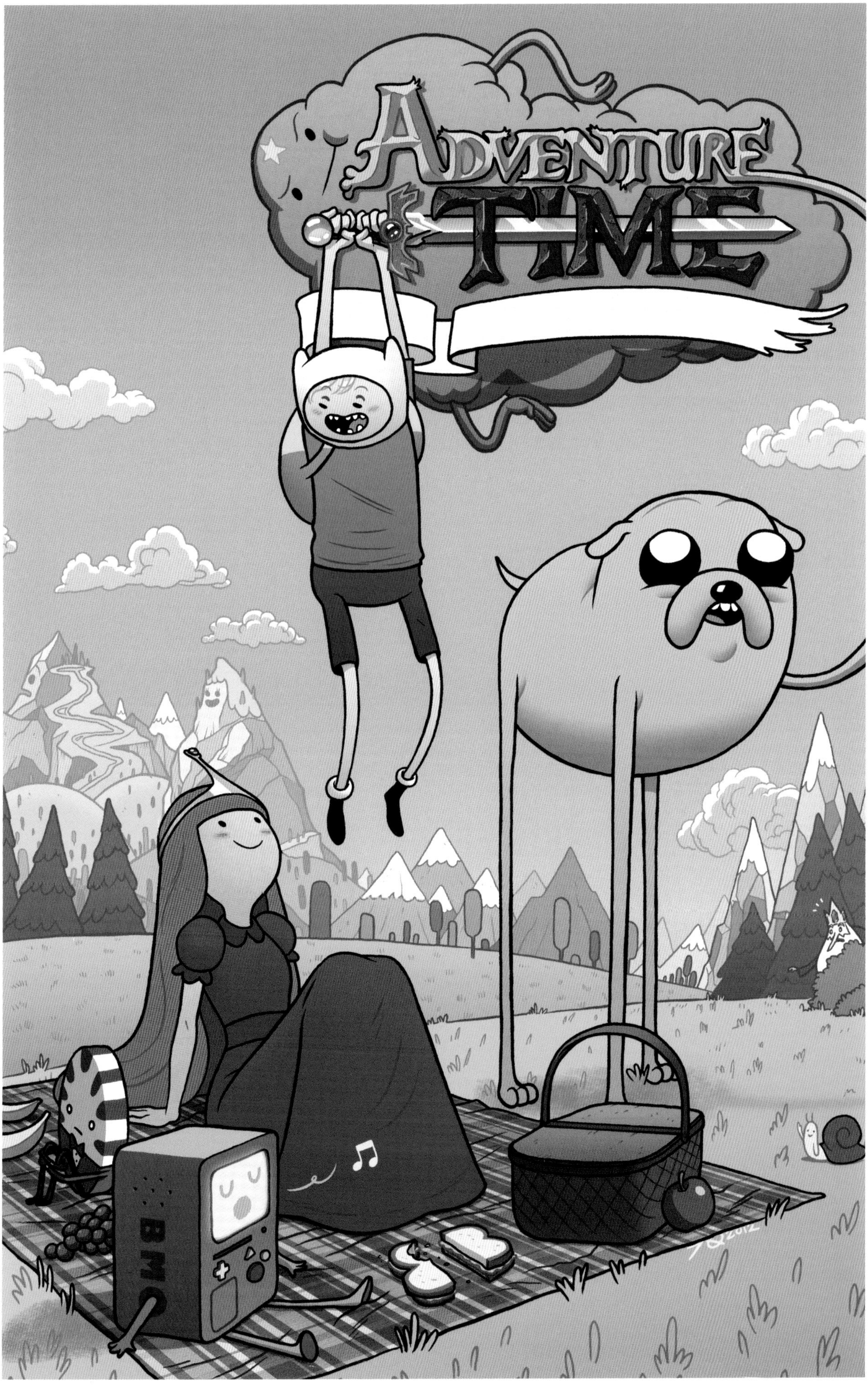
ADVENTURE TIME
BMO

ISSUE NINE | JOE QUINONES

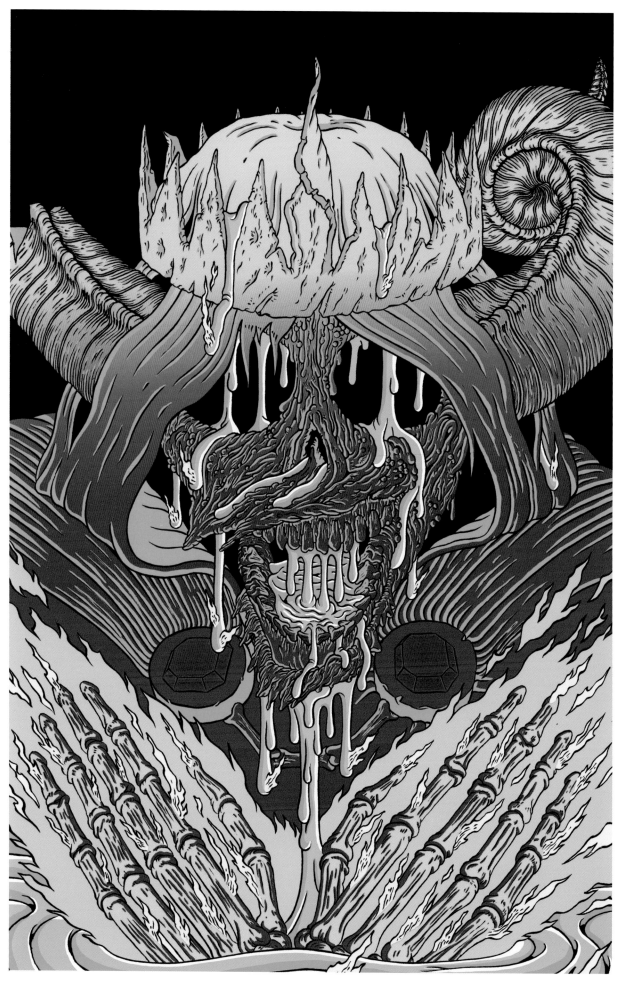

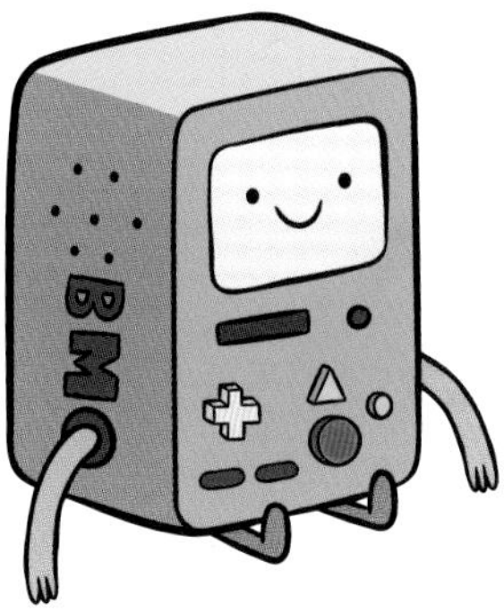
BMO

ISSUE TEN

"ICE KING, HAVE YOU EVER
CONSIDERED HOW EASY AND
AWESOME THINGS WOULD BE IF
YOU WEREN'T A SELFISH
PA-TOOT ALL THE TIME?"

- FINN

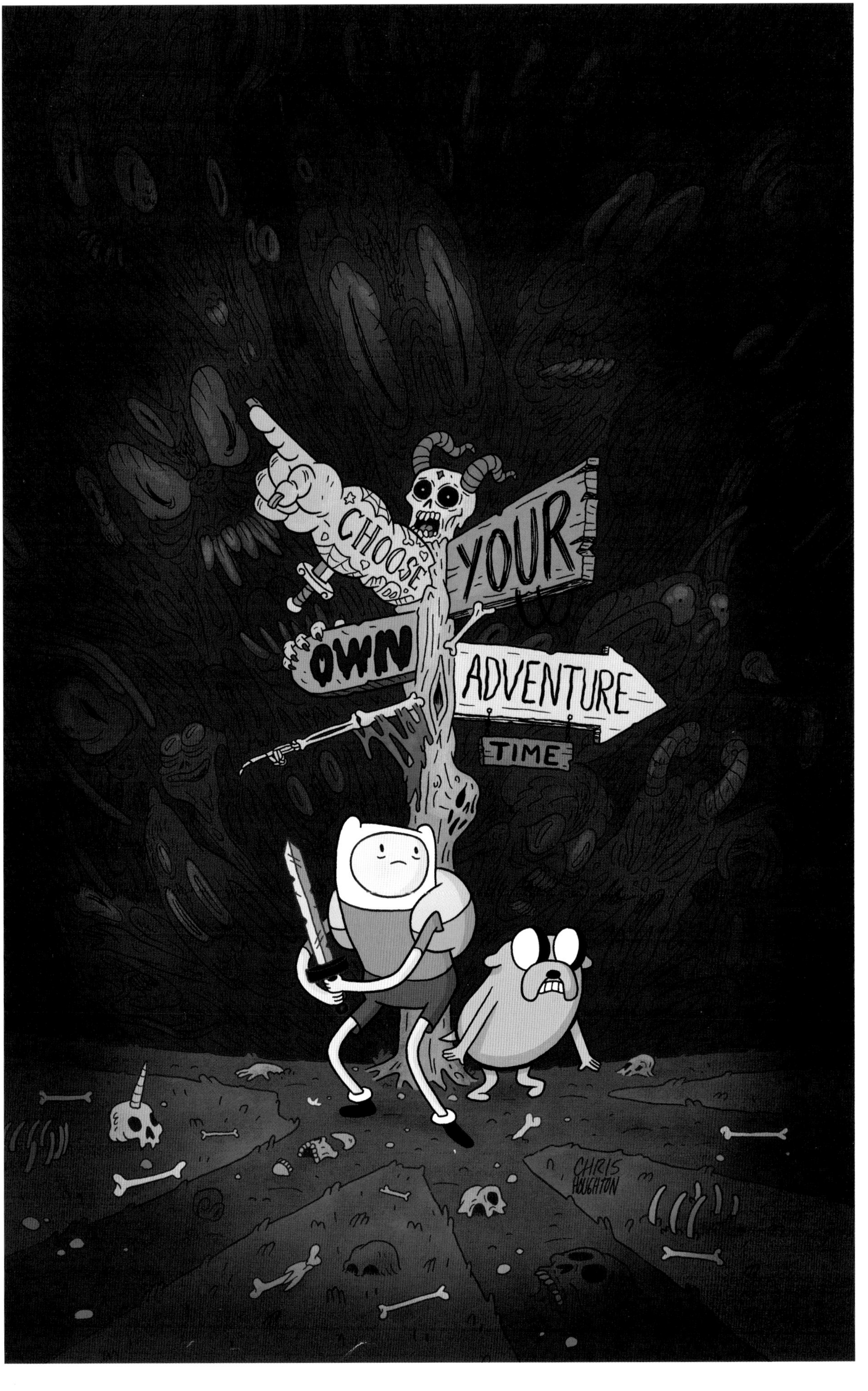
CHOOSE
YOUR
OWN
ADVENTURE
TIME
CHRIS HOUGHTON

ISSUE TEN | CHRIS HOUGHTON | COLORS BY KASSANDRA HELLER

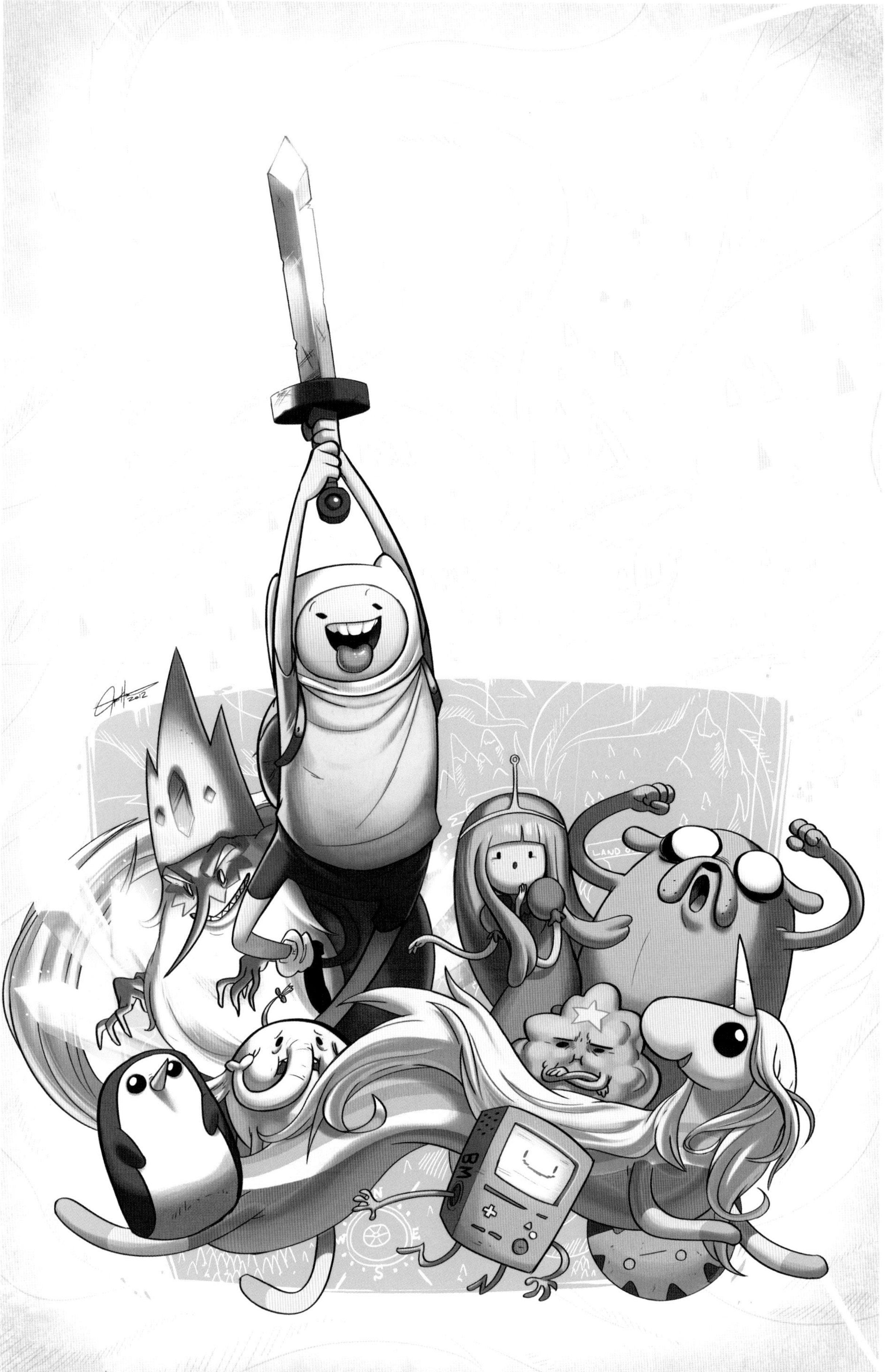
LAND
BMO
W
E
S

ISSUE TEN | TYSON HESSE

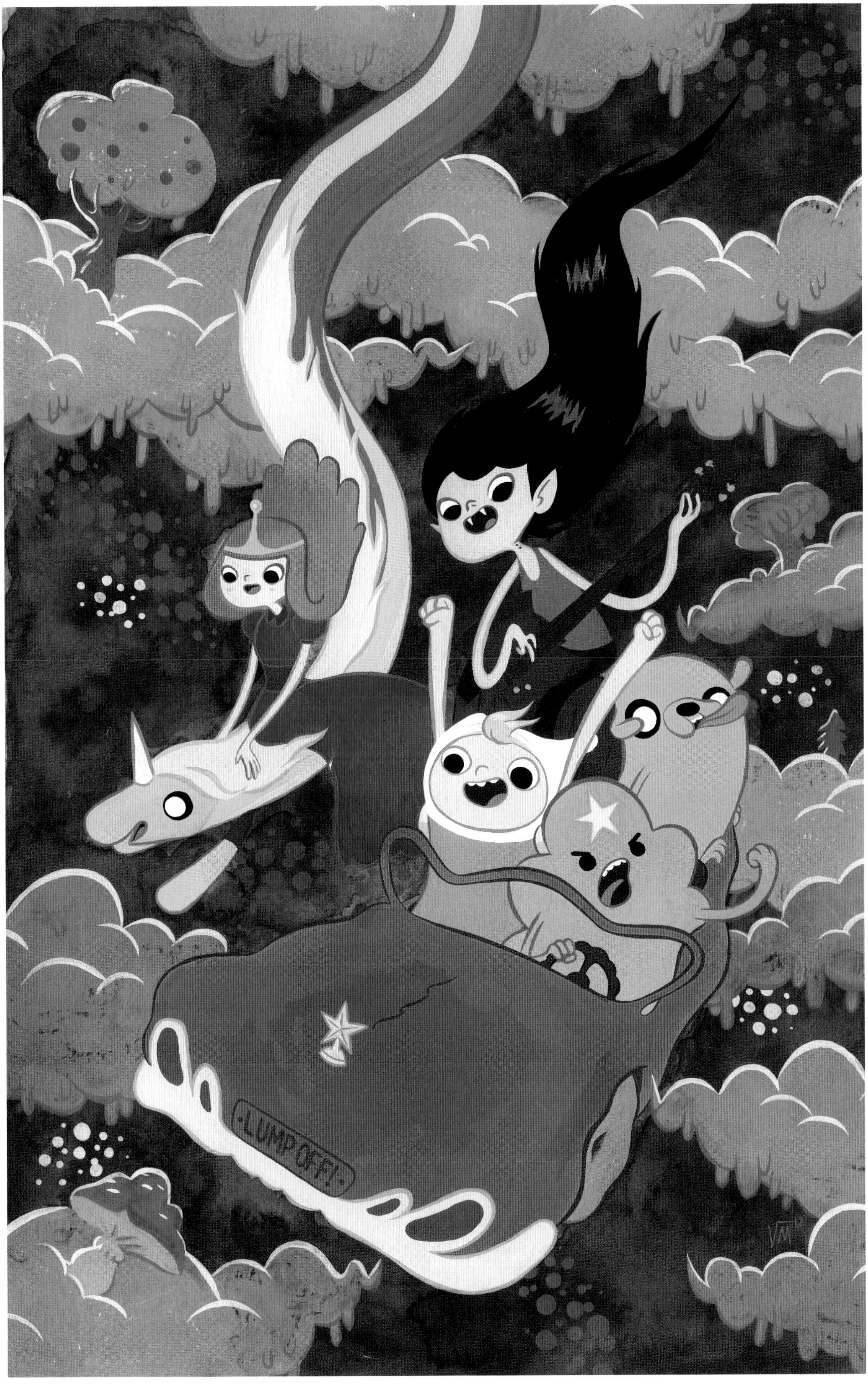

·LUMP OFF!·
VM

ISSUE TEN | VICTORIA MADERNA

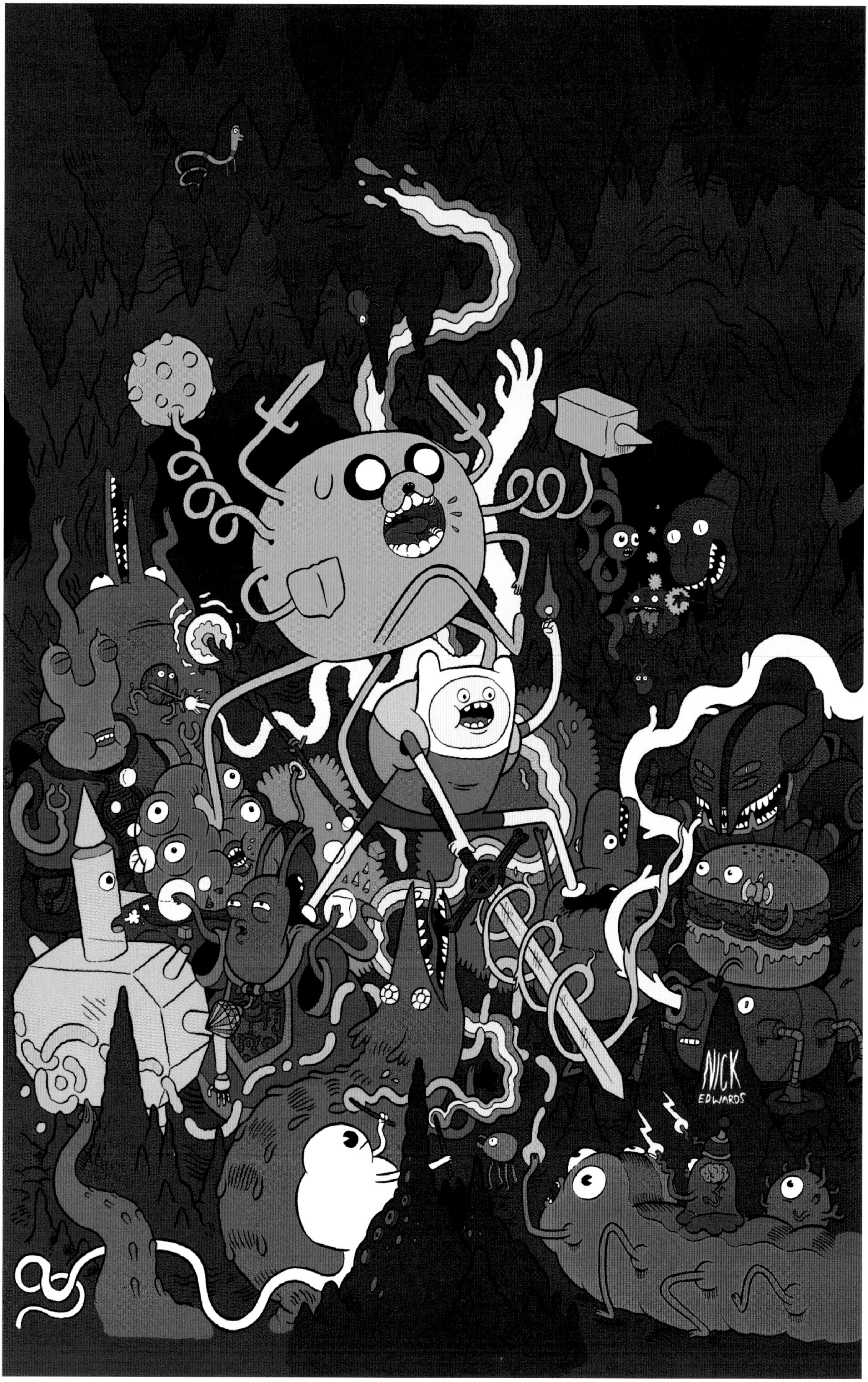
NICK
EDWARDS

ISSUE TEN | NICK EDWARDS

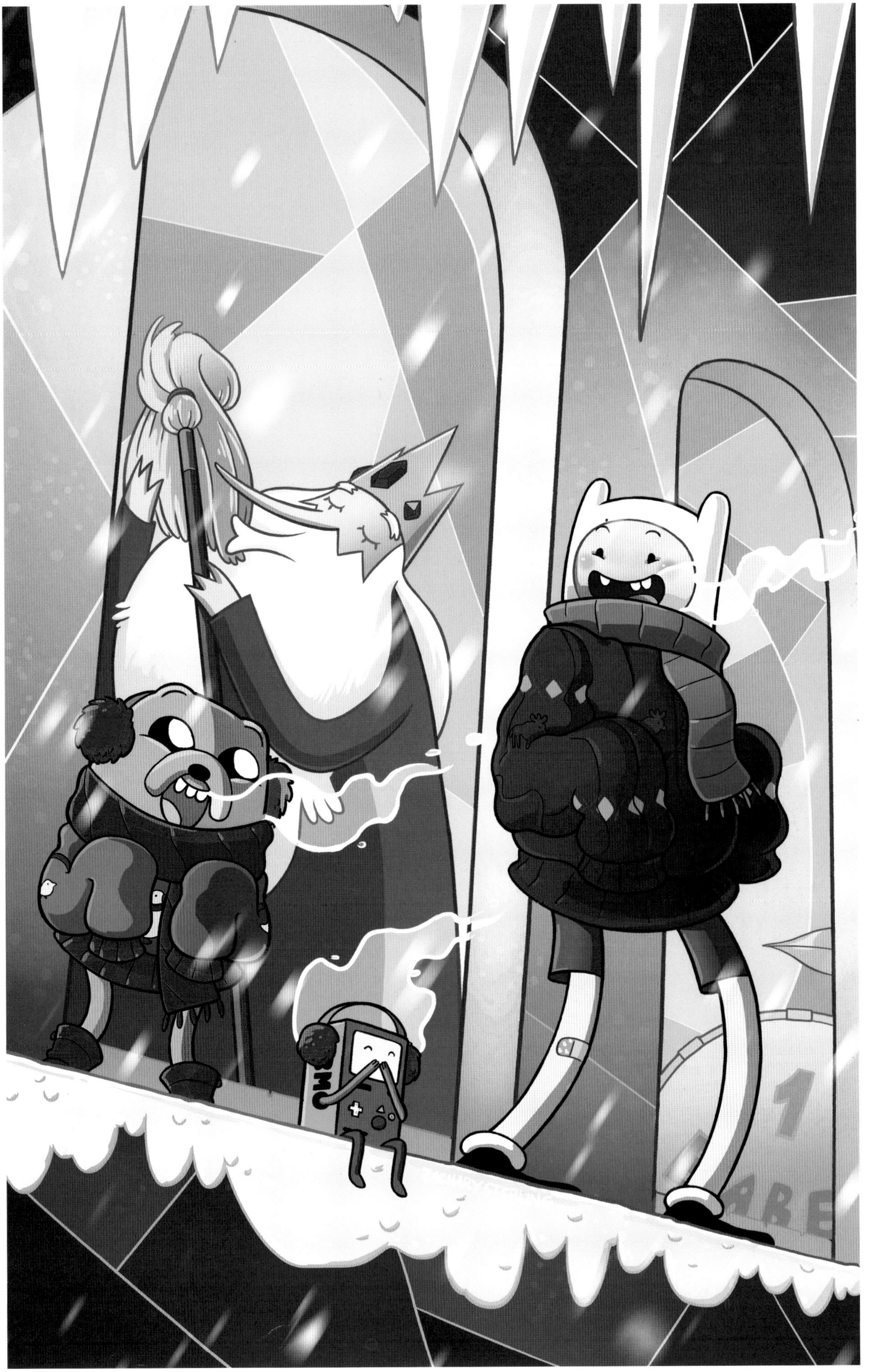

ISSUE TEN HASTINGS EXCLUSIVE | ZACK STERLING

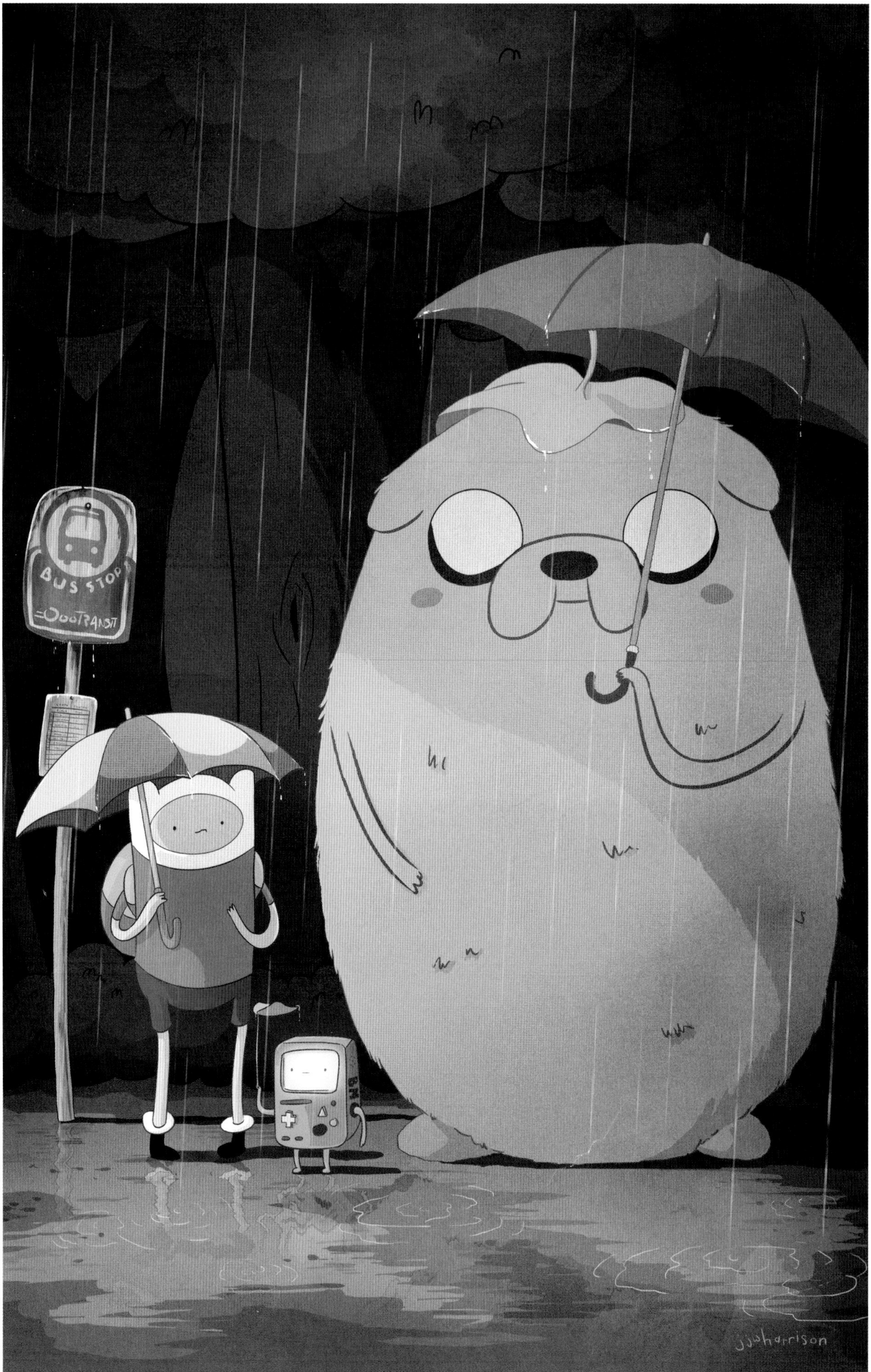
BUS STOP
=OooTRANSIT
jjharrison

ISSUE TEN DYNAMIC FORCES EXCLUSIVE | JJ HARRISON

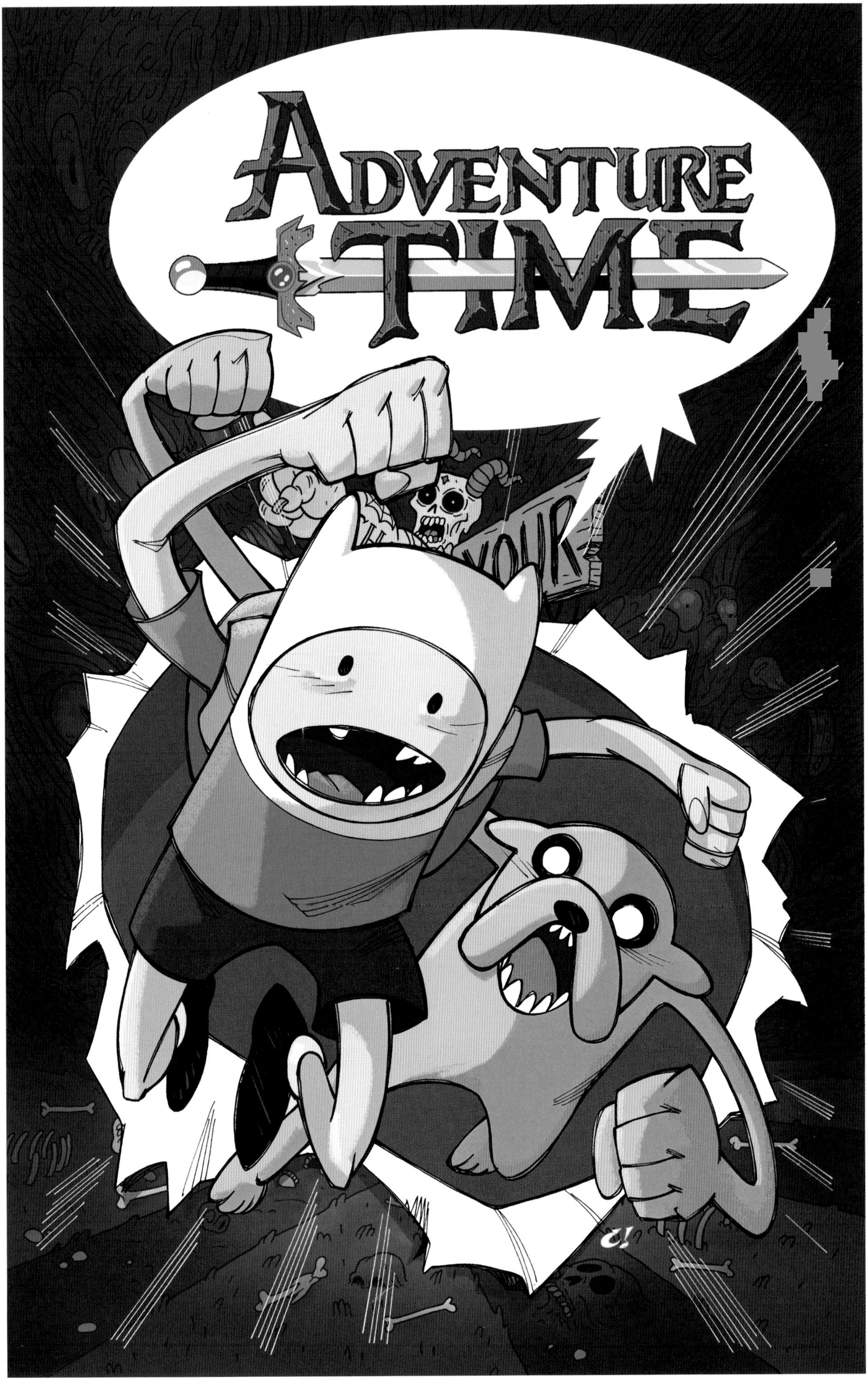
ADVENTURE TIME
YOUR

ISSUE TEN CARDS, COMICS AND COLLECTIBLES EXCLUSIVE | CRAIG ROUSSEAU

ISSUE ELEVEN

"WELL, ANYWAY, LET'S FIND
SOME GUTS TO PUNCH."

- MARCELINE

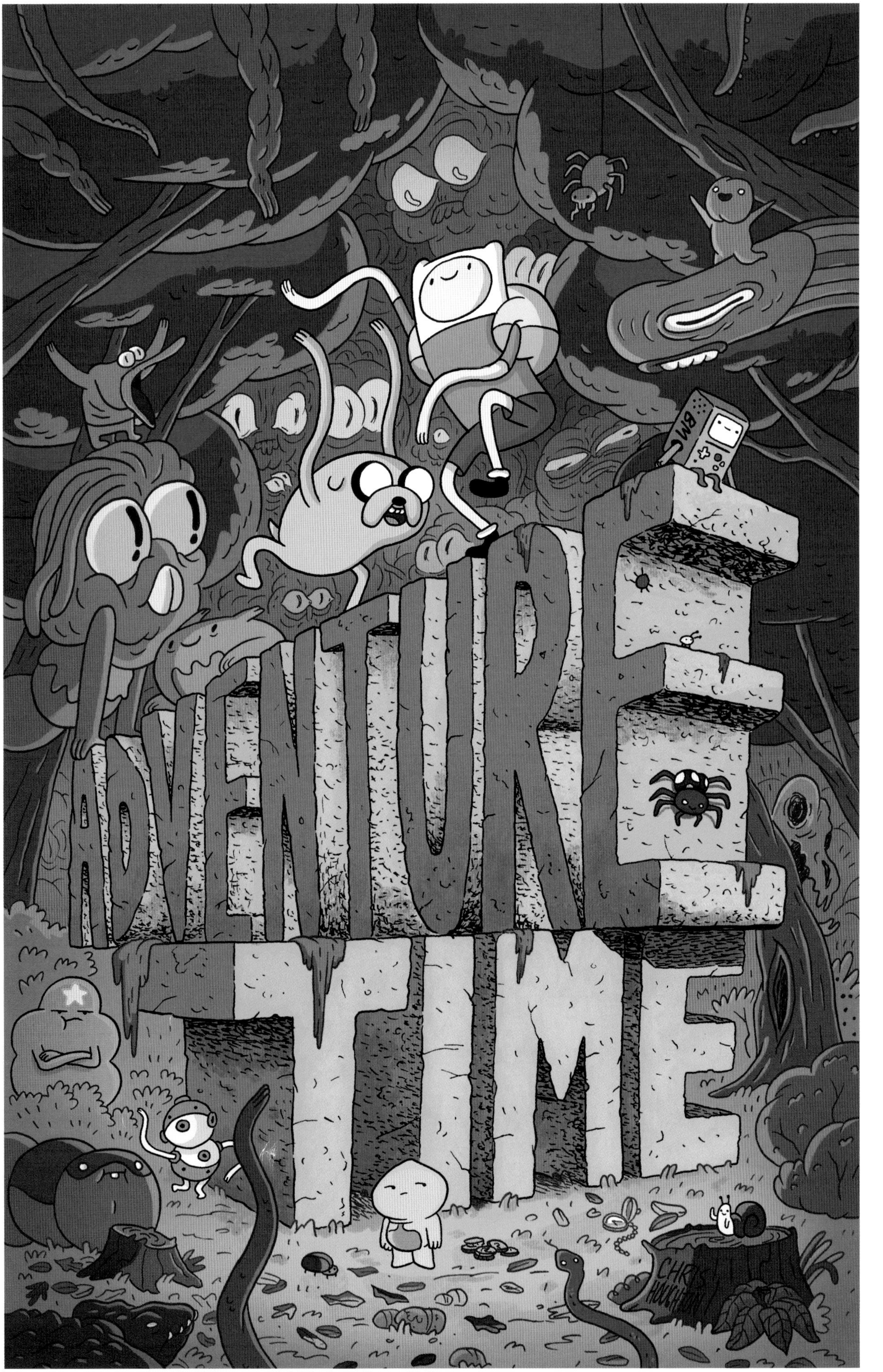
ADVENTURE
TIME
BMO
CHRIS HOUGHTON

ISSUE ELEVEN | CHRIS HOUGHTON | COLORS BY KASSANDRA HELLER

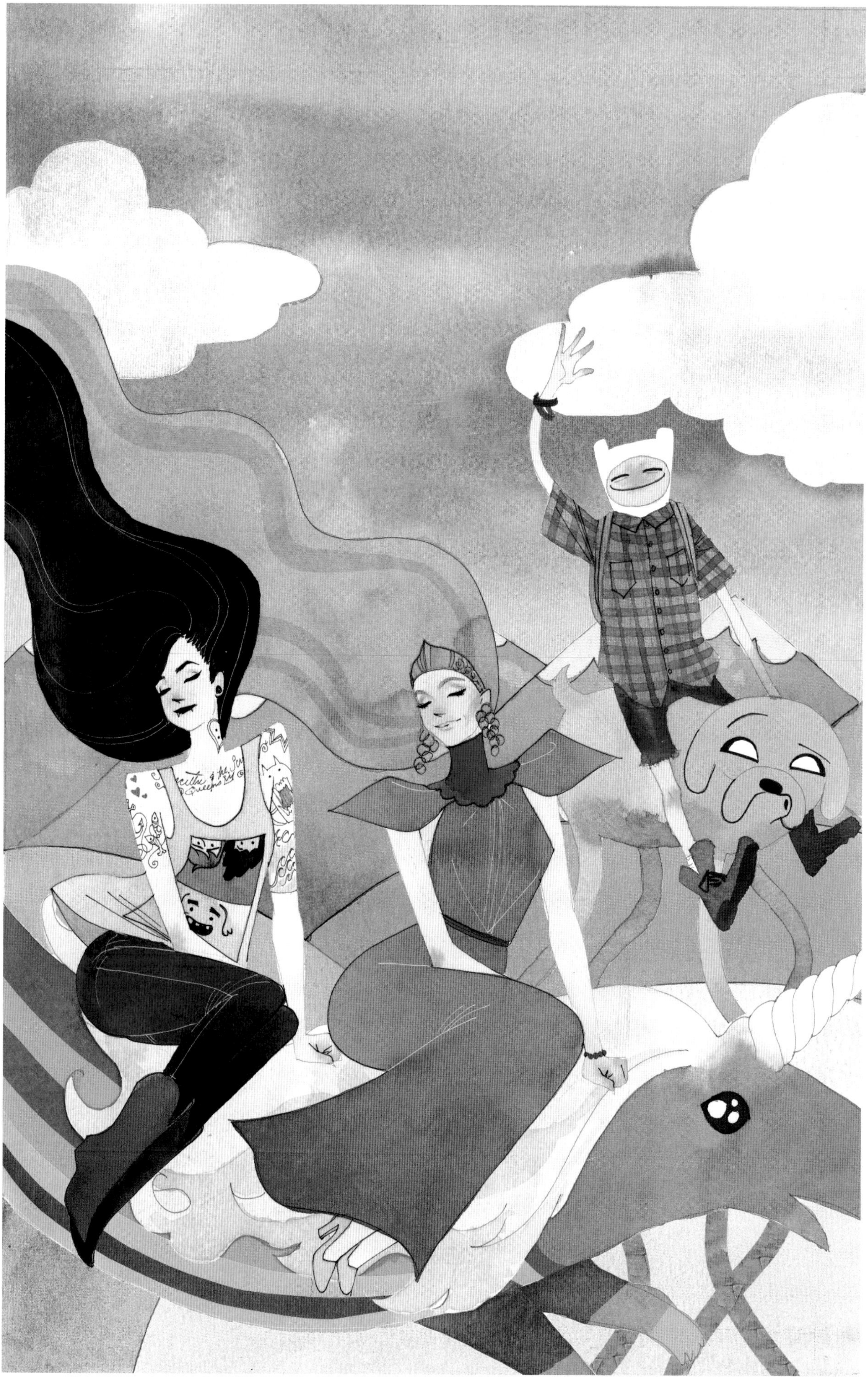

ISSUE ELEVEN | KEVIN WADA

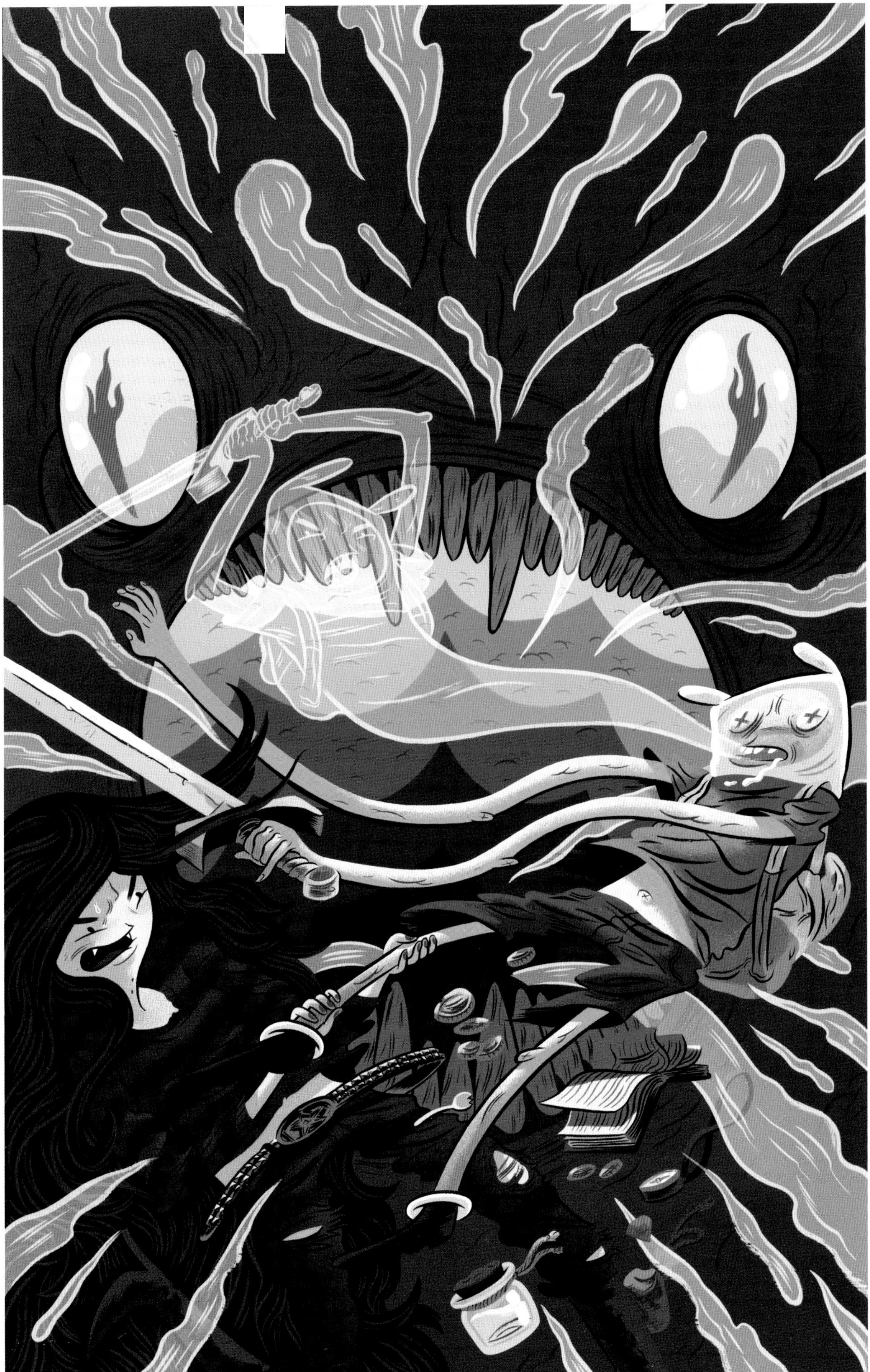

ISSUE ELEVEN | LOGAN FAERBER

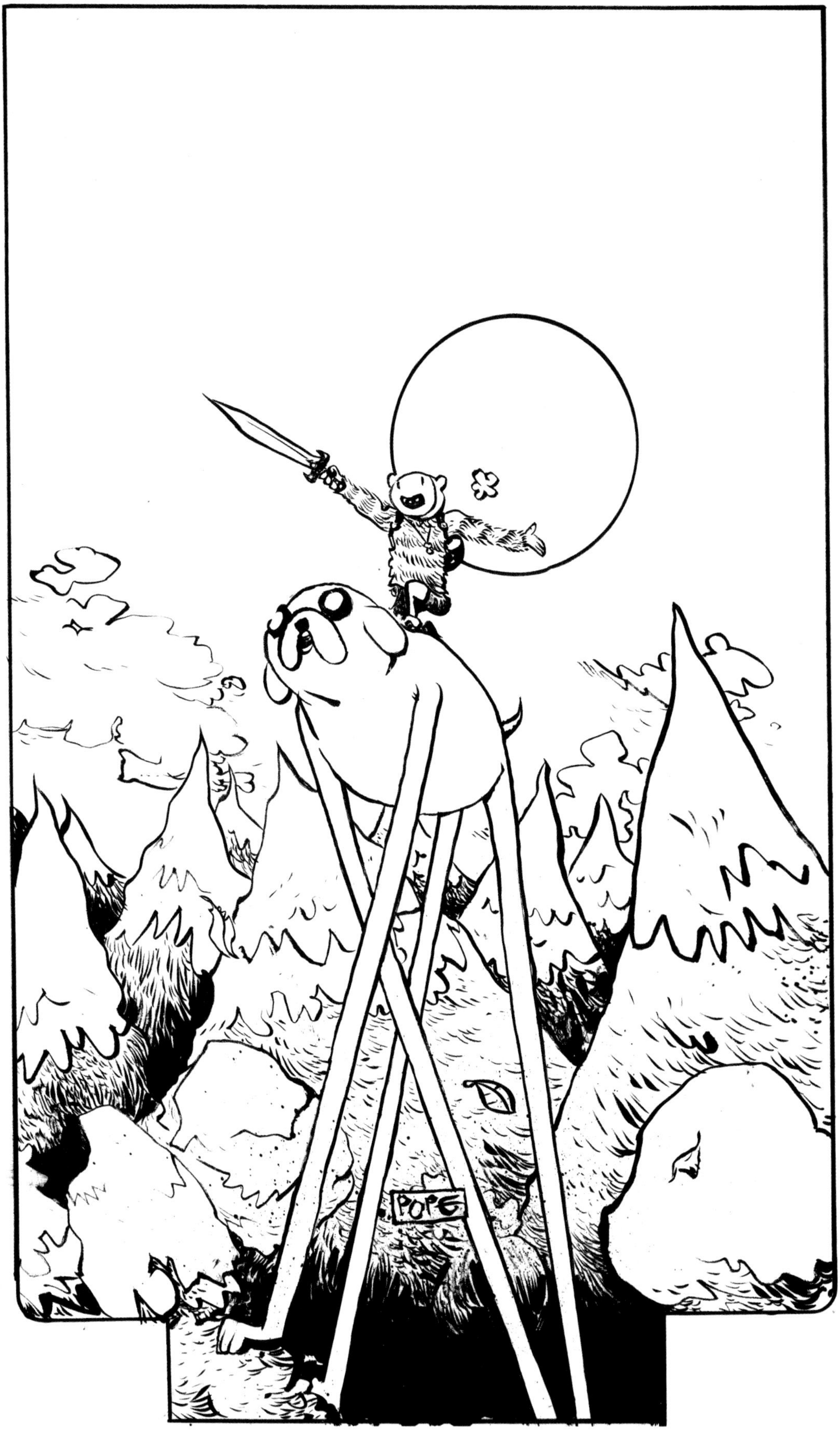
POPE

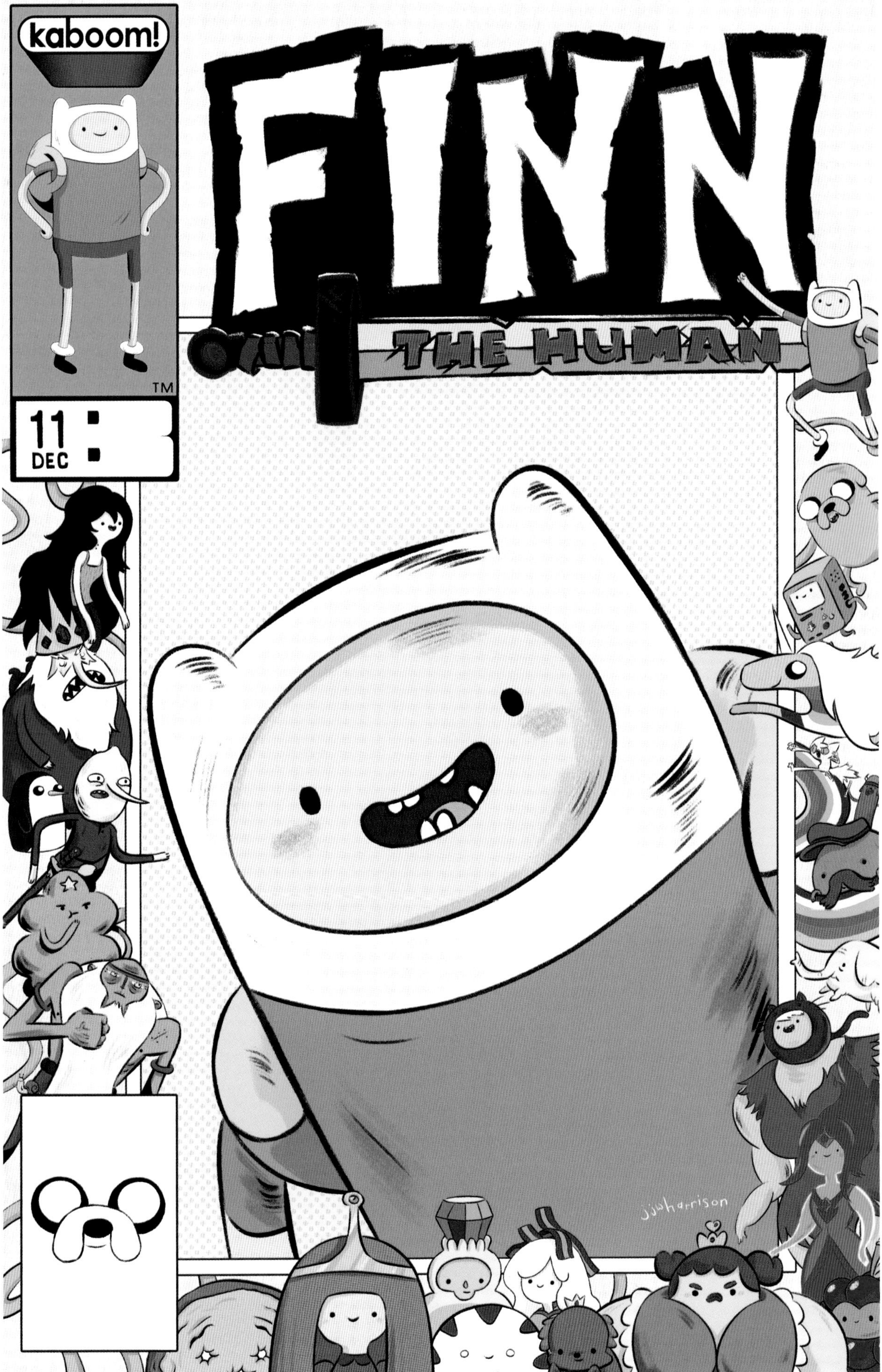
kaboom!
FINN
THE HUMAN
TM
11
DEC
jjwharrison

ISSUE ELEVEN BRETT'S COLLECTOR'S EXCLUSIVE | JJ HARRISON

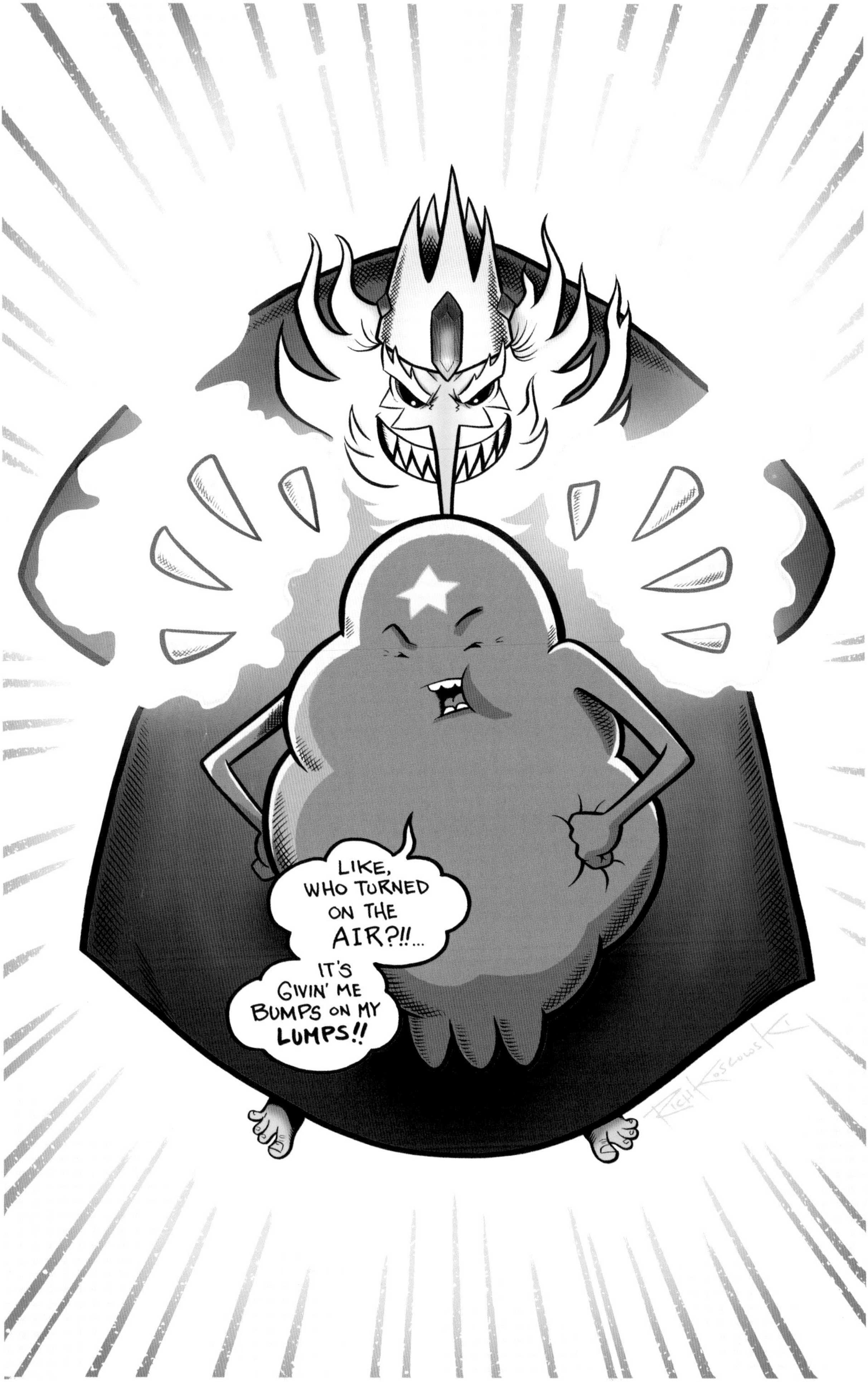
LIKE, WHO TURNED ON THE AIR?!!...
IT'S GIVIN' ME BUMPS ON MY LUMPS!!
RICH KOSCOWSKI

ISSUE ELEVEN DYNAMIC FORCES EXCLUSIVE | RICH KOSLOWSKI

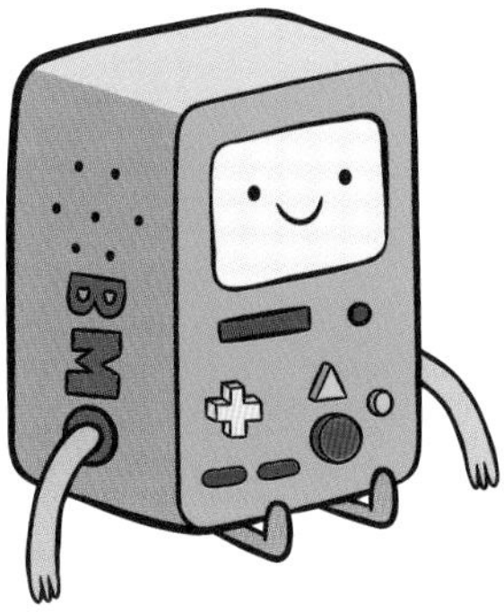
BMO

ISSUE TWELVE

"DEAR DIARY: RAW DISPLAYS OF
EMOTION AND FREE FOOD?
BEST VISIT TO FINN AND JAKE'S PLACE EVER!!"

- LUMPY SPACE PRINCESS

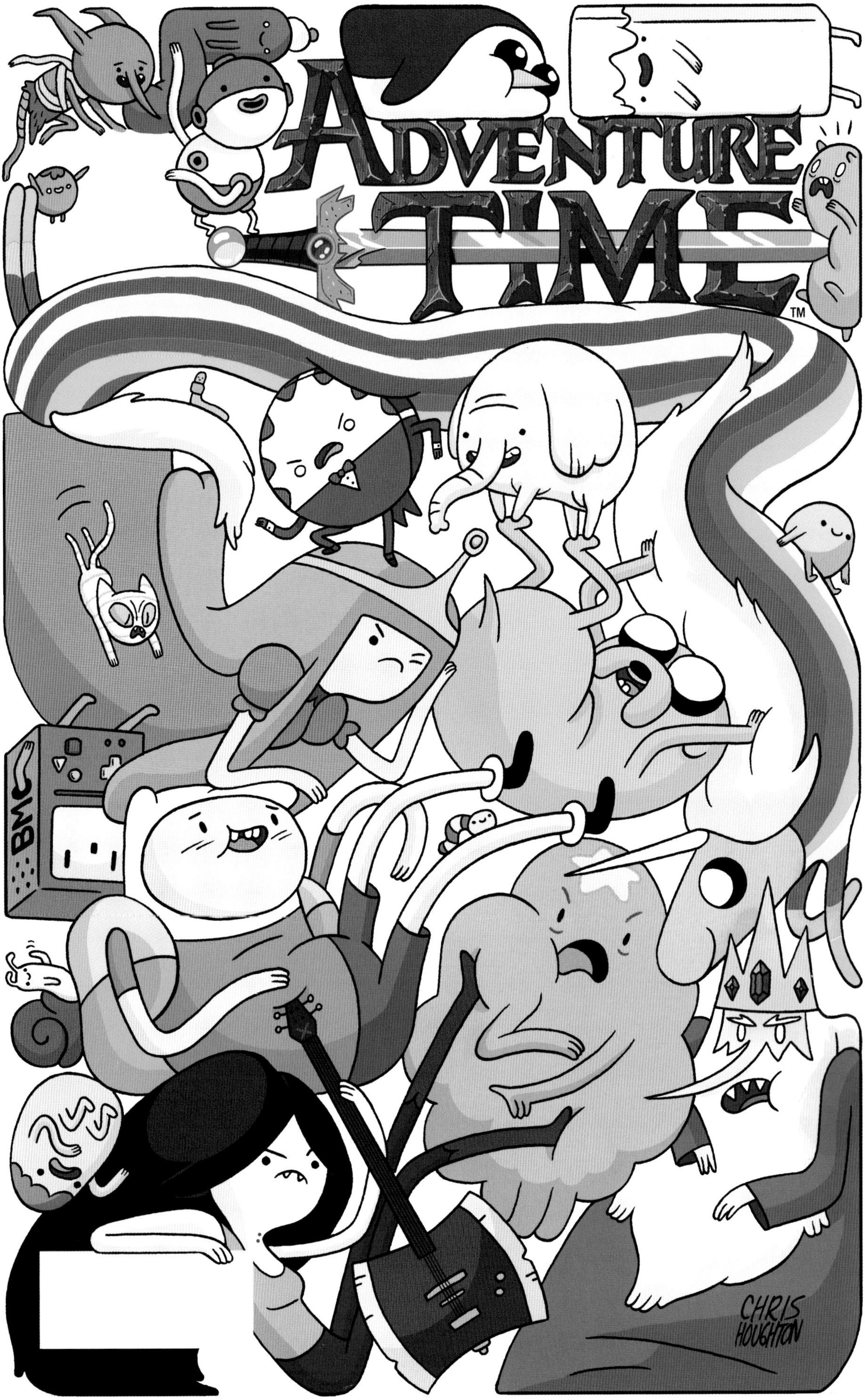
ADVENTURE TIME
TM
BMO
CHRIS HOUGHTON

ISSUE TWELVE | CHRIS HOUGHTON | COLORS BY KASSANDRA HELLER

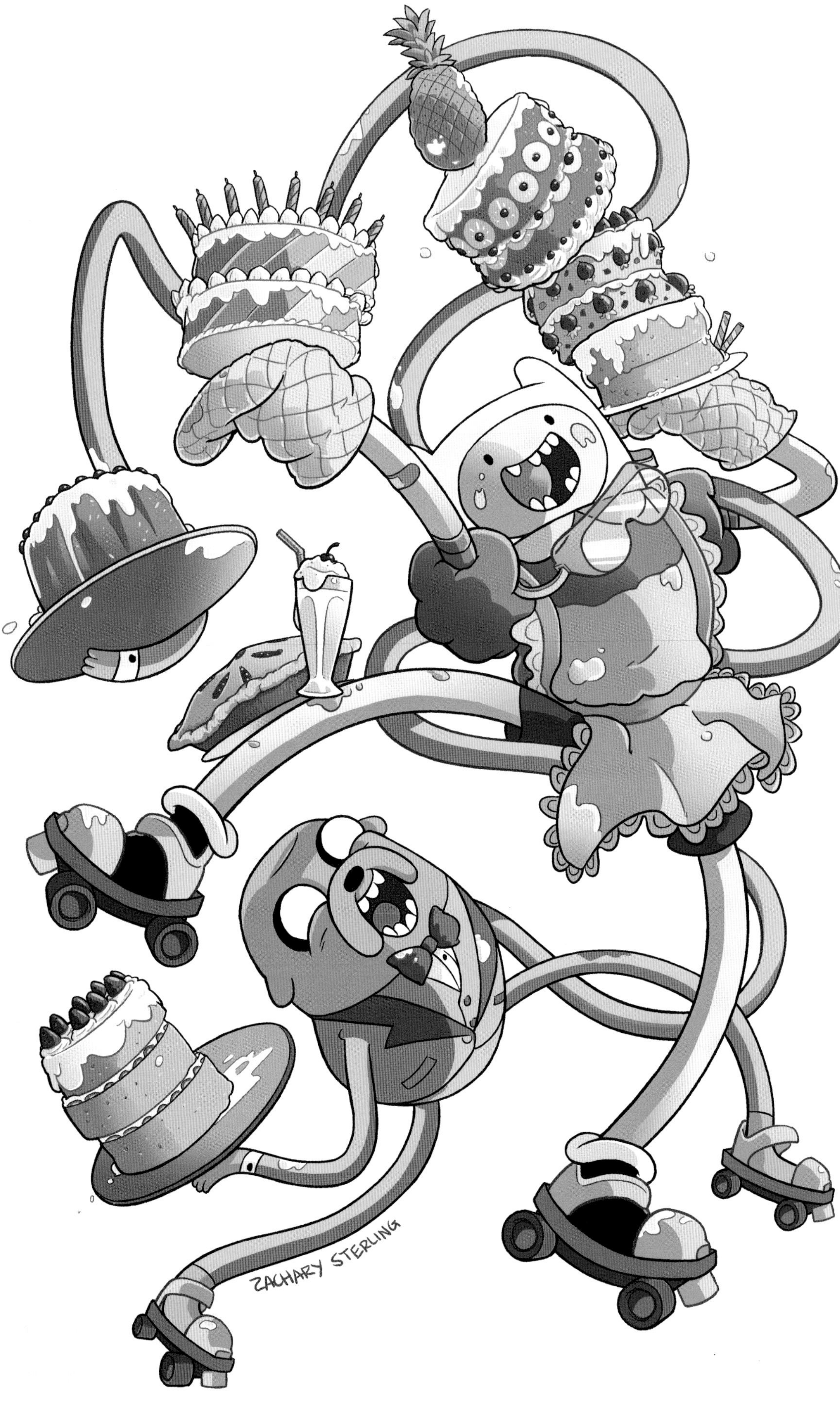
ZACHARY STERLING

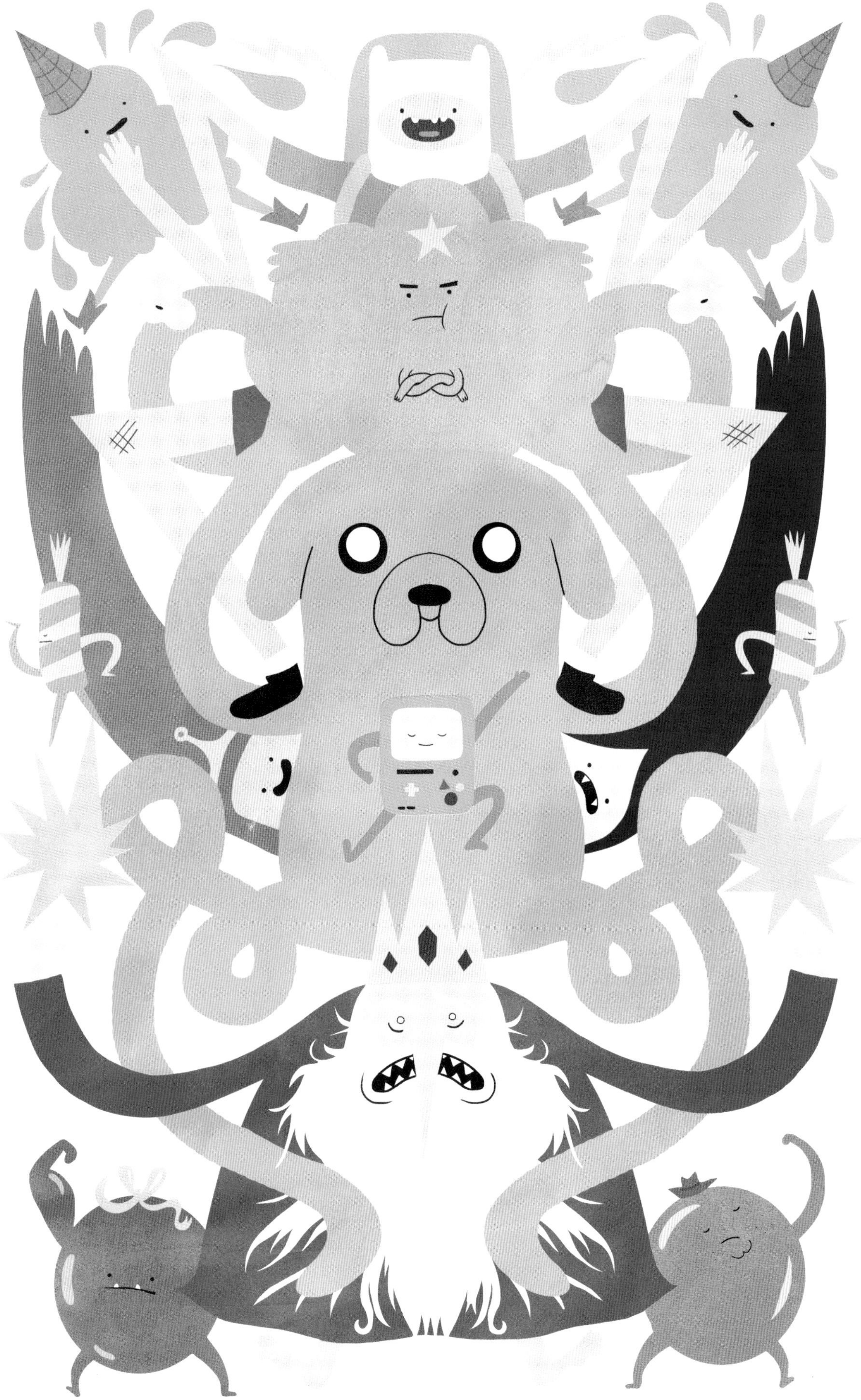

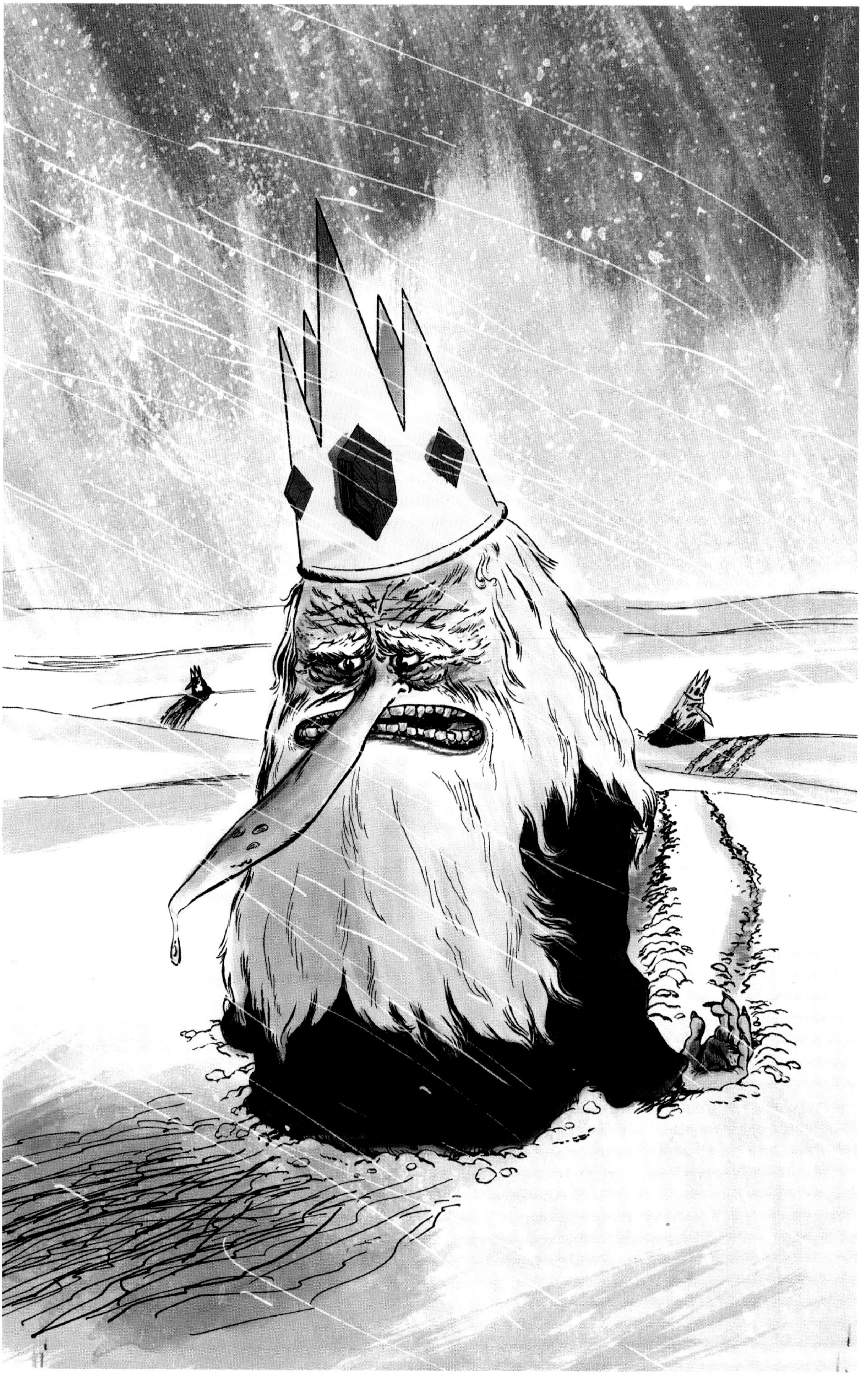

ISSUE TWELVE | DAVID KING

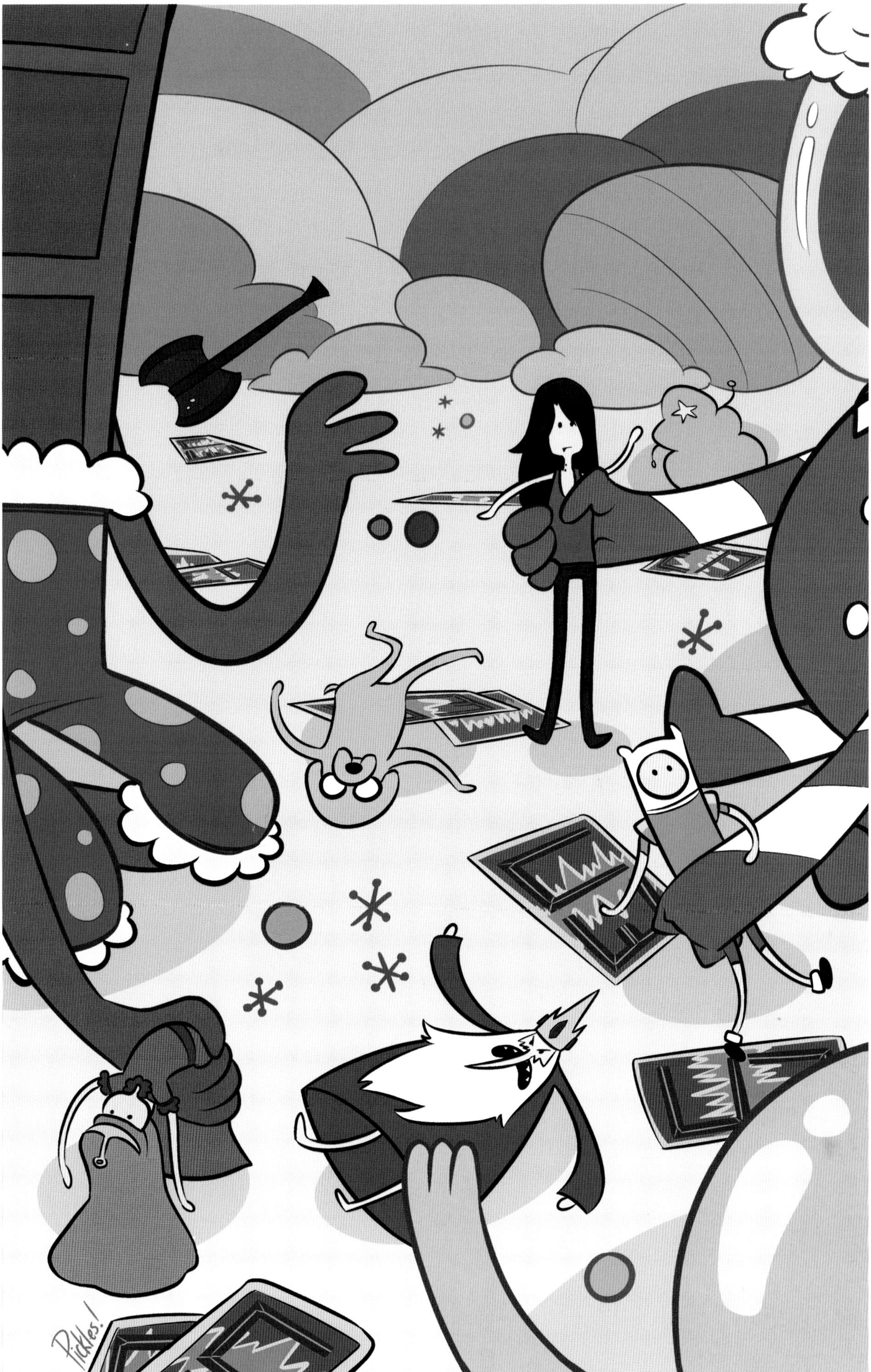
Pickles!

ISSUE TWELVE DYNAMIC FORCES EXCLUSIVE | SARAH "PICKLES" DILL

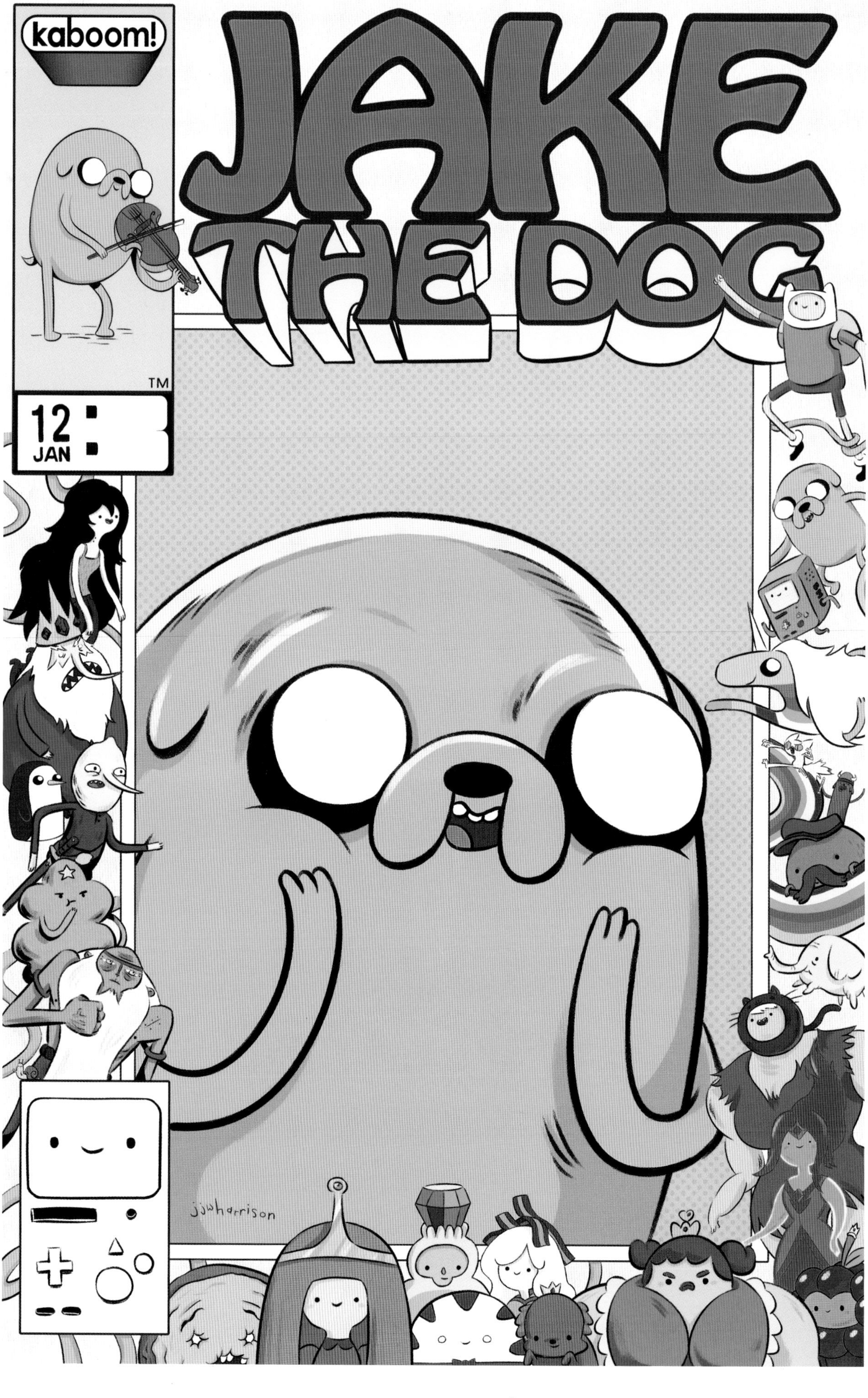
kaboom!
JAKE THE DOG
TM
12
JAN
jjwharrison

ISSUE TWELVE BRETT'S COLLECTOR'S EXCLUSIVE | JJ HARRISON

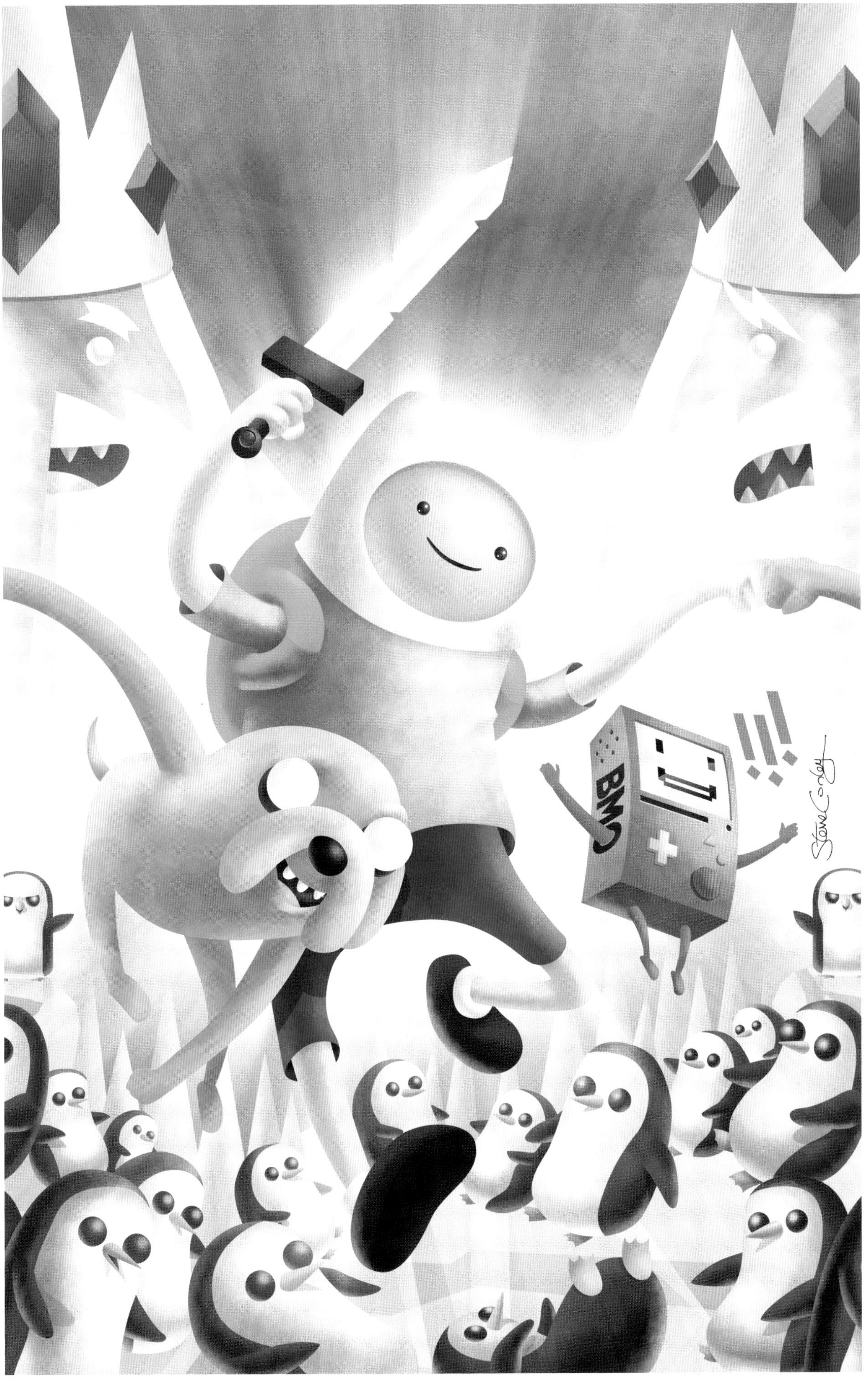
BMO
!!!
Steve Conley

ISSUE TWELVE CARDS, COMICS AND COLLECTIBLES EXCLUSIVE | STEVE CONLEY

ISSUE THIRTEEN

"I LOVE IT WHEN A SENSIBLE BEDTIME PAYS OFF."

– FINN

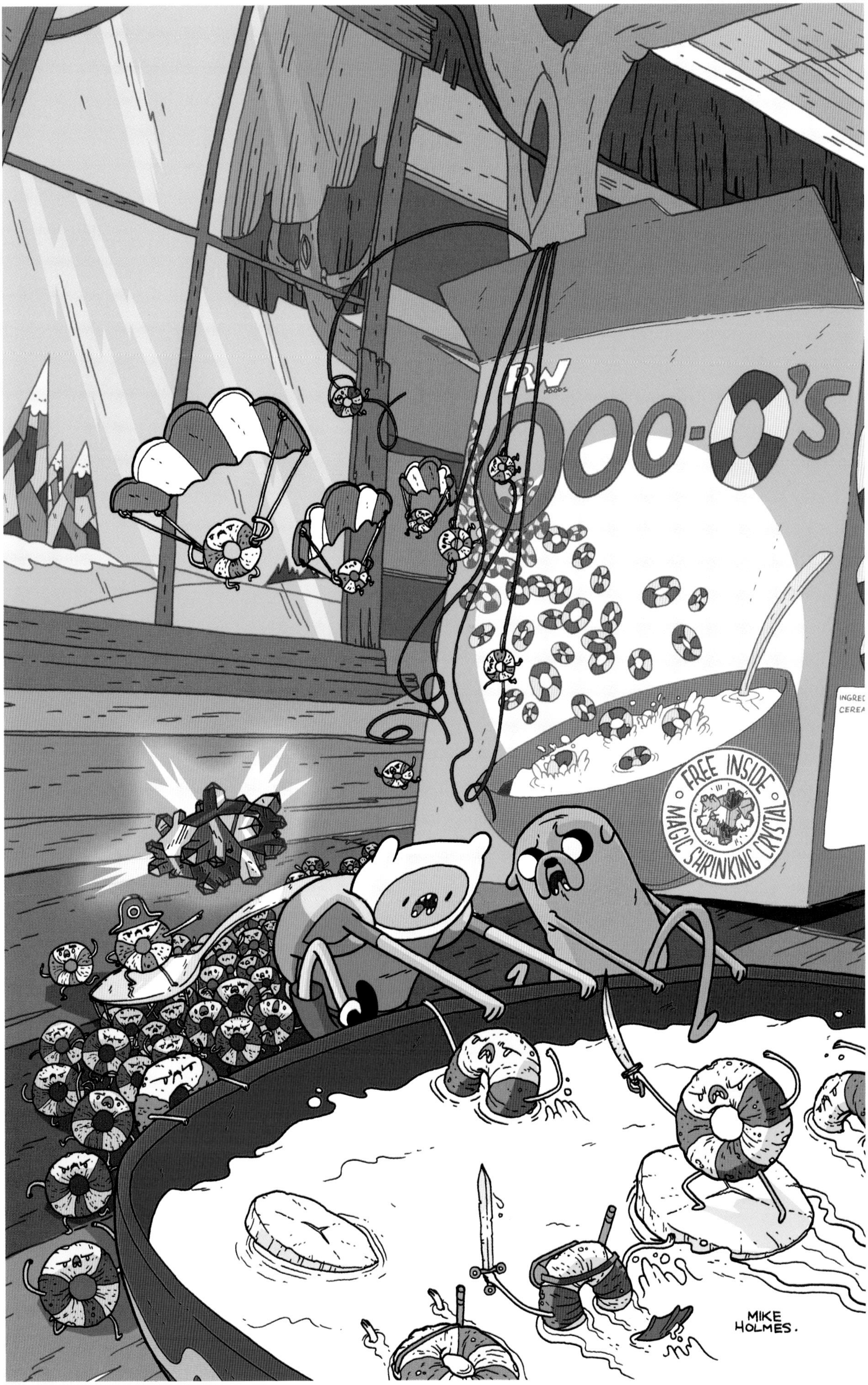
RW FOODS
OOO-O'S
FREE INSIDE
MAGIC SHRINKING CRYSTAL
INGRED
CEREA
MIKE HOLMES.

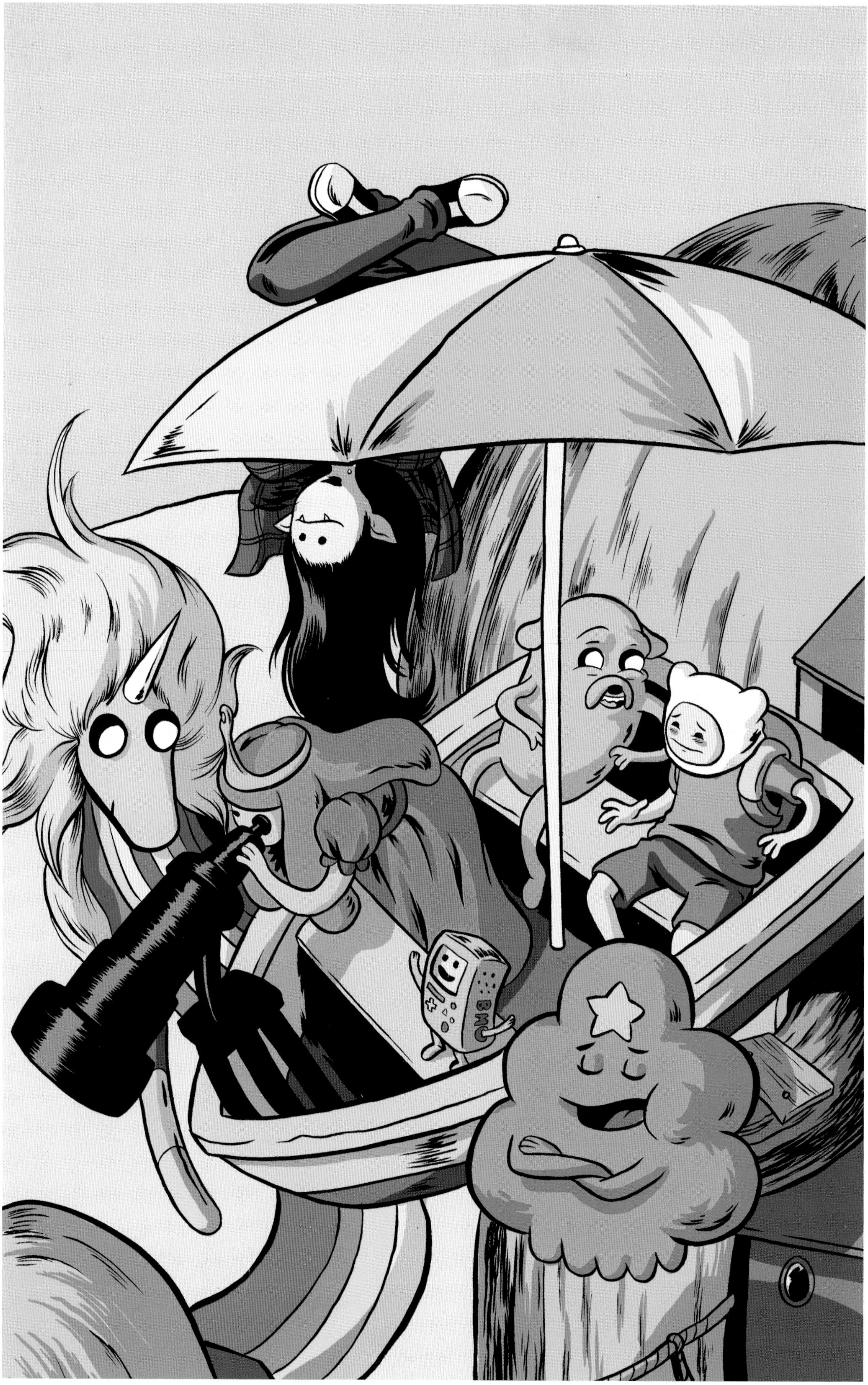
BMO

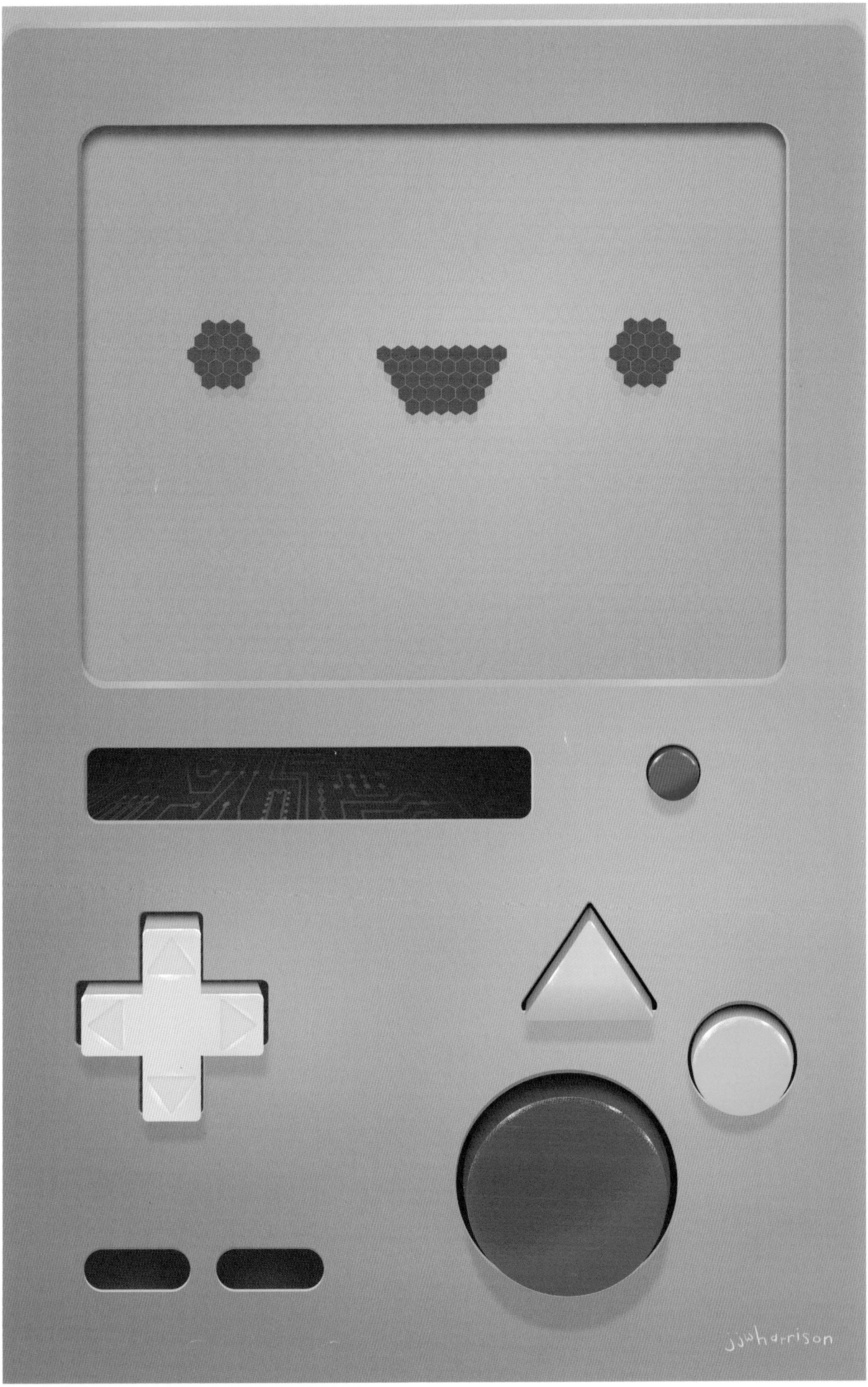
jjwharrison

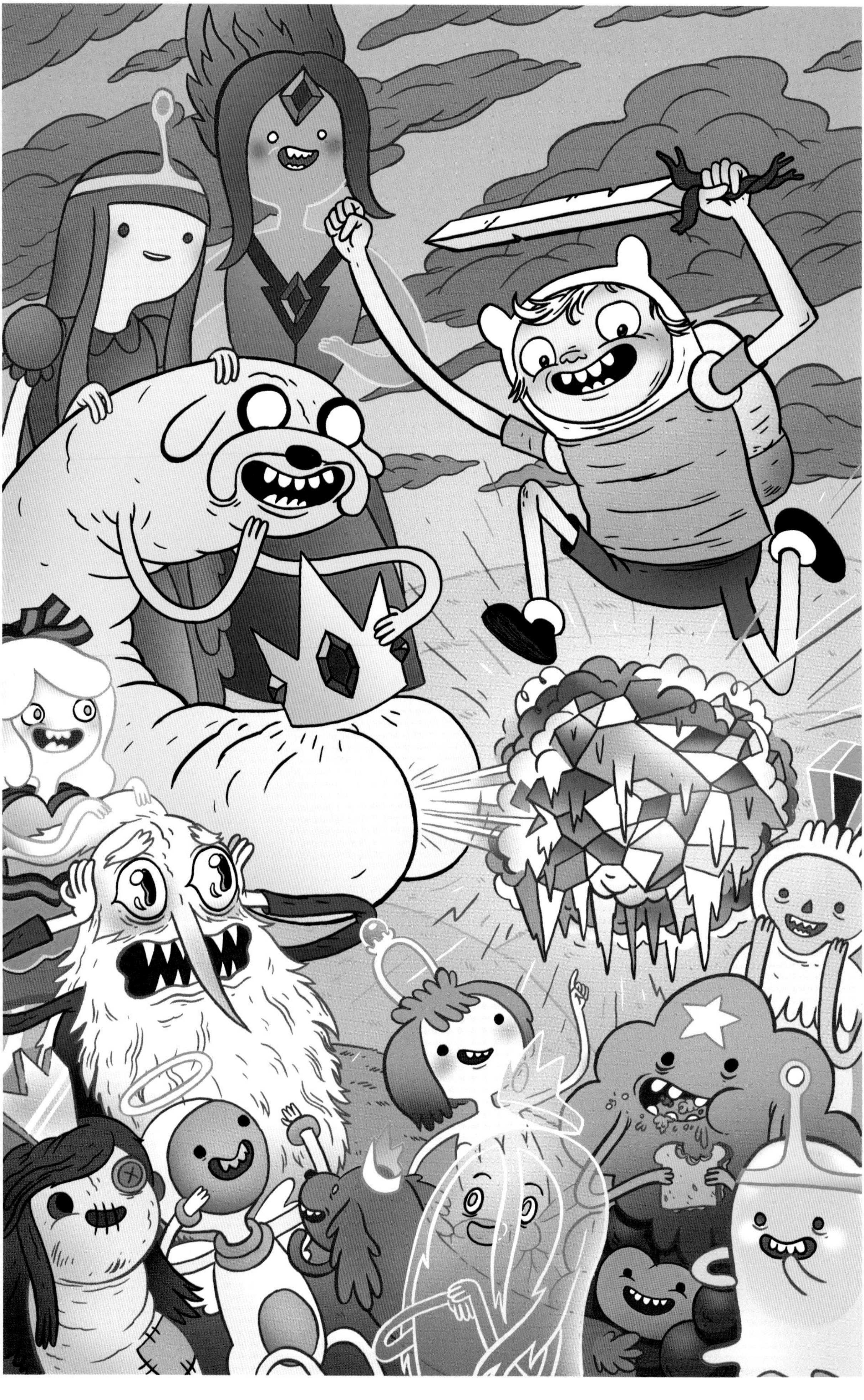

ISSUE THIRTEEN | MIKE BERTINO

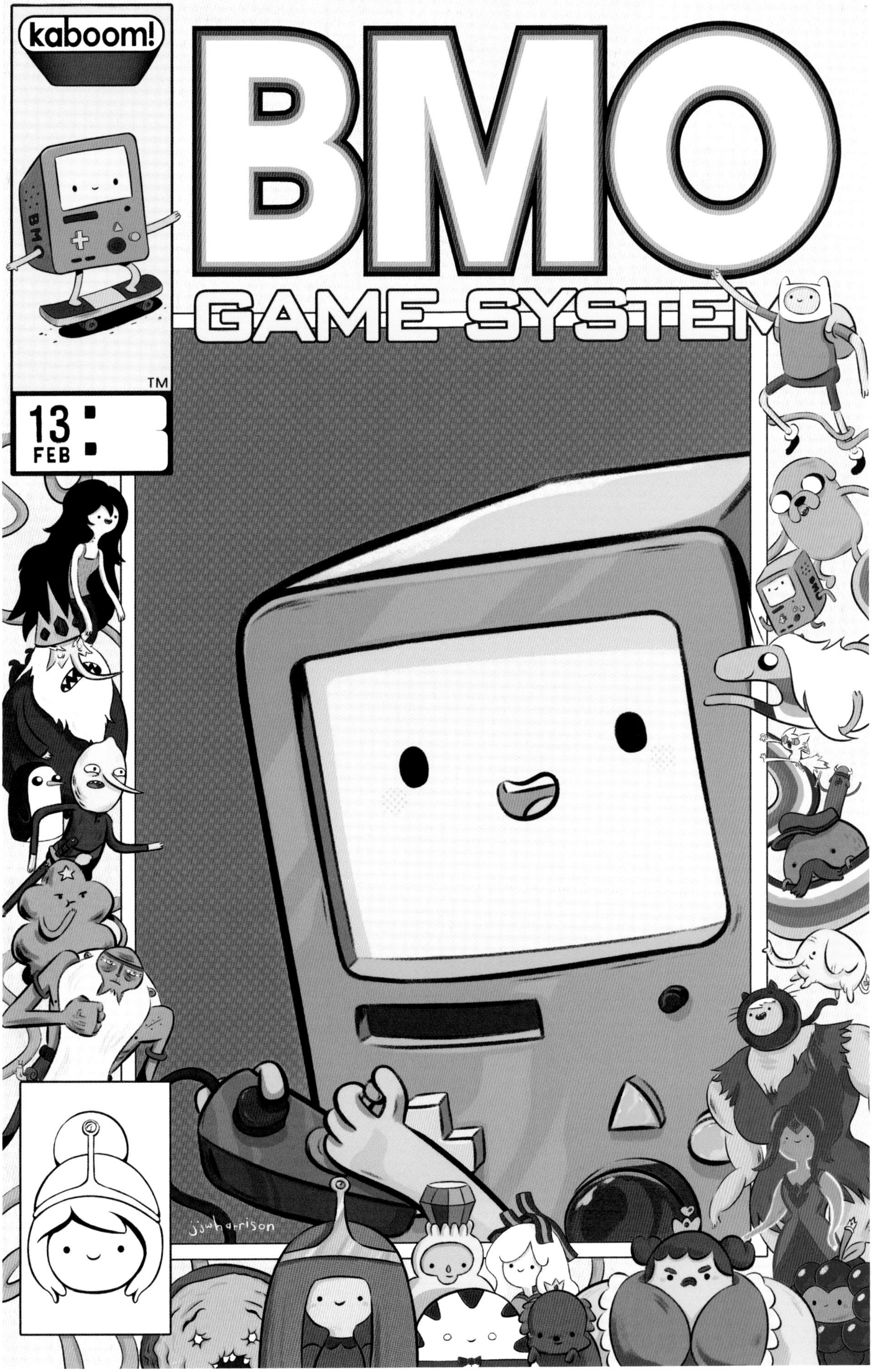
kaboom!
BMO
GAME SYSTEM
TM
13
FEB
jjwharrison

ISSUE THIRTEEN BRETT'S COLLECTOR'S EXCLUSIVE | JJ HARRISON

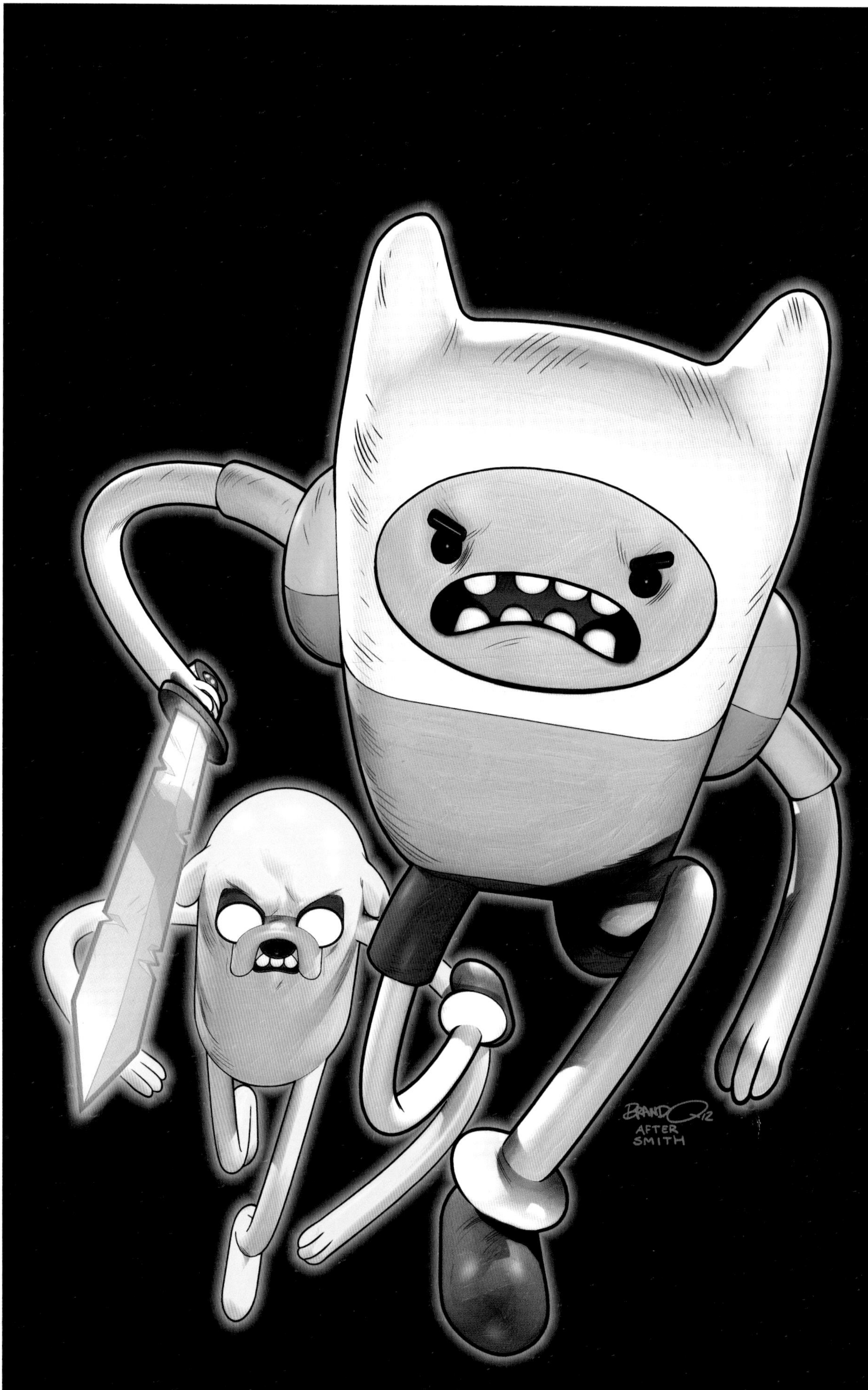
BRANDO '12
AFTER
SMITH

ISSUE THIRTEEN CARDS, COMICS AND COLLECTIBLES EXCLUSIVE | BRANDON PETERSON

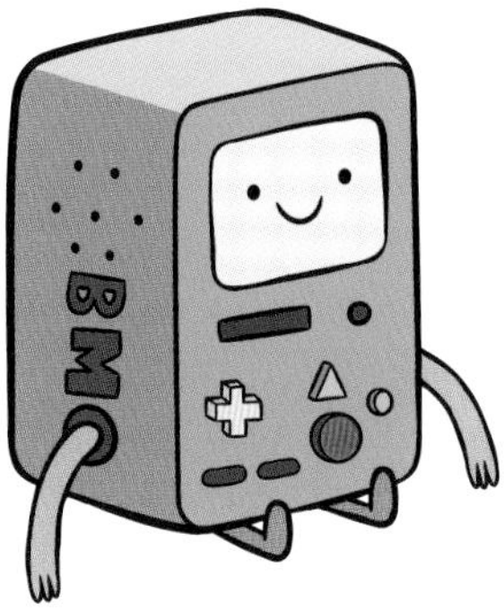
BMO

ISSUE FOURTEEN

"DUDE, THE BELLY OF THE BRO
MANEUVER WAS A COMPLETE SUCCESS!"

– FINN

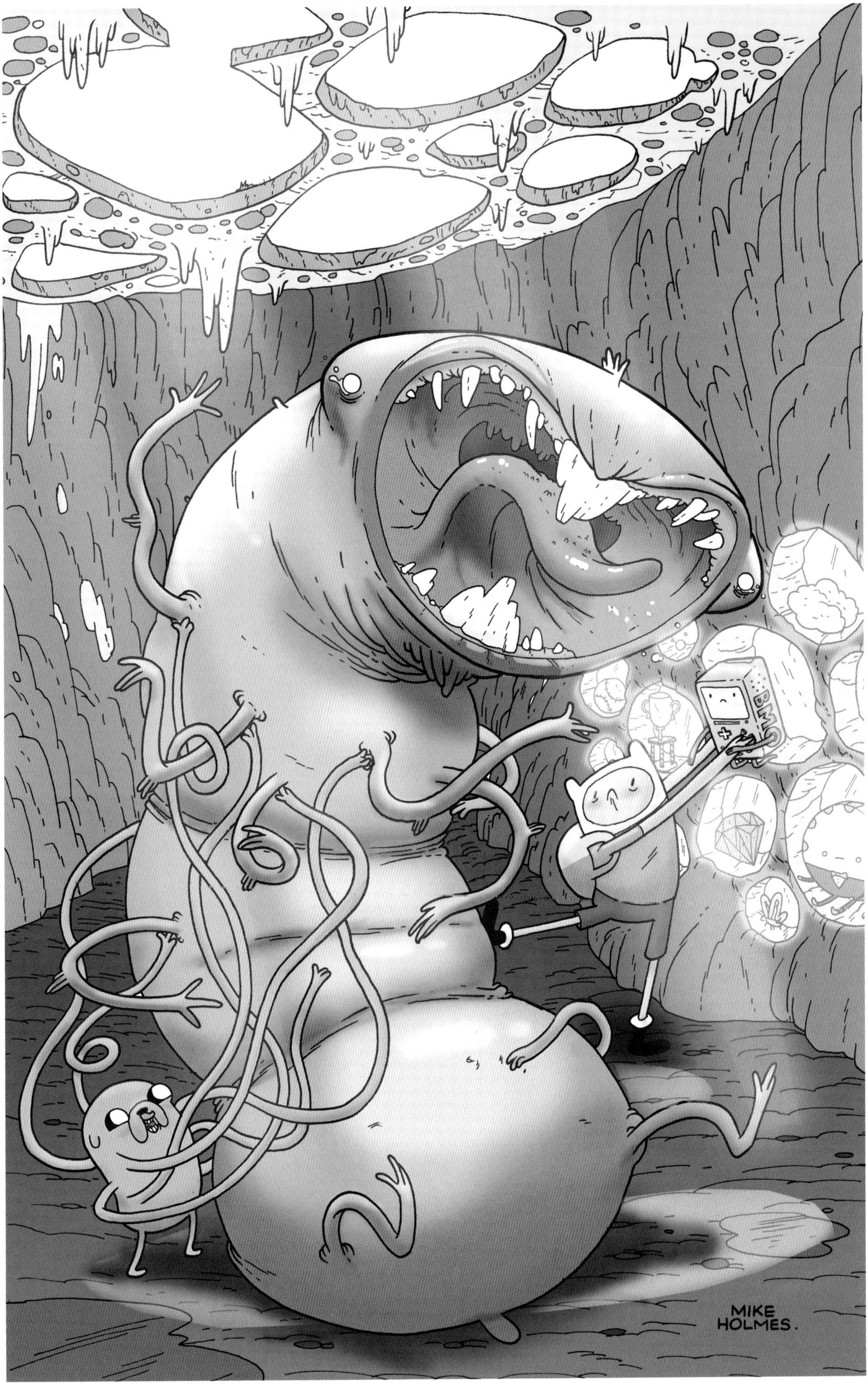
BMO
MIKE
HOLMES.

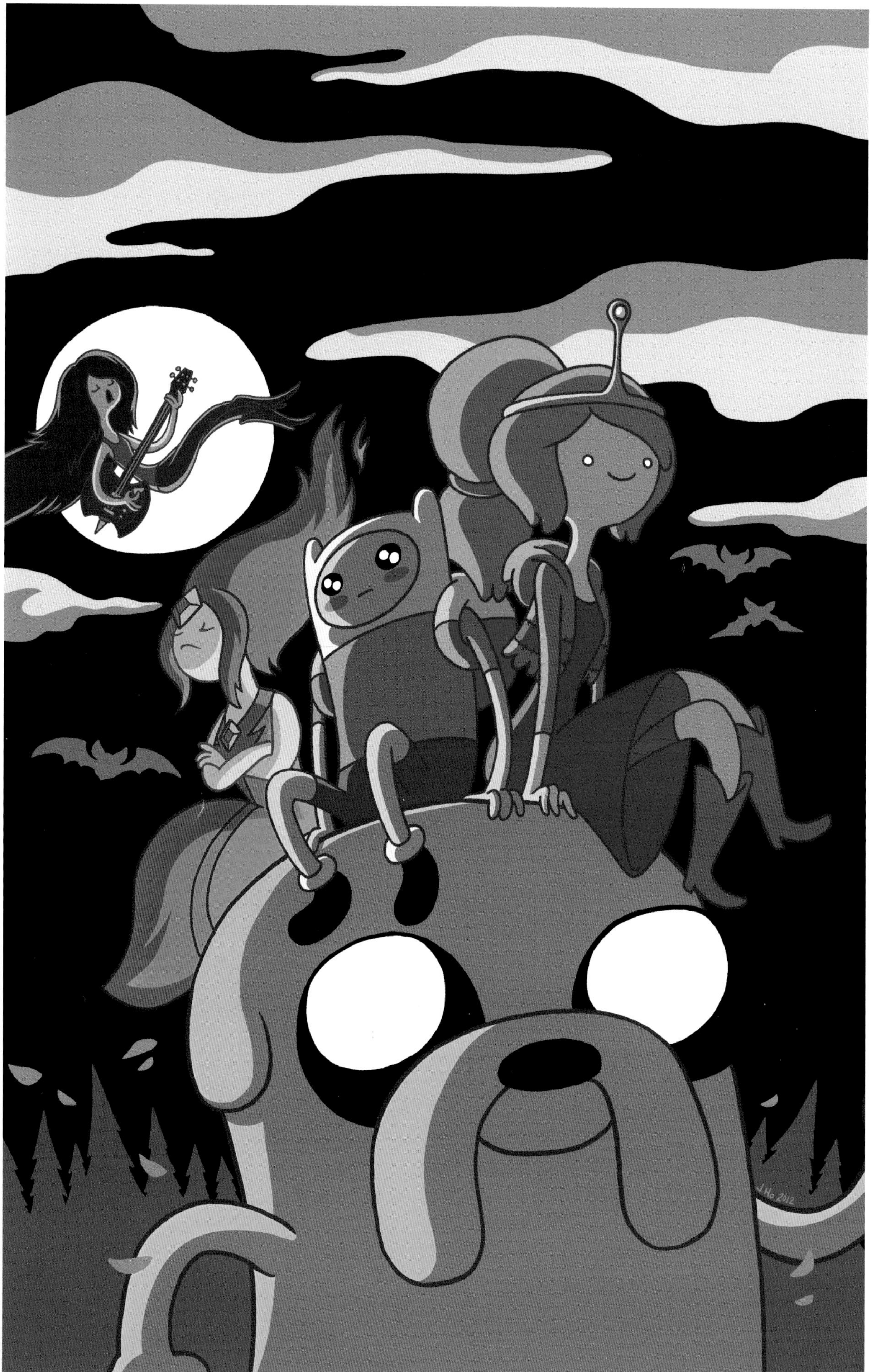
J.Ho 2012

ISSUE FOURTEEN | JASON HO

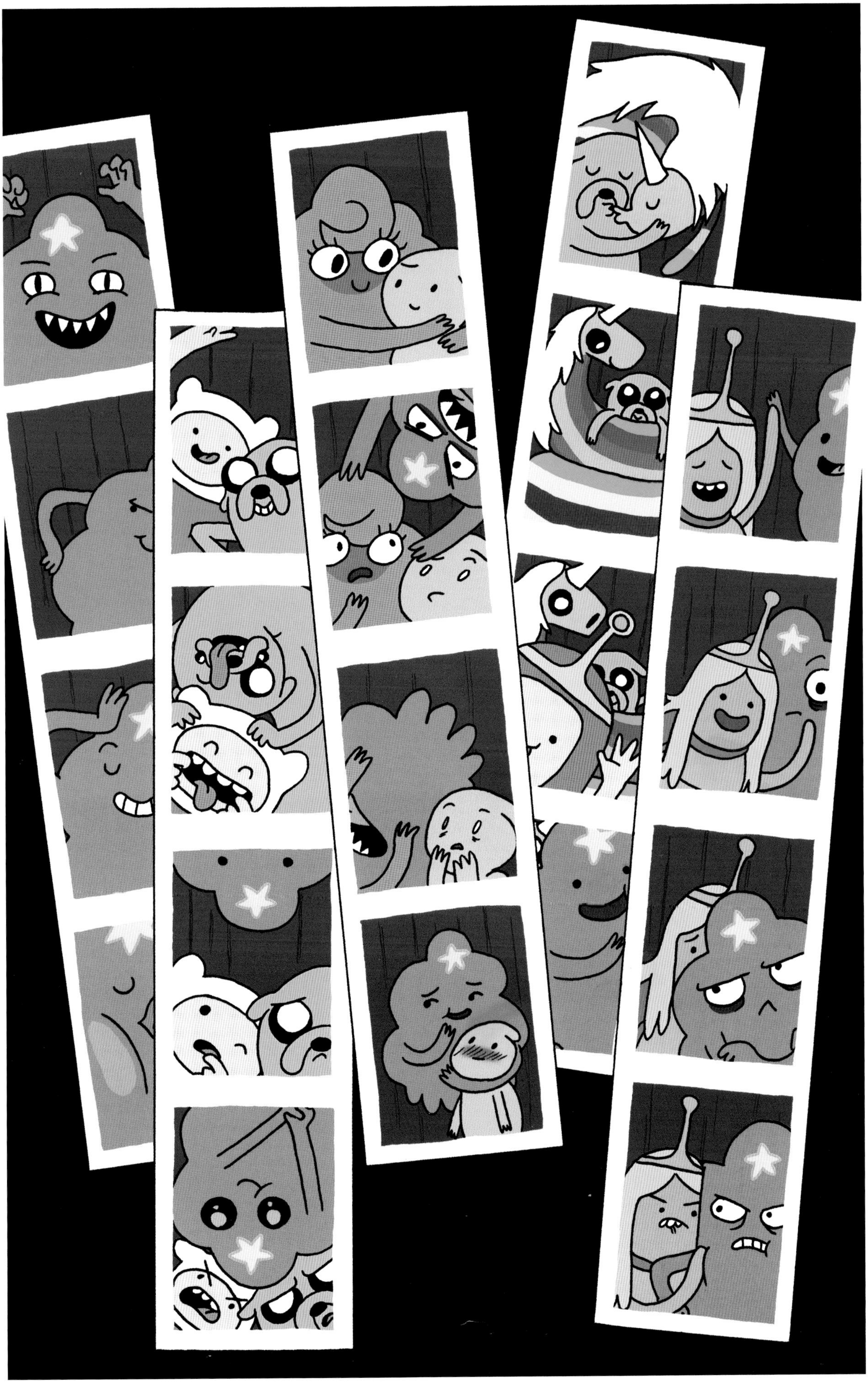

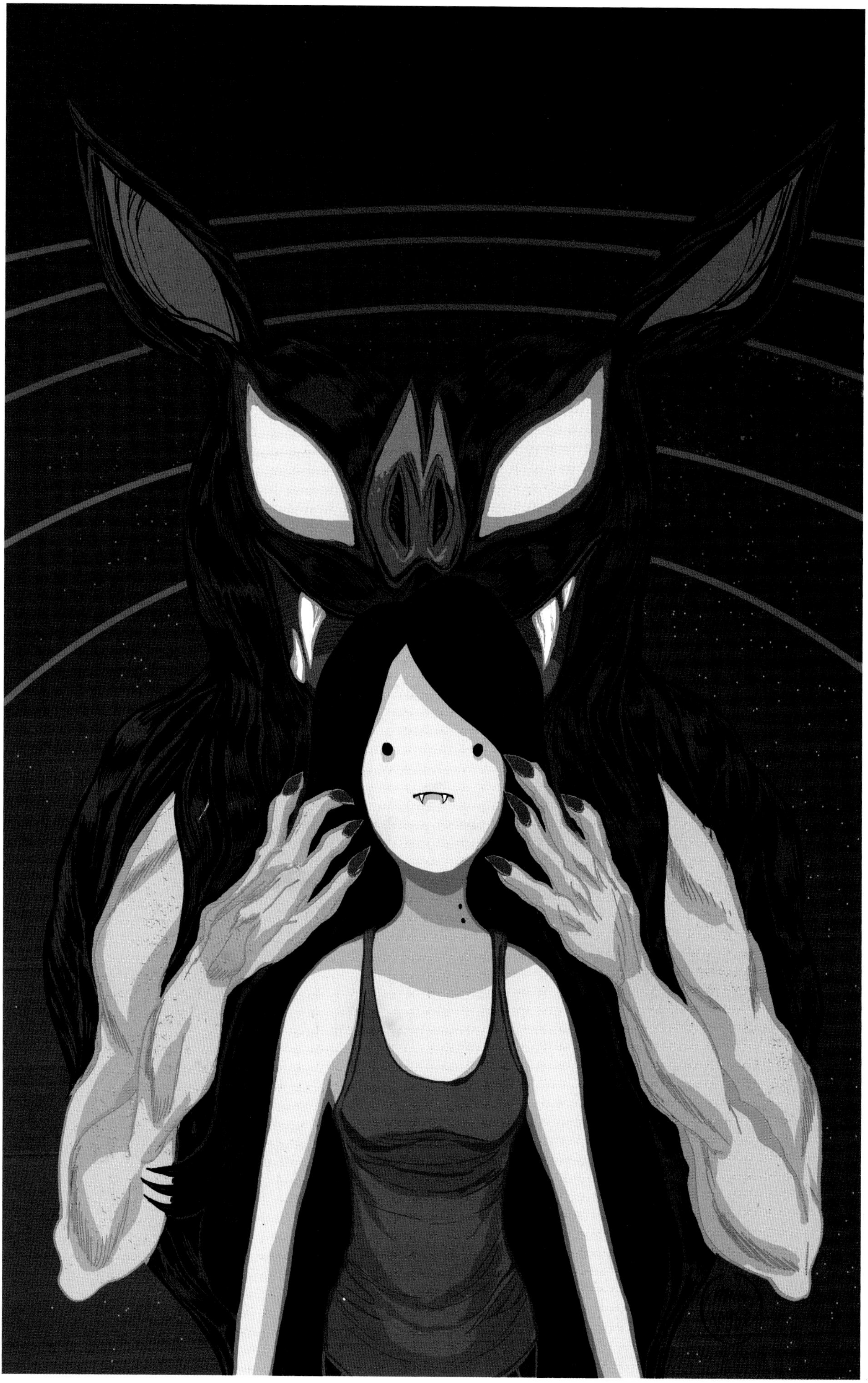

ISSUE FOURTEEN | MING DOYLE

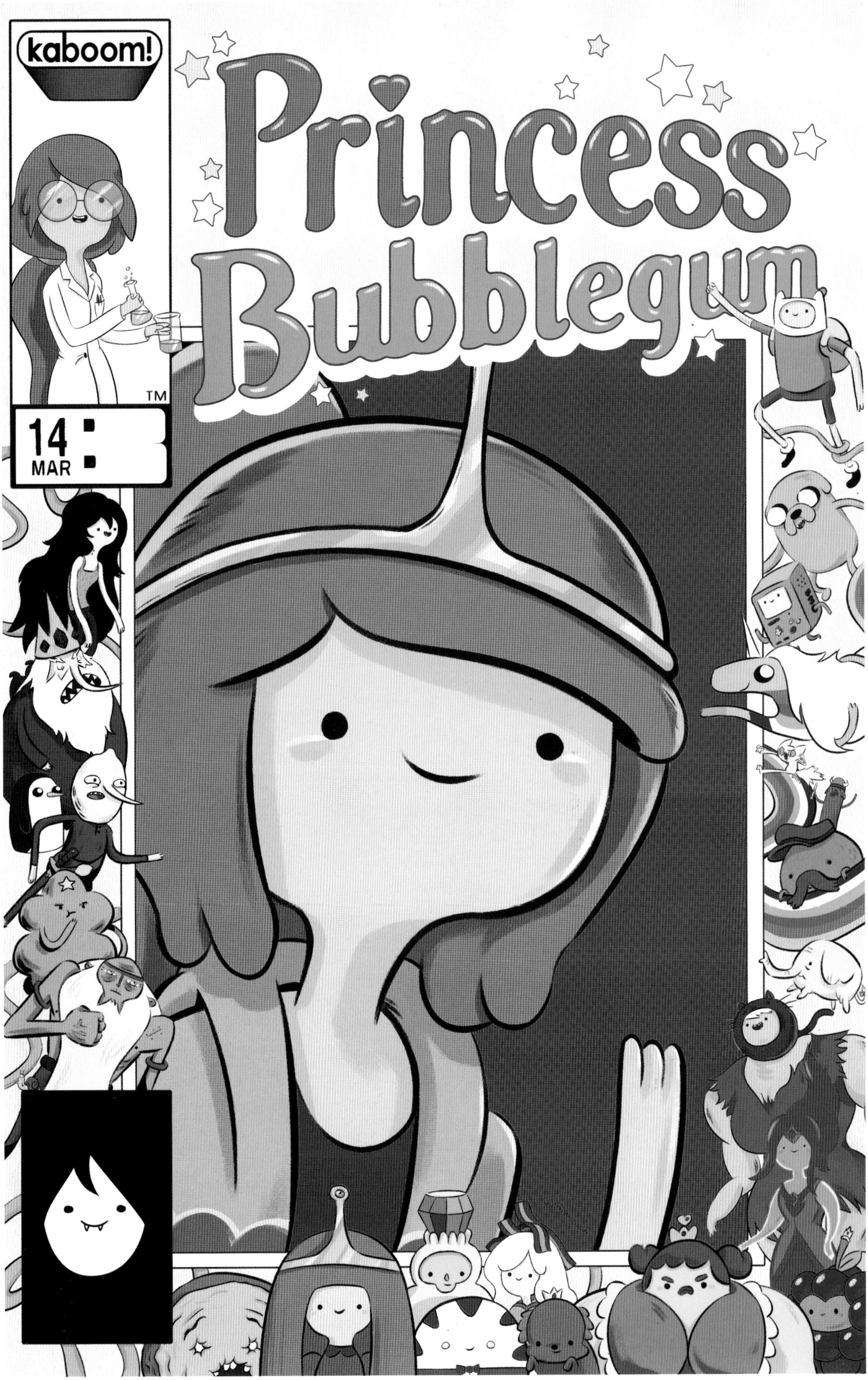
kaboom!
Princess Bubblegum
TM
14
MAR

ISSUE FOURTEEN BRETT'S COLLECTOR'S EXCLUSIVE | JJ HARRISON

ISSUE FIFTEEN

"CRASH? WHY BUBBLEGUM,
THAT SOUNDS PERFECTLY DELIGHTFUL.
MAAAAAAGIC!"

- MAGIC MAN

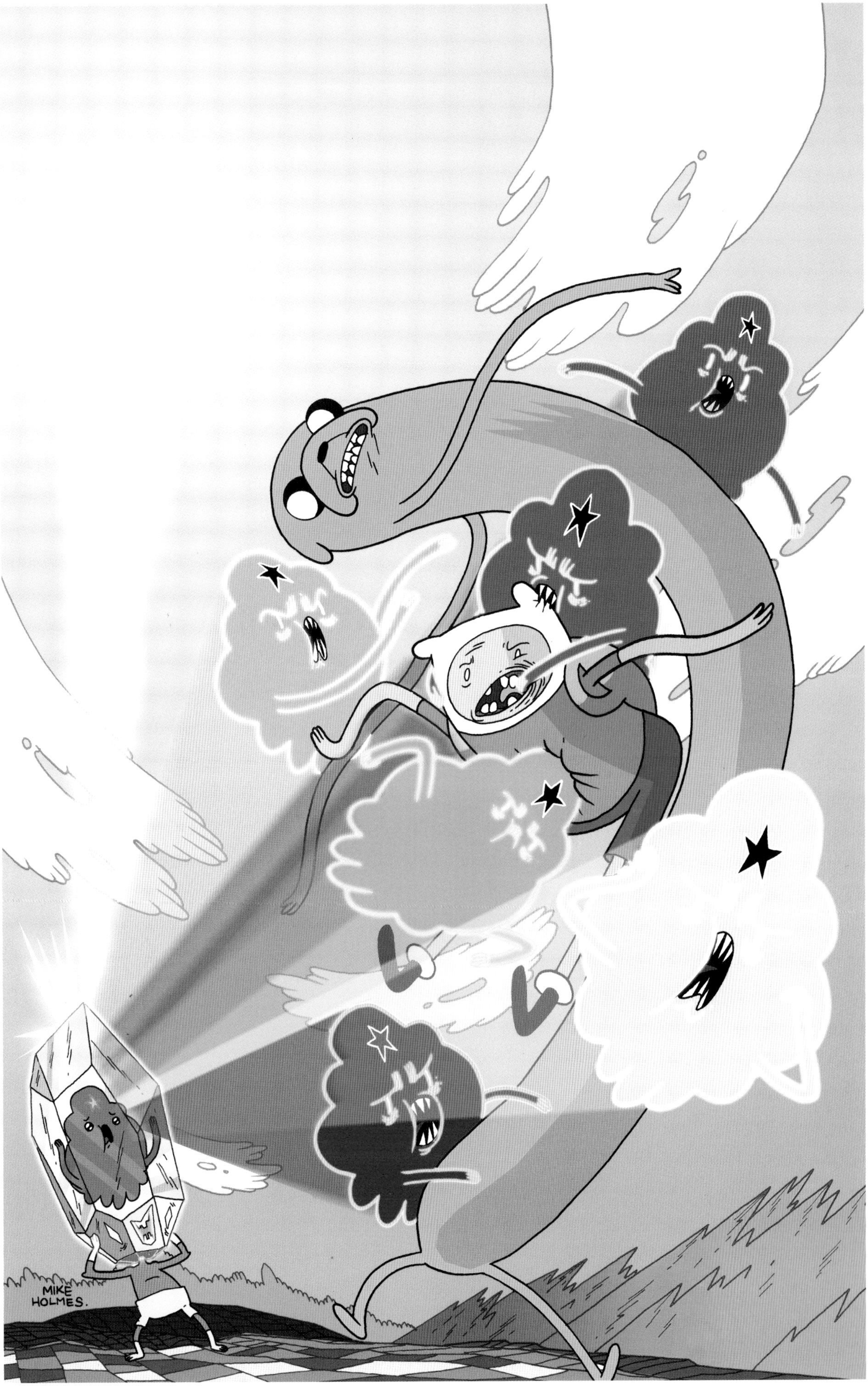
MIKE HOLMES.

ISSUE FIFTEEN | MIKE HOLMES

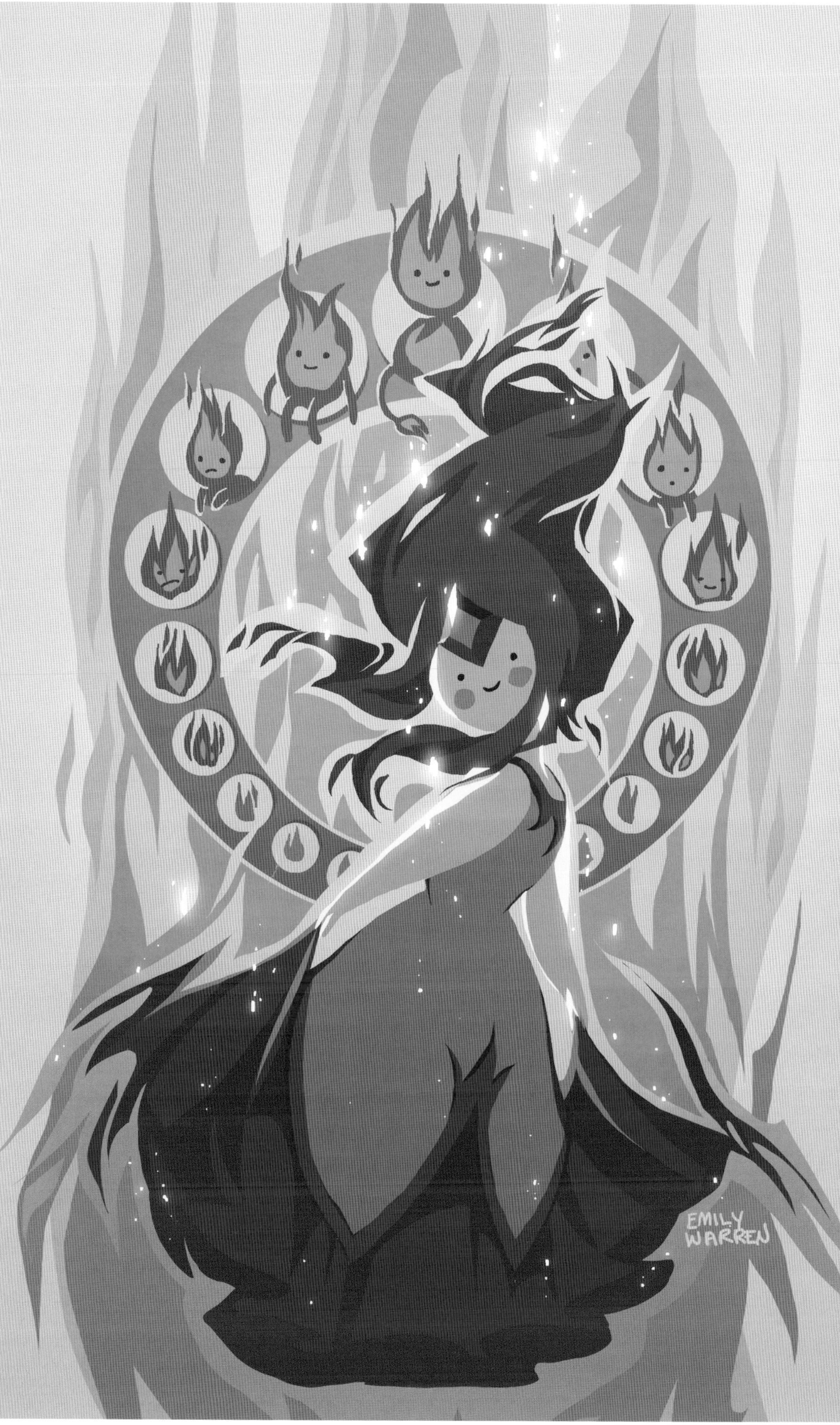
EMILY
WARREN

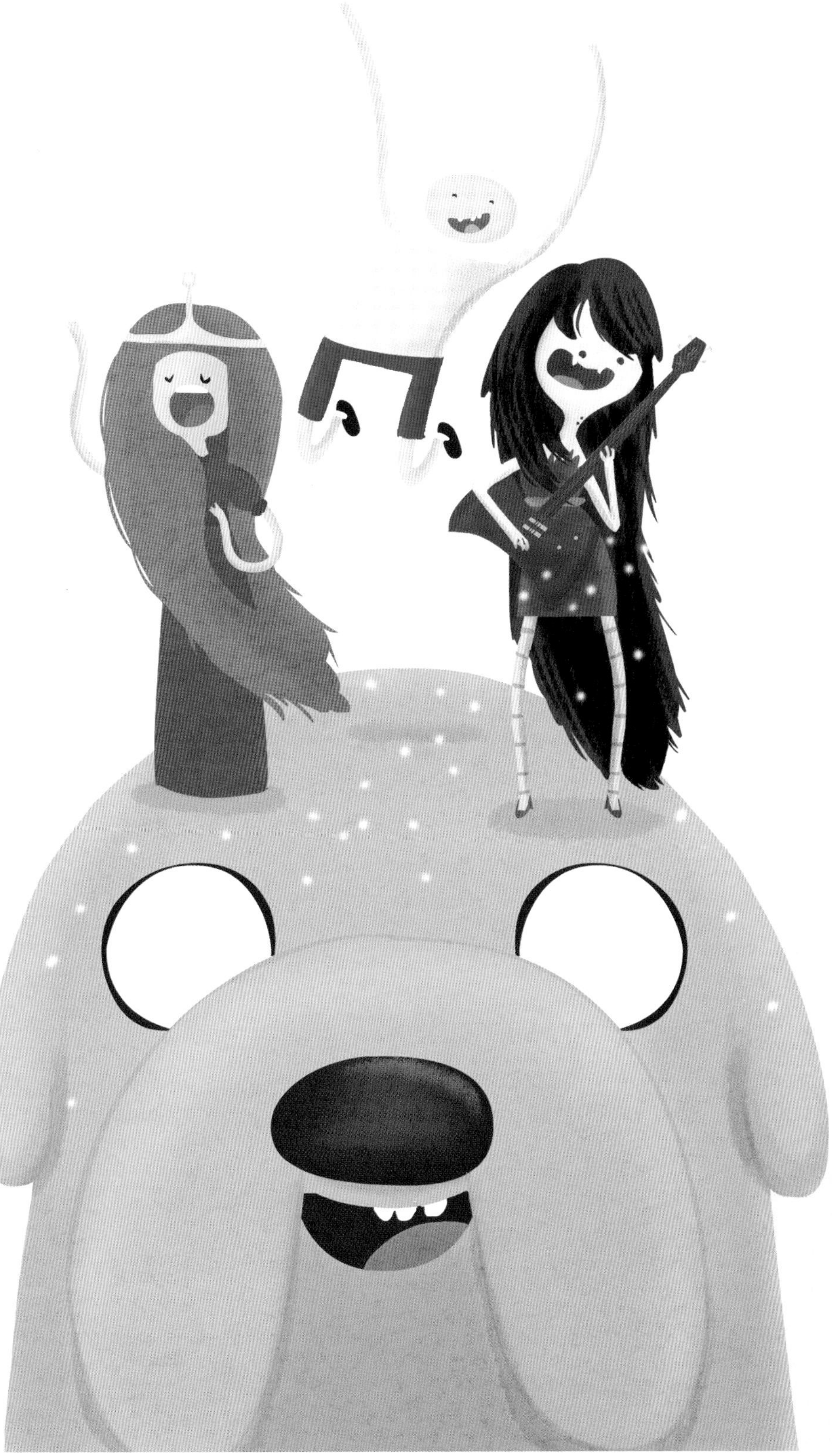

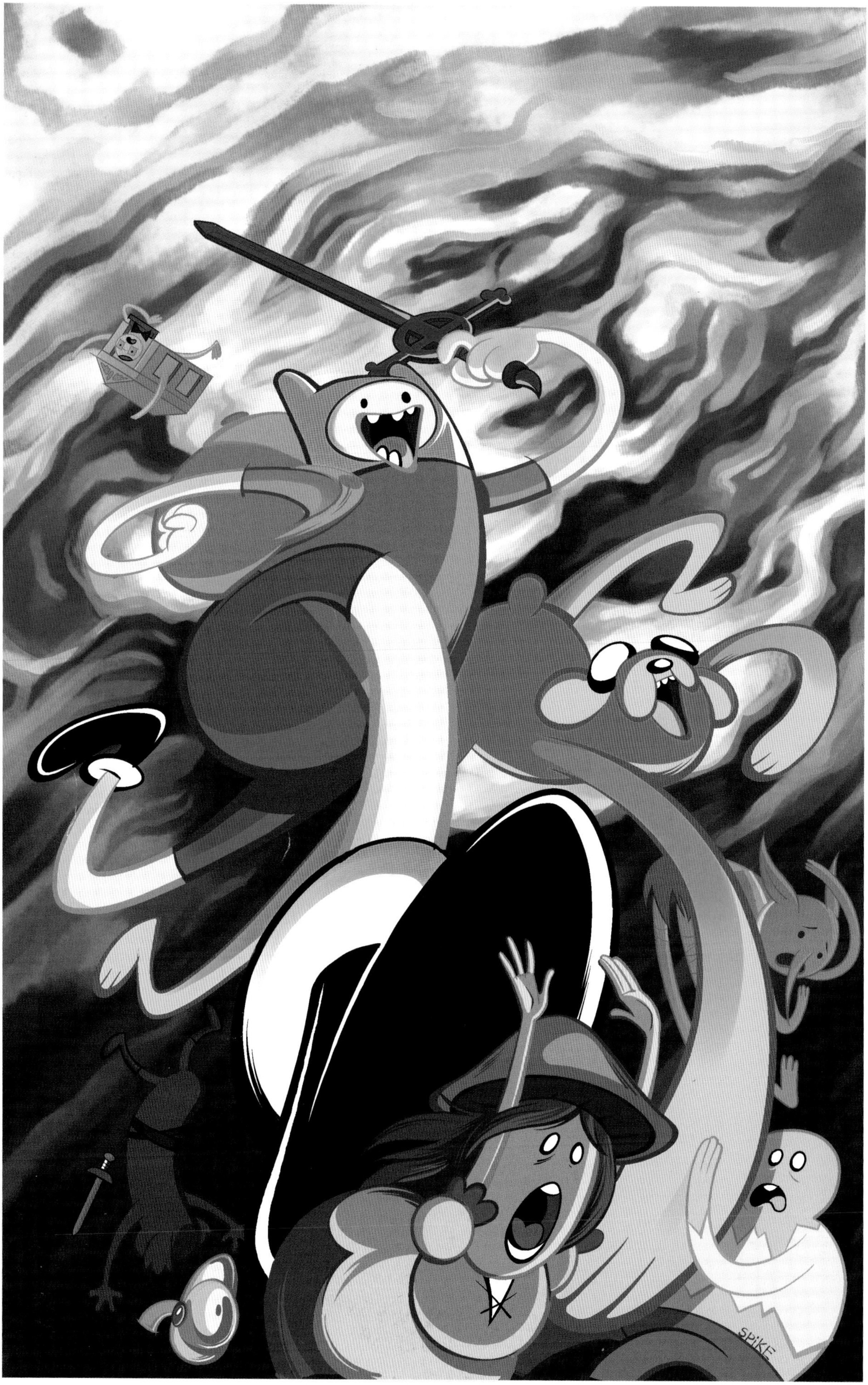
SPIKE

ISSUE FIFTEEN | SPIKE TRAUTMAN

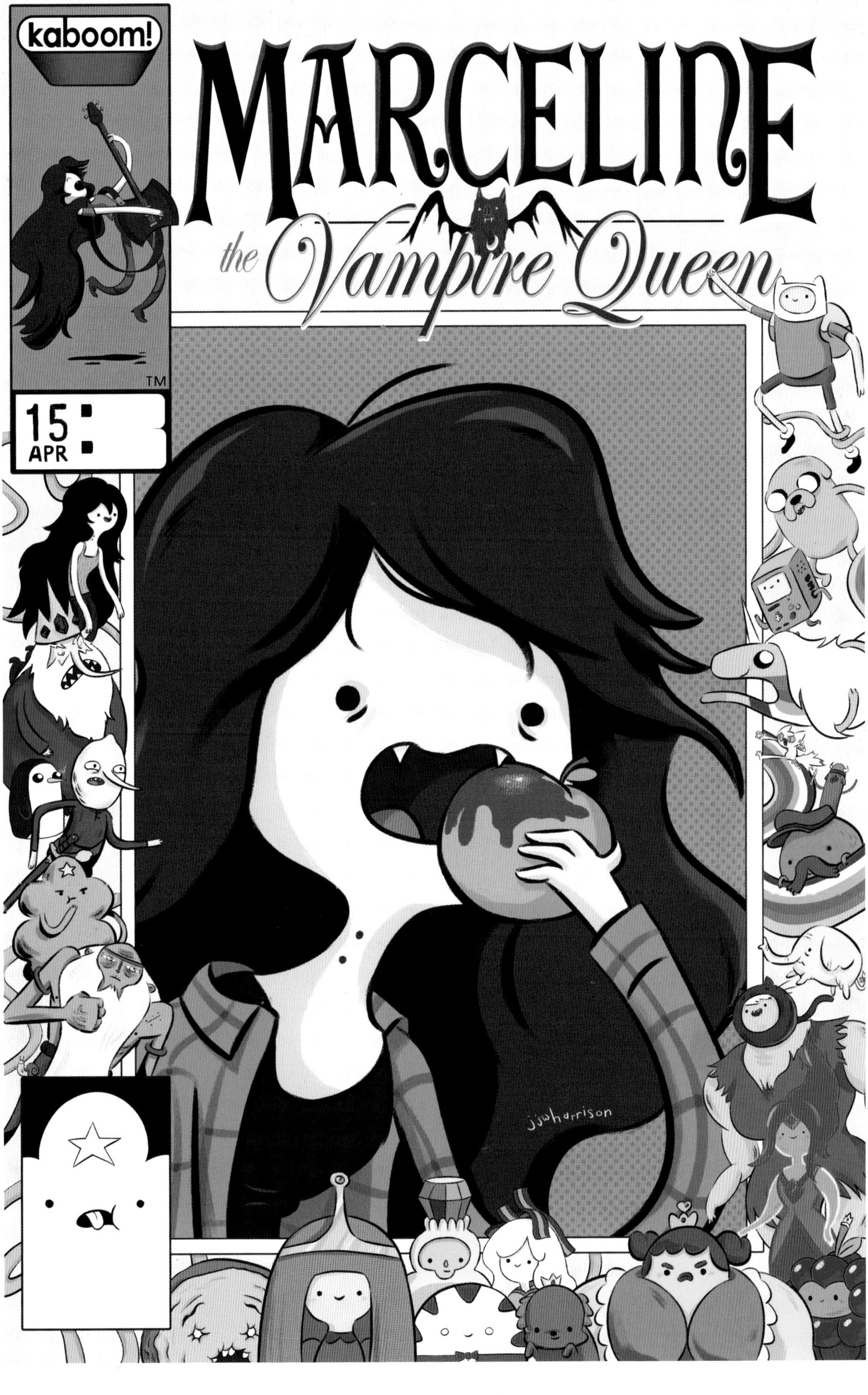
kaboom!
MARCELINE
the Vampire Queen
TM
15
APR
jjwharrison

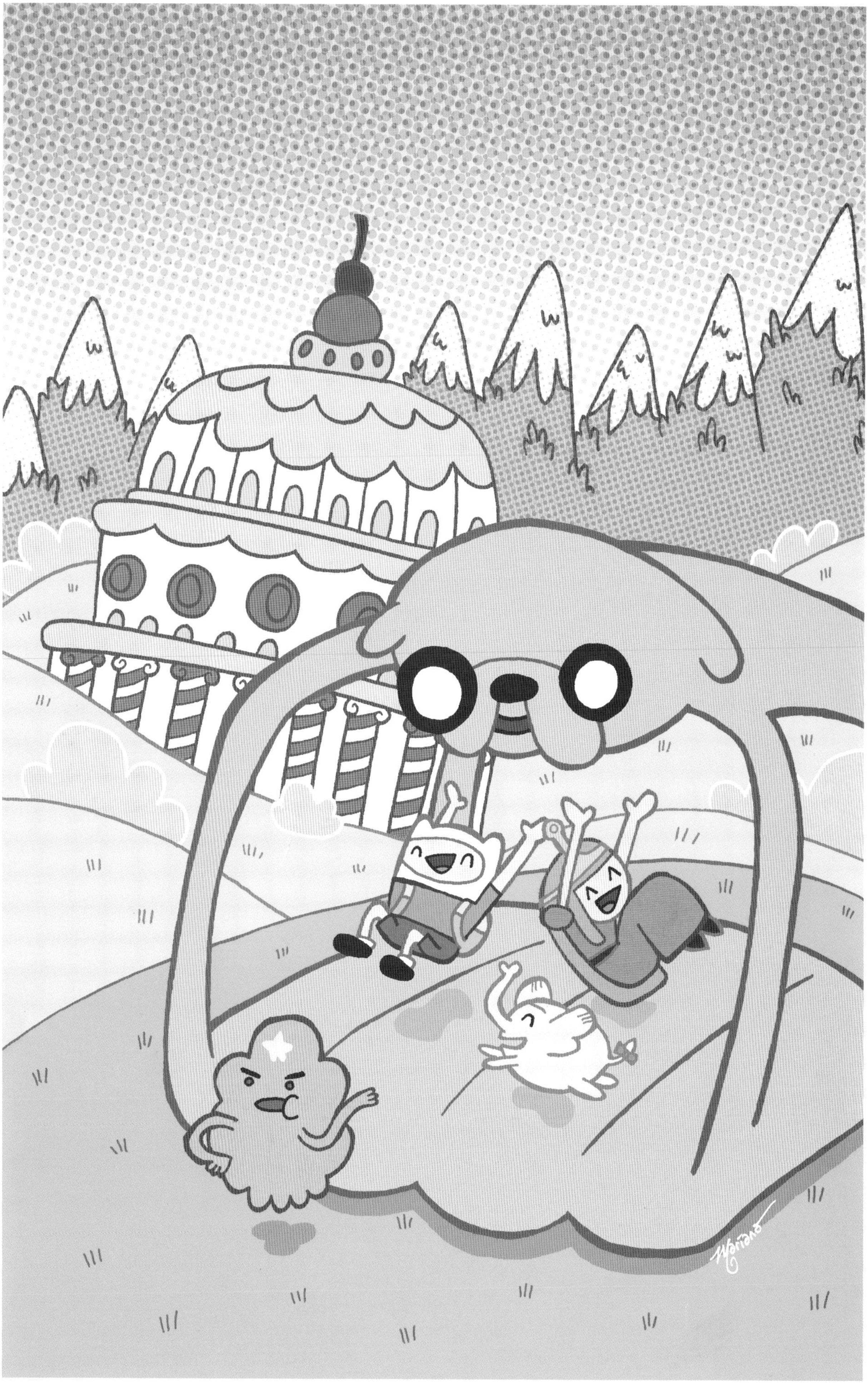
Mariano

ISSUE FIFTEEN AWESOME CON EXCLUSIVE | MARK MARIANO

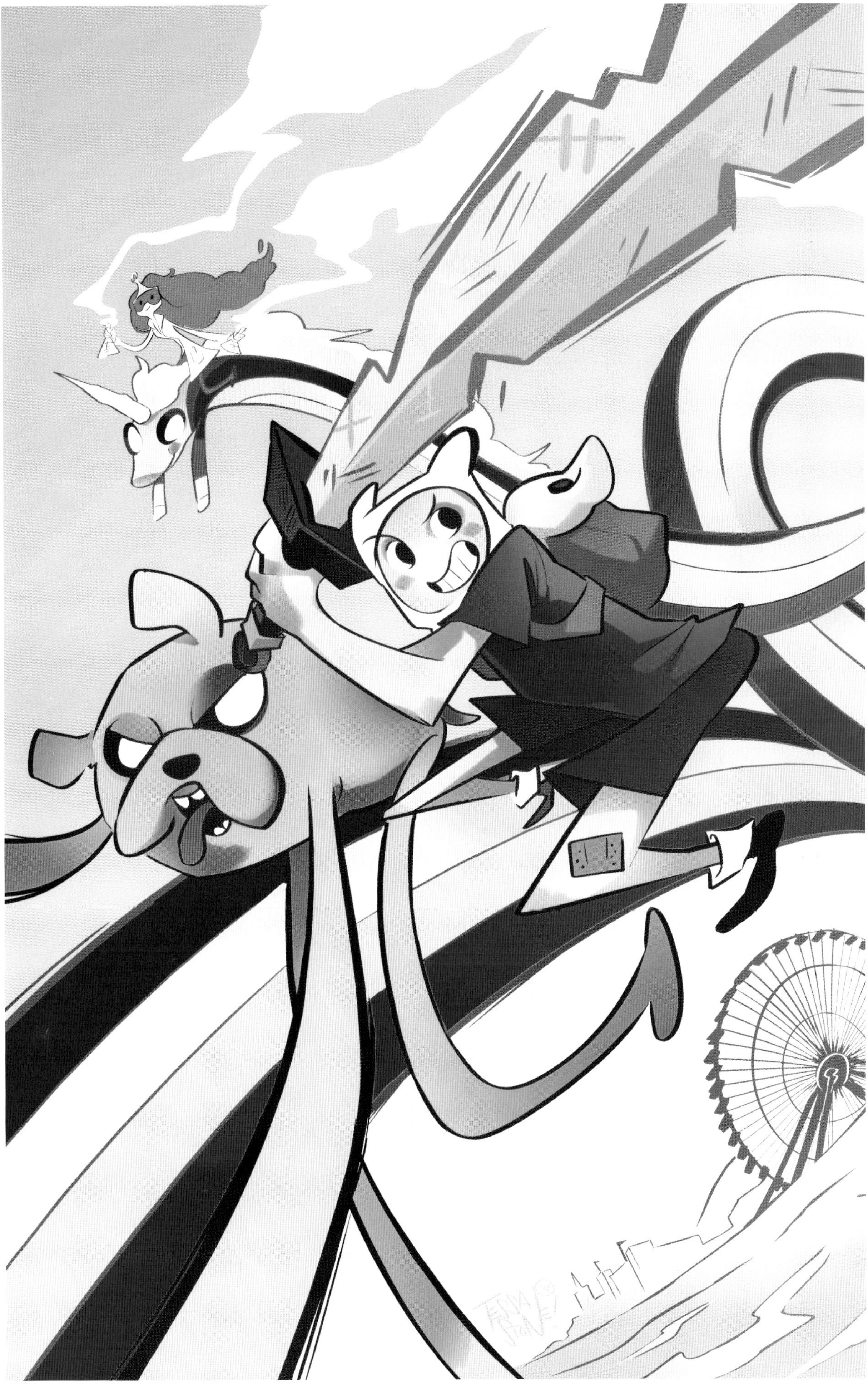
TESSA STONE

ISSUE FIFTEEN C2E2 EXCLUSIVE | TESSA STONE

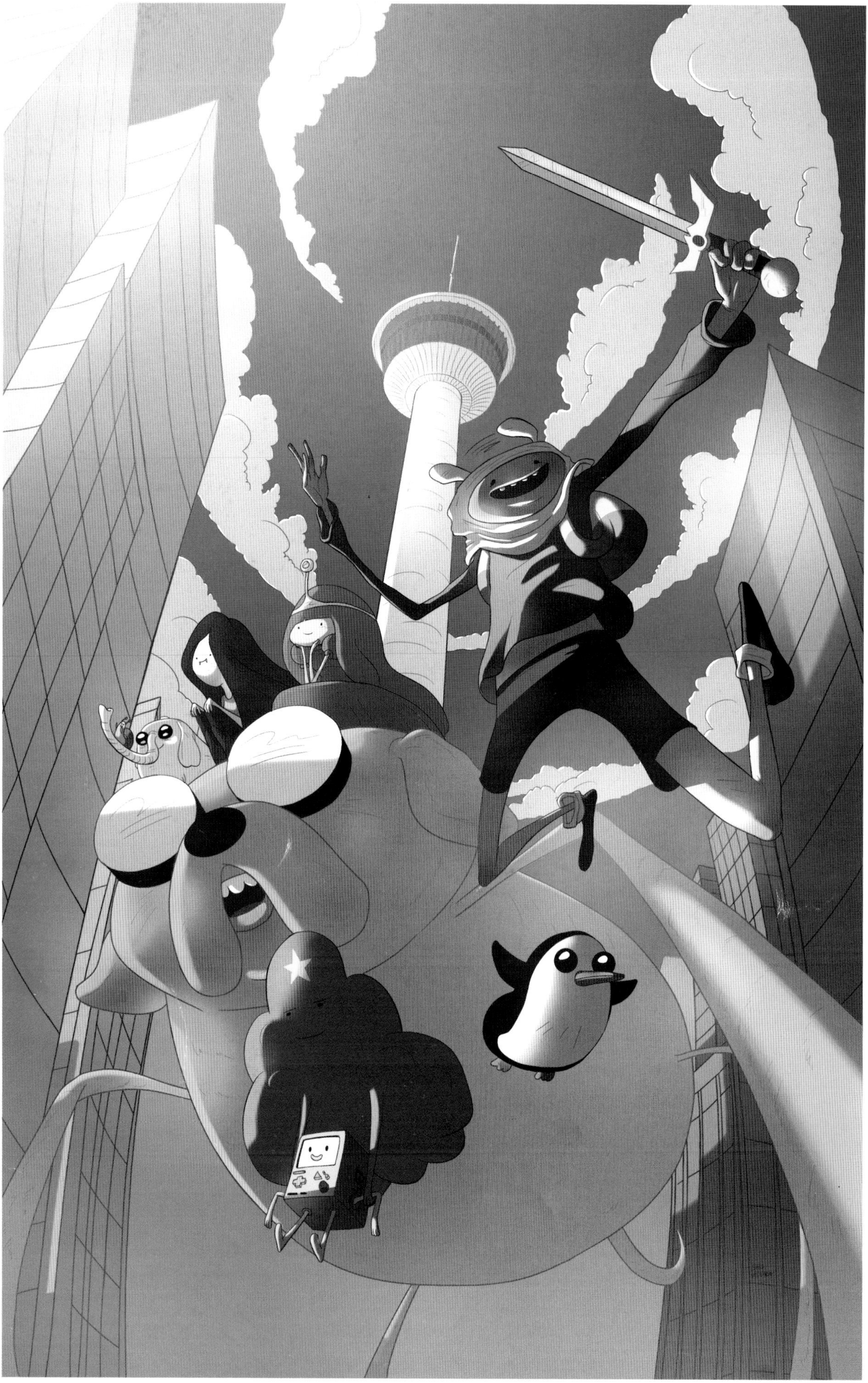

ISSUE FIFTEEN CALGARY COMICS AND ENTERTAINMENT EXPO EXCLUSIVE | SHOICHI UEHARA

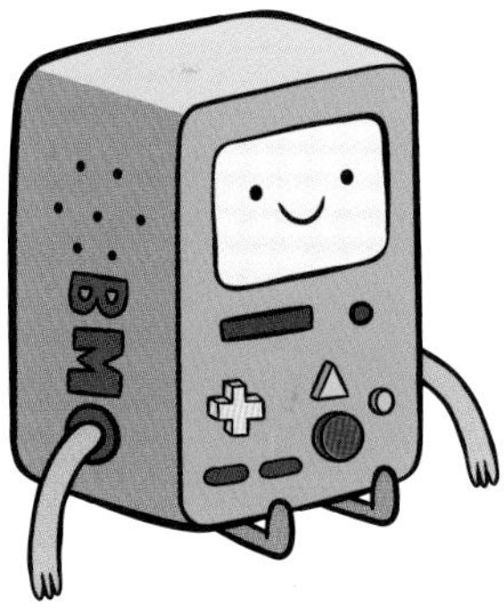
BMO

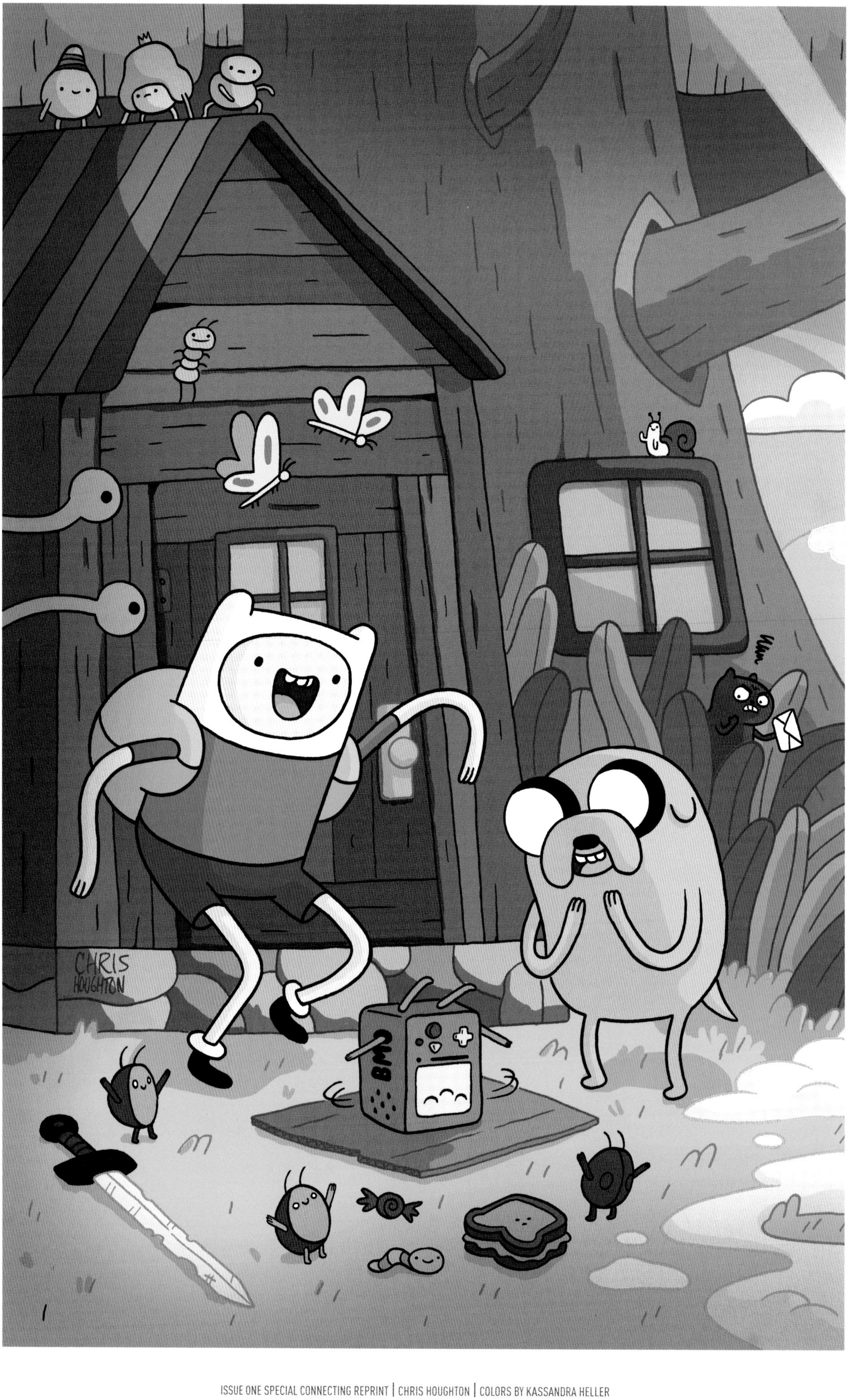
CHRIS HOUGHTON
BMO

ISSUE ONE SPECIAL CONNECTING REPRINT | CHRIS HOUGHTON | COLORS BY KASSANDRA HELLER

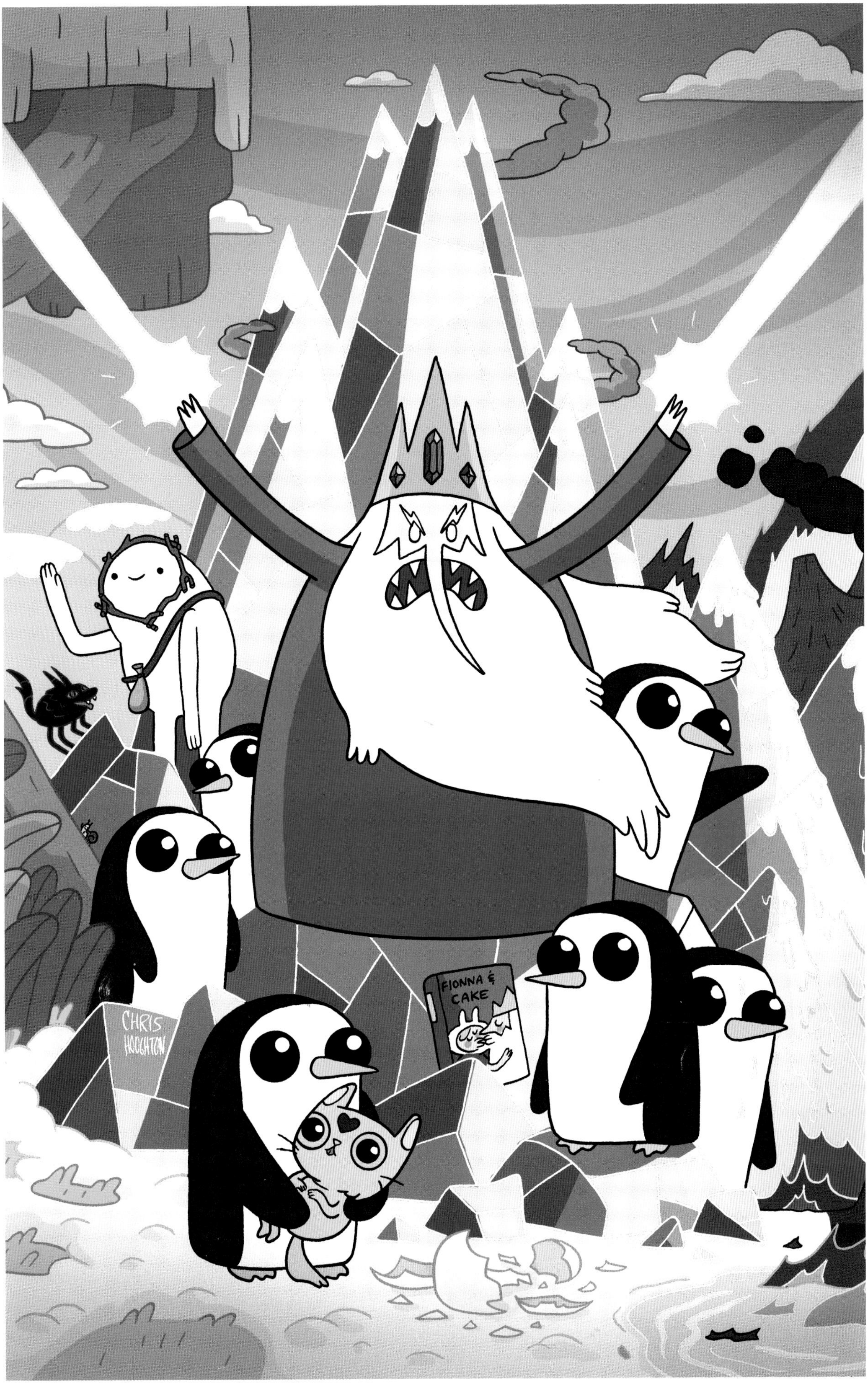
CHRIS HOUGHTON
FIONNA & CAKE

ISSUE TWO SPECIAL CONNECTING REPRINT | CHRIS HOUGHTON | COLORS BY KASSANDRA HELLER

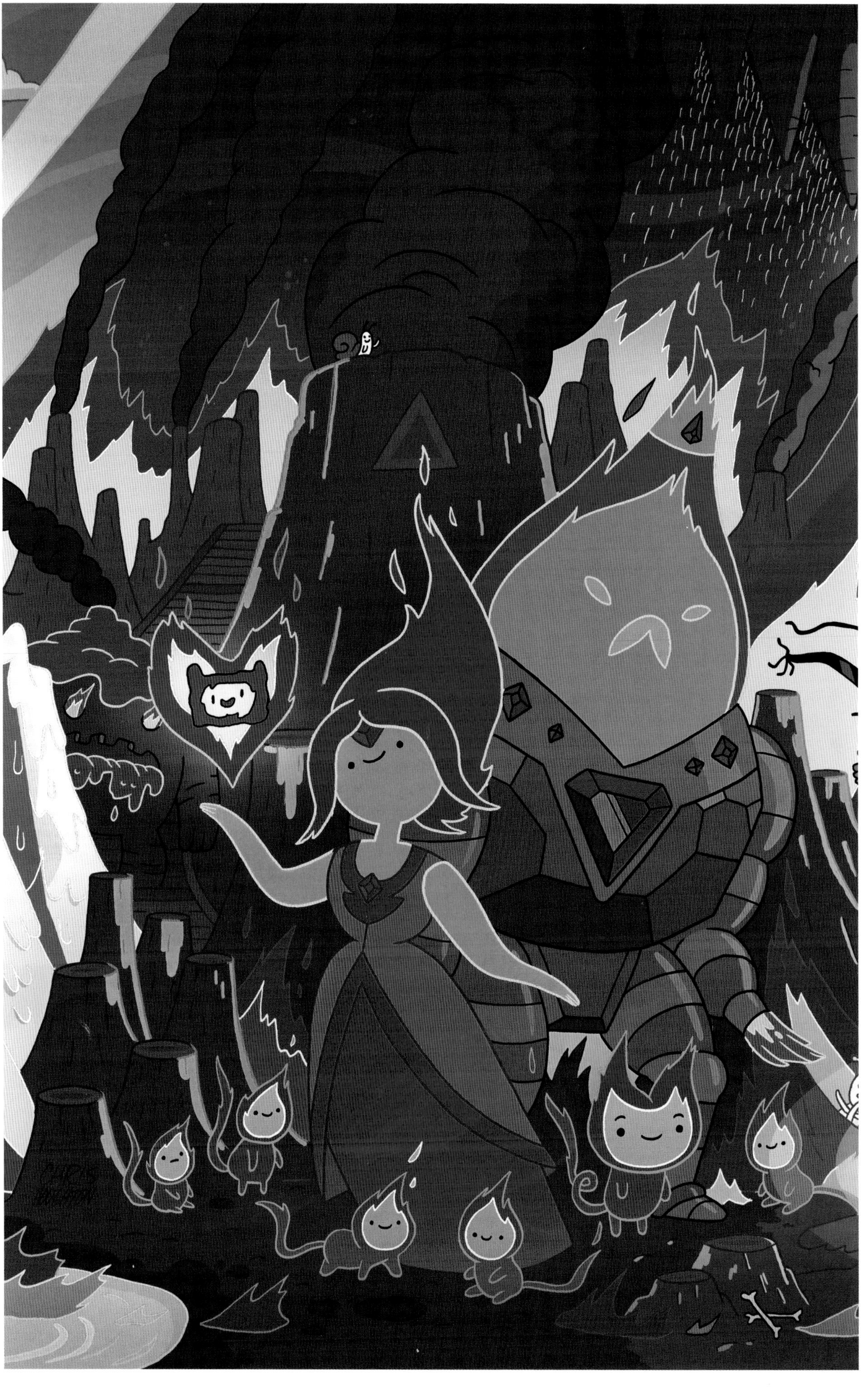

ISSUE THREE SPECIAL CONNECTING REPRINT | CHRIS HOUGHTON | COLORS BY KASSANDRA HELLER

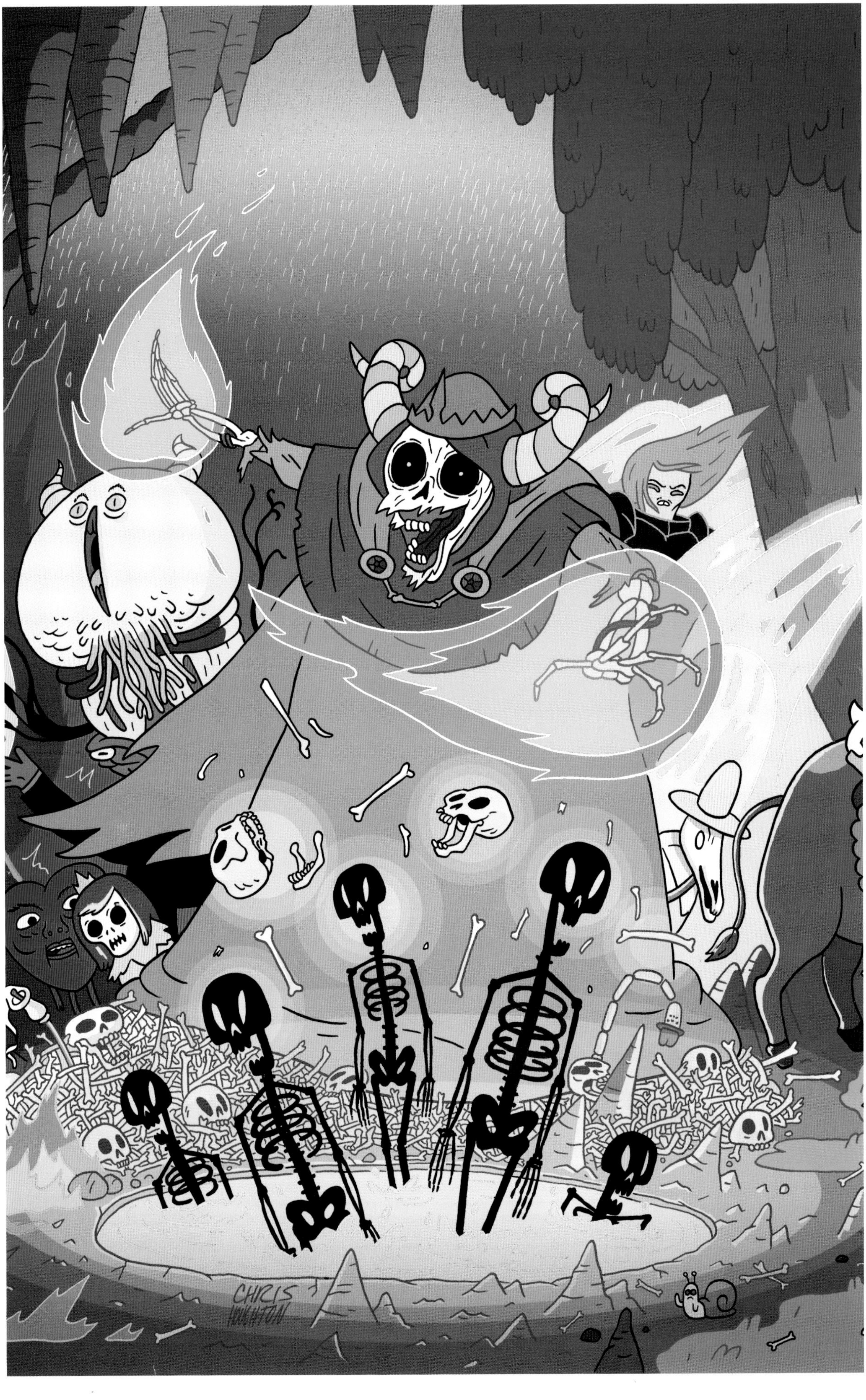
CHRIS HOUGHTON

ISSUE FOUR SPECIAL CONNECTING REPRINT | CHRIS HOUGHTON | COLORS BY KASSANDRA HELLER

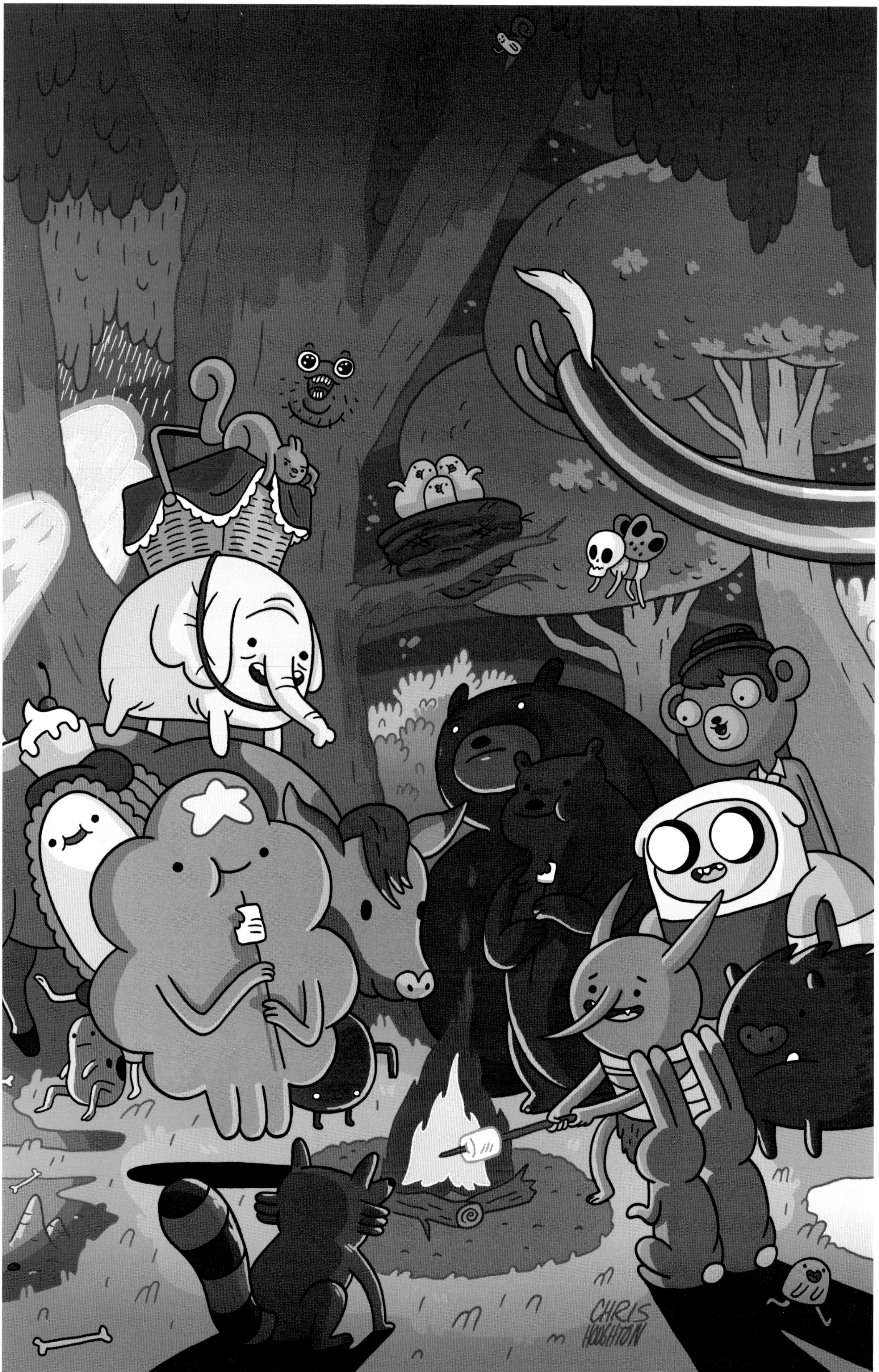
CHRIS HOUGHTON

ISSUE FIVE SPECIAL CONNECTING REPRINT | CHRIS HOUGHTON | COLORS BY KASSANDRA HELLER

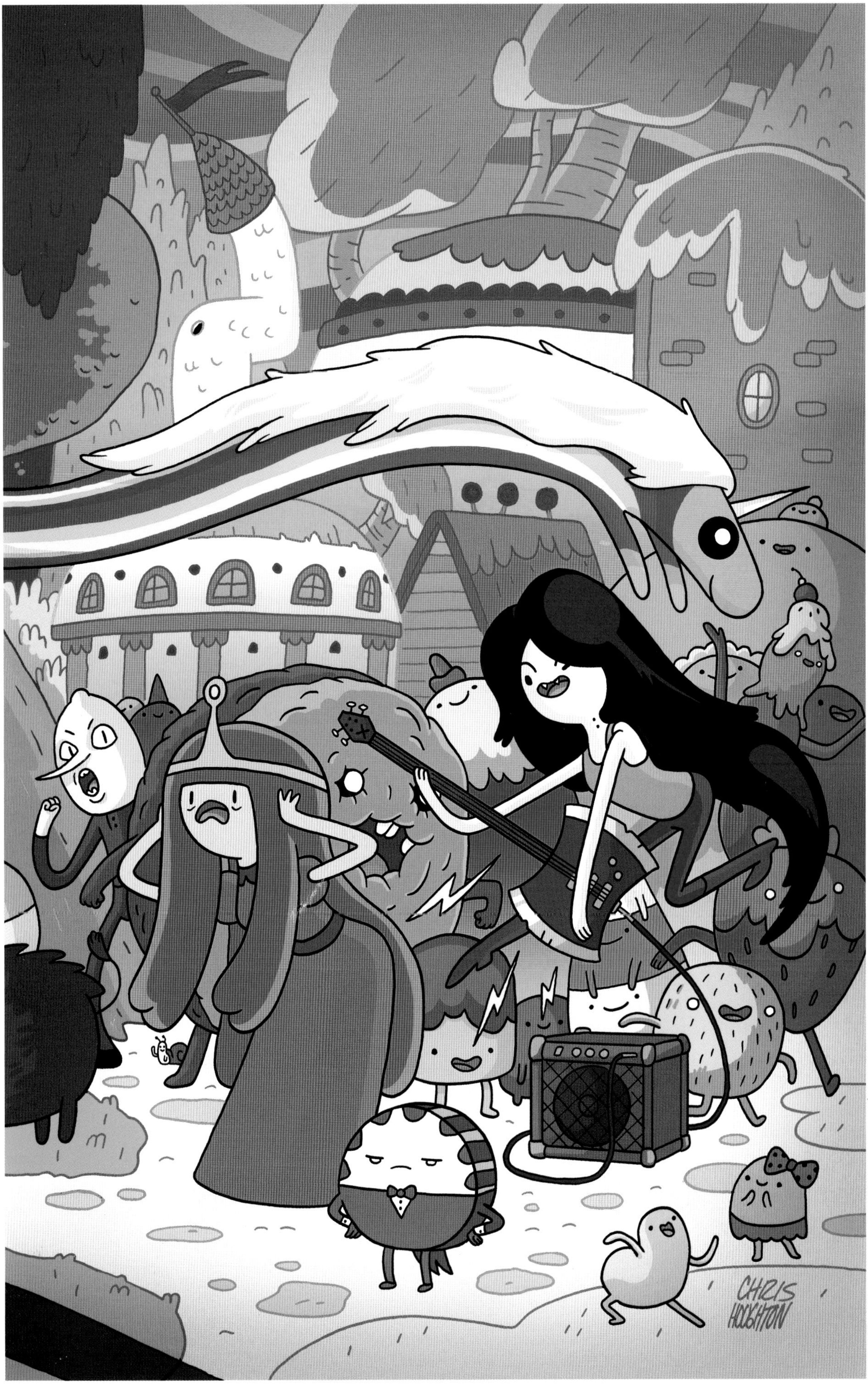
CHRIS
HOUGHTON

ISSUE SIX SPECIAL CONNECTING REPRINT | CHRIS HOUGHTON | COLORS BY KASSANDRA HELLER

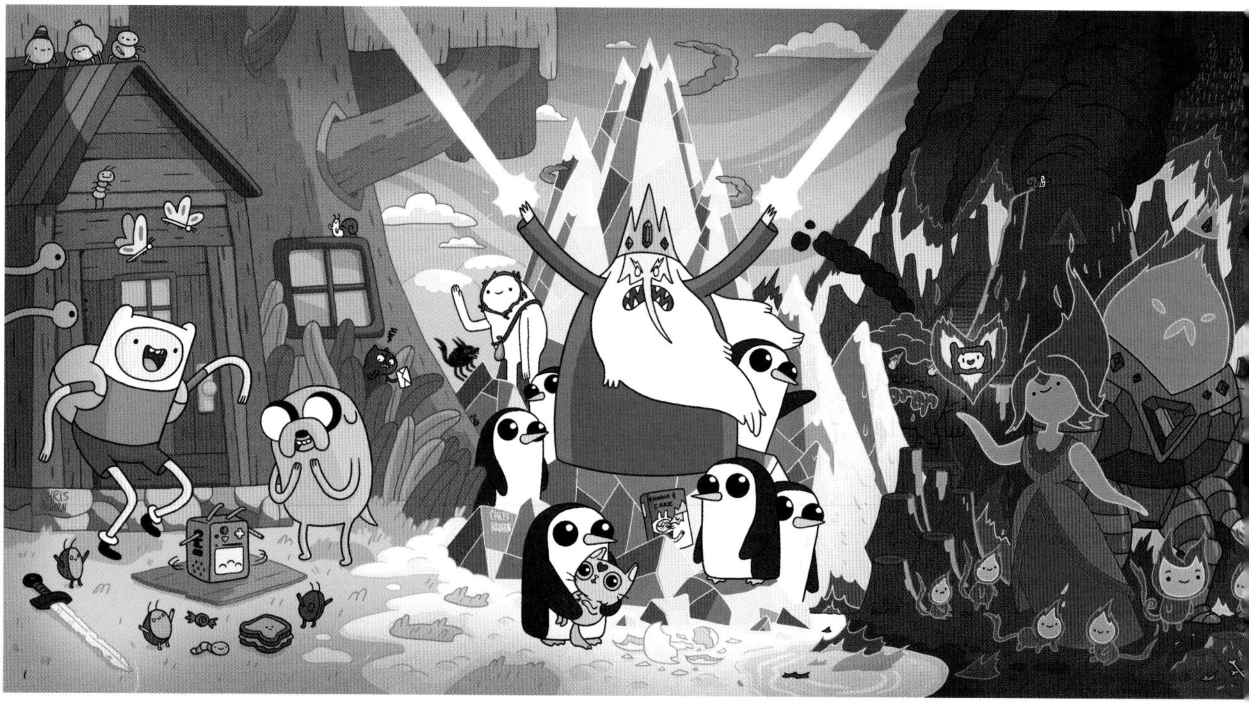
FIONNA & CAKE

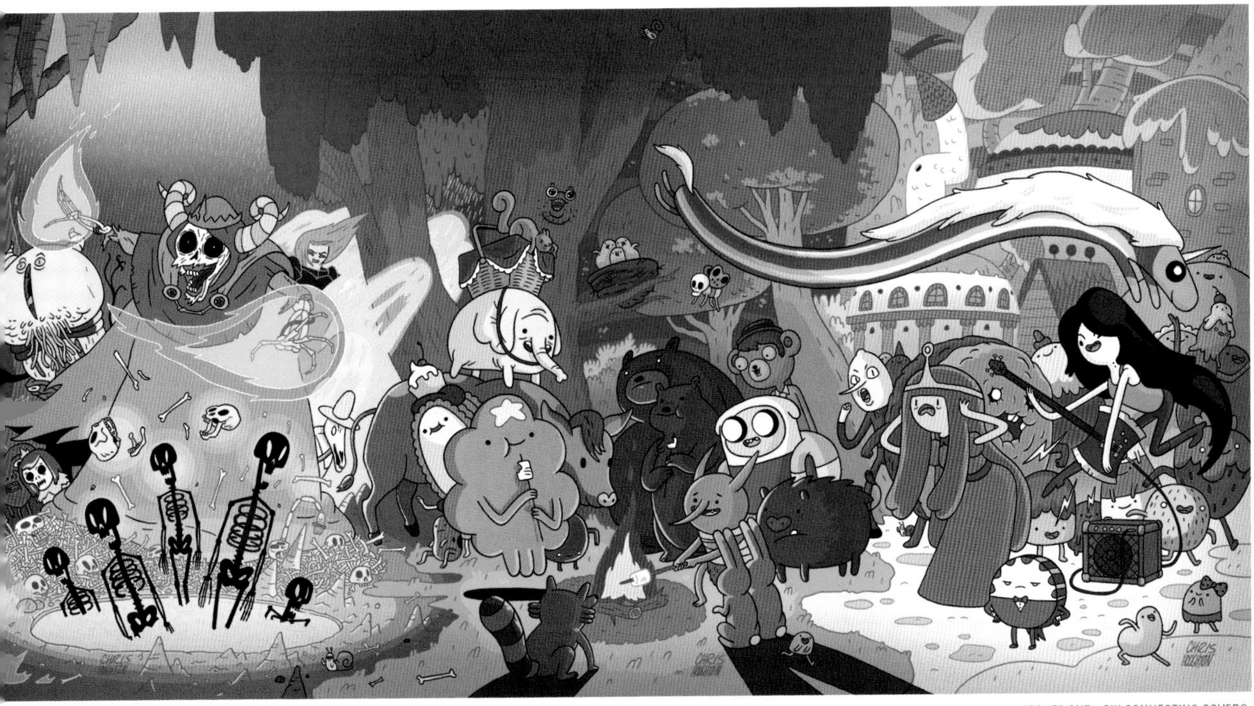

ISSUES ONE - SIX CONNECTING COVERS

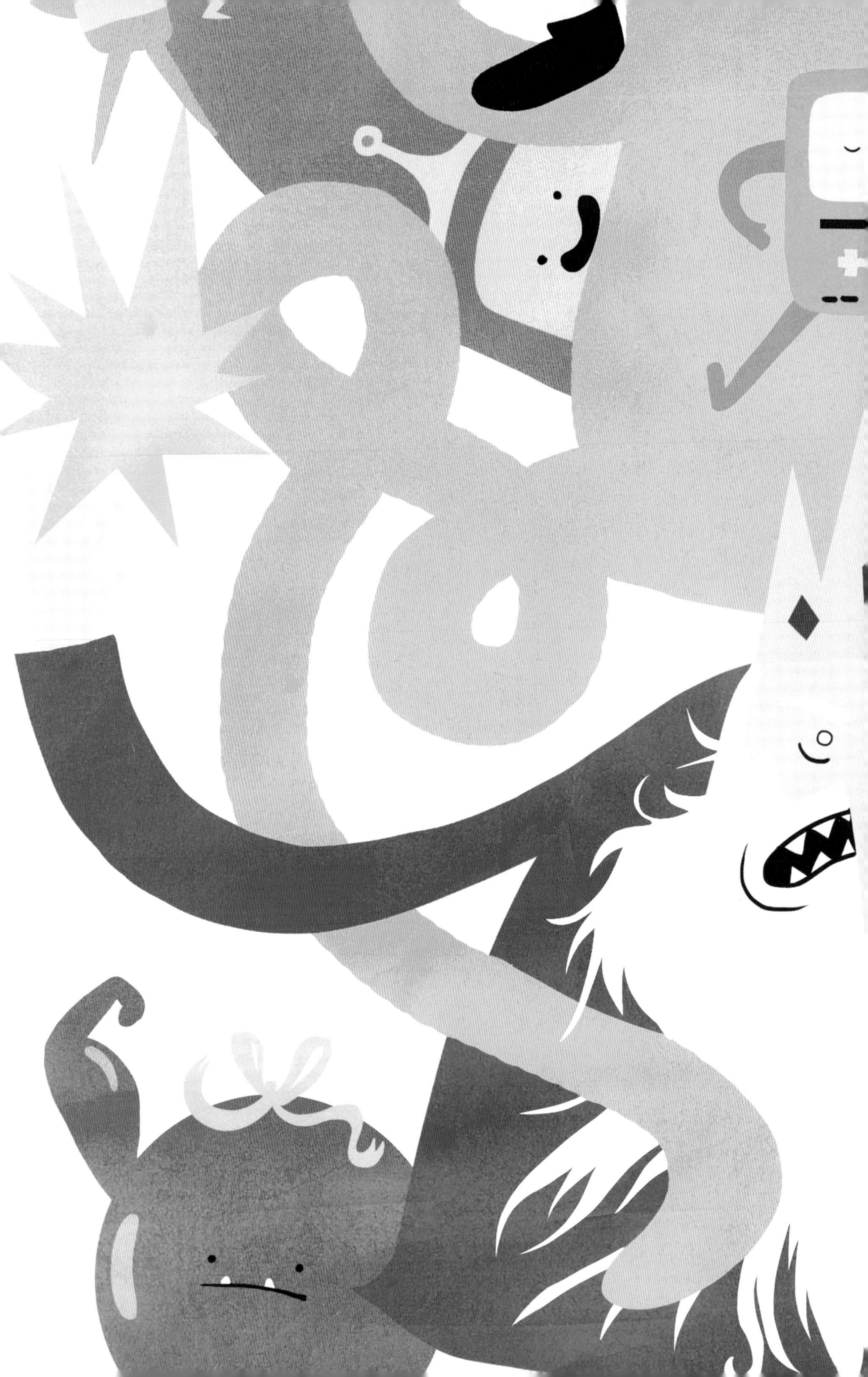

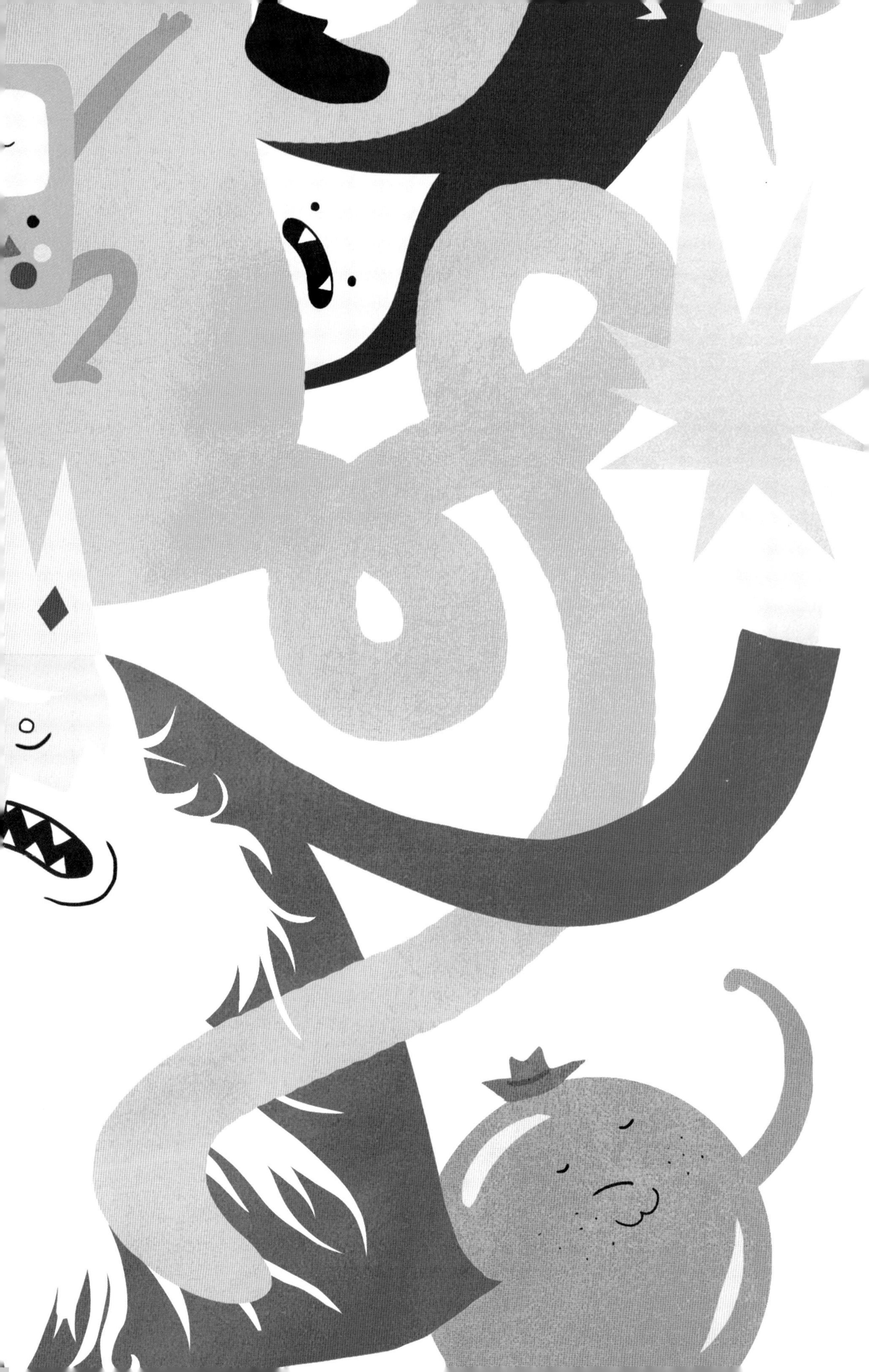

EYE CANDY

VOLUME TWO

COMING 2014

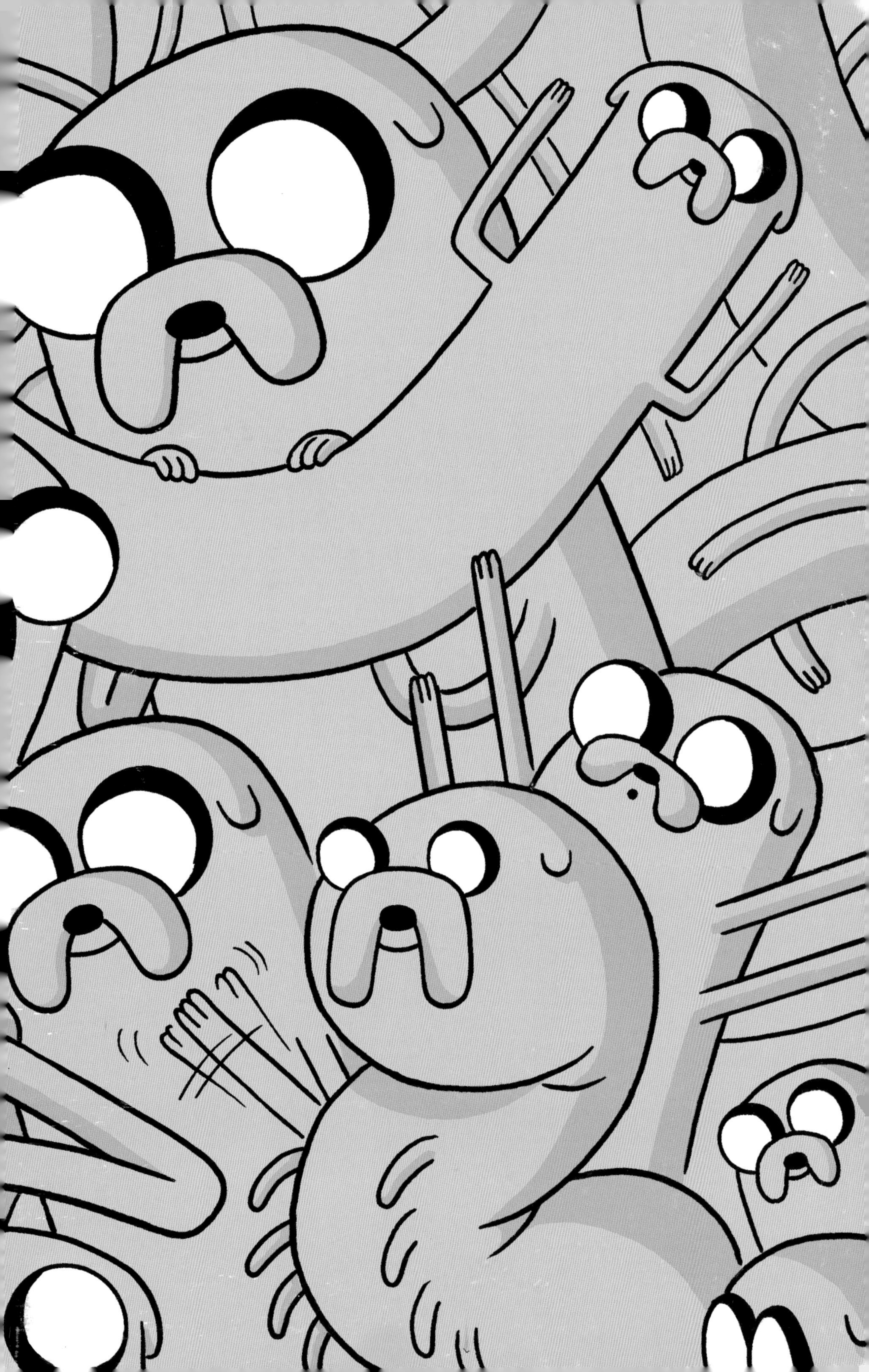